PAX ROMANA

THE RISE OF SEREN

To Kim, with thanks for all your help. Michael Thomas

Michael Thomas

LifeRich Publishing is a registered trademark of
The Reader's Digest Association, Inc.

LifeRich Publishing books may be ordered through booksellers or by contacting:

LifeRich Publishing
1663 Liberty Drive
Bloomington, IN 47403
www.liferichpublishing.com
1 (888) 238-8637

ISBN: 978-1-4897-0615-7 (sc)
ISBN: 978-1-4897-0616-4 (hc)
ISBN: 978-1-4897-0614-0 (e)

Library of Congress Control Number: 2015920544

Print information available on the last page.

LifeRich Publishing rev. date: 01/04/2016

PAX ROMANA - Latin for "Roman Peace." About two hundred years (1st and 2nd centuries A.D.) of uneasy peace in the Mediterranean world following a century of relentless Roman conquest.

"Quandiu stabit Colyseus—stabit et Roma; quando cadet Colyseus—cadet et Roma; quando cadet Roma—cadet et mundus." Beda Venerabili
"While the Coliseum stands, Rome shall stand; when the Coliseum falls, Rome shall fall; when Rome falls, the world shall fall." – Venerable Bede (c. 673-735, quoting a prophecy by Anglo-Saxon pilgrims).

"Terrified by her torment, they will stand afar off and cry, 'Alas, alas, Babylon! O great and mighty city, for in one hour your doom has come!'" – Revelation 18:10

PART I

—1—

THE CHOLERIC CHIEFTAIN

It is almost dawn on the Spanish coast near Valencia as Captain Mark Knutson turns his *Prochain Mirage* fighters to reverse course back east. Mark leans forward on the joystick, causing the warplanes to plummet like dive bombers. At the last possible moment, he pulls back on the stick, redirecting the fighters skyward and accelerating, creating a G-force within the cockpit that pulls at his facial skin.

"Yeeeeeeee-haaaaaah!" he yells as the warplanes ascend. He doesn't yank and bank often, but when he does, it just brings out the Oklahoma cowboy in him.

As Mark eases back on the joystick, the fighters level off and resume a patrol altitude above the Haze.

"Wings in, Mach 5." At this command the warplanes streamline and accelerate exponentially, streaking eastward across the Mediterranean Sea. On Mark's starboard side at three hundred meters flies a drone daughter craft that mirrors his every movement with flawless precision.

In a low voice, Mark transmits a routine communication to European Federation Security Headquarters, EuroSecure. "FPC-462. Initiating eastward run. All clear."

The response comes, "Acknowledged. Voiceprint verified."

While listening to the New World Symphony, Mark munches on a chocolate power bar, sips on a Coke, and watches instruments and scanners glowing before him in the faint early morning light.

Just one pilot commands both warplanes simultaneously. Both respond to his orders with perfect accuracy and superhuman swiftness. Planes and pilot are in every respect a human fighting machine. The drone daughter craft that flies alongside copies the mother craft, linked to her by an umbilical beam. In combat, they are two potent weapons controlled by a single human will.

The warplanes continue on an eastward course, maintaining Mach 5. The Mediterranean is unusually choppy this morning. Mark notices more turbulence than usual, as if a Rogue Storm were approaching. These are the most destructive and violent of all storms, an irregular phenomenon occurring worldwide, but only in the last five years or so. Rogue Storms kill and destroy everything in their path. They are enormous, hellish, erratic, monstrous, and feared wherever they strike.

But Mark's attention is focused to the south. His ongoing mission is to protect European Federation shipping from raids by pirates and to alert Federation forces to potential territorial incursions. He has made this same run hundreds of times, but today, something is different, wrong. He just can't figure out what.

As he ponders this, he moves his joystick slowly, first to the left and then to the right, following the Dvorak symphony in four-four time. The planes follow suit as they dance in synch and sway gracefully in the morning light while speeding straight toward the rising sun.

Icarus made invincible. Prometheus unbound.

Mark notices on his scanners some unusual activity to the south, and he immediately receives a communication from EuroSecure headquarters: "UFO uncloaking. Approaching buffer zone. 32.733°N 15.538°E. Possible drone decoy or fighter. Engage."

"FPC-462, responding."

As quickly as he acknowledges the order, Mark turns his warplanes to intercept. They respond instantly, easily, dropping altitude and reducing speed as they approach the southern zone, racing to investigate the blurry blip that appears on his forward screen. *They're using an old smoke-screen technique*, he thinks.

The blip suddenly turns back south.

"They're on to us. Daughter, engage target," he commands. "Mother, scan for other possible energy signatures."

The drone daughter craft separates herself from the mother, turns, and accelerates to pursue the fleeing warplane, which has recloaked and is creating ghosts that register on Mark's sensors. He watches the chase on various screens, occasionally looking out his cockpit window.

"Daughter, identify the energy signature."

"Father, scans reveal that the warplane is a drone decoy, remotely controlled. It is unarmed. It cannot escape me. Shall I kill?"

"Kill," orders Mark.

In the blink of an eye, the image vanishes from the forward scan screen. Minutes later, the daughter drone returns to her previous position.

"Report kill to HQ."

But just as the Federation warplanes are about to return to their patrol route, Mark notices on his rear sensor screen new contacts coming out of cloak. Enemy fighters are in pursuit and are multiplying as holograms, also producing more ghost sensor contacts. Five blips become ten, then twenty but then fifteen again as the original five planes go back into cloak. In his rear camera screen, he now can visually confirm fifteen pursuing holoplanes.

"Ex-cel-lent," Mark whispers slowly. He thinks, *I love dogfights!*

Mark is pumped. "Looks like they've really improved their cloak-and-dagger technology. Let the chess game begin!"

He commands mother and daughter, "Cloak and holograph, glider mode. Eject holopods in four-directional array."

At these instructions, mother and daughter shut down all detectable power and disappear from the view of human and electronic eyes. Mark's fighters eject small holopods that in turn project new pseudo warplanes that also produce ghost sensor contacts on to the open sky, first four, then eight. The enemy warplanes, or what appear to be warplanes, open fire on the virtual Federation fighters, which suffer no damage whatsoever.

After the hostiles' initial burst, Mark initiates his *BattleNet* program and eight additional sets of ash-gray Federation patrol fighters appear directly behind the pursuing warplanes and also seem to begin firing flash-plasma bursts on Mark's pursuers, which are virtual rather than actual. The sky is ablaze with pseudo-lightning.

While in silent glider mode, Mark observes the aerial combat between his holograms and the enemy holograms. He patiently waits for a telltale burst of measurable energy to appear, and the enemy warplanes, he assumes, are looking for the same from him. While each waits, the bogus battle laces the upper atmosphere with mock rockets and make-believe plasma. The warplanes are flying, firing, dodging, and angling so fast that the whole illusory storm is a near blur to the naked eye.

Up to this point, it's like a hologame, warfare at its best: dogfights, drama, and derring-do, but no destruction and no death.

"What's the best option for stepping this up?" Mark wonders out loud.

The mother craft analyzes the situation and responds, "High-intensity pan-burst from both mother and daughter followed immediately by a 180-degree evasive maneuver."

Mark commands, "Execute in five seconds. Secure Foam."

The cockpit instantly fills with Secure Foam, which will cushion Mark from injury during the radical reversal.

In exactly five seconds, both mother and daughter discharge a powerful torrent of disruptive energy plasma into the faux battle and blast off quickly in the opposite direction to a safe distance. Federation holograms disappear first; then, following several real explosions, all enemy holograms vanish. The pan-burst has hit and severely damaged three cloaked enemy fighters, which are now visible and spinning out of control to earth. Two slightly crippled but still functioning fighters immediately turn south in a desperate attempt to escape.

"Will these people never learn?" Mark muses to himself as he directs the pursuit, increasing speed. *This is going to be easy*, he thinks.

"Fangs out. Lock on." At this command, several weapons systems begin clicking and whirring, infallibly targeting their wounded prey.

A message alert appears on Mark's screen in bright red: "WARNING: YOU HAVE CROSSED INTO THE AIRSPACE OF THE AFRICAN CONTINENT. DANGER IMMINENT."

"This will only take a second," reasons Mark as he prepares to fire.

Suddenly one of the wounded warplanes veers away, drastically dropping altitude and hugging an irregular surface of impossibly large sand dunes.

"Daughter, pursue fleeing target." The drone daughter craft turns to the southeast, initiating a high-speed chase.

Mark continues in pursuit of the second target. He knows the first is no match for his daughter.

The second target also suddenly decreases speed and descends to a dangerously low altitude, repeatedly veering and disappearing into massive dunes and deep valleys and then reappearing, winding its way through the small mountains of sand. Mark likewise decreases airspeed and struggles with his controls for another lock-on. *They're jamming me,* Mark thinks.

Just when Mark is about to abandon the chase and return to the sea, he notices dozens of white dots on the surface of the rolling dunes ahead. Scores of human figures cloaked in white are positioned below in successive valleys.

It's a trap.

"Pull up!" Mark shouts.

Many below are raising what look like RPG launchers. They fire en masse just as Mark's warplane comes into view. Most of the grenade explosions miss, but some find their mark. *"I hate low-tech,"* Mark thinks.

On screen in bold red letters Mark sees: "VITAL SYSTEMS DAMAGED. RECOMMEND EJECT." A warning siren blares.

"Eject!" he shouts.

A controlled explosion blasts Mark out of the cockpit into the open air. After about a minute, he is on the sand, struggling to free himself from his seat and chute, dragging himself along with his hands. For some reason, he cannot stand up or use his legs.

He is suddenly powerless—just a man, not a god—completely helpless unless plugged into something far greater than himself.

As Mark strains to look around him, fear sweeps over him like a hot desert wind. He keeps trying to stand and run, but then he realizes that his legs have been paralyzed by the eject explosion. *Impossible!* he thinks. He reaches for his side arm..., but his holster is empty. *Impossible!*

Without warning, he is surrounded, not by holograms, but by living, hostile men who hold his life in their hands. They are wearing flowing white robes and a headpiece with a slit, revealing only their eyes. Together, they look like a kind of mystical mirage created by the desert heat. The silent assembly gathers around him in a circle and stands motionless.

After a moment a figure mounted on a shiny black Arabian stallion slowly rides into view from behind a nearby dune. He is robed in royal purple, wearing a chain and a large golden medallion around his neck. *"A chieftain of some sort,"* Mark thinks. The rider dismounts and advances slowly toward him.

The chieftain bends over Mark's body. Only his bushy eyebrows and angry, dark eyes are visible through the opening on his headpiece. He produces a flat, hand-held electronic device and presses it on to Mark's forehead. *No way do they have access to our personnel database.* He can only wonder what will happen next.

After studying the read-out from the device, the chieftain spits on Mark's face and abruptly shouts something angrily in a language that Mark does not recognize. *Why is Universal Translator not working?* After the furious outburst, the chieftain reaches inside his garment, and draws out a gleaming scimitar with an ornately jeweled handle and a wide, curved blade. He grasps the handle with both hands and raises it high above his head...

—2—

BIRTH OF VENUS

"Wake up, Mark!"

Ten-second pause.

"Wake up, Knutson!!!" Same voice, several decibels louder.

Ten-second pause.

Then, as programmed, the sound of a blaring bugle playing reveille.

At this, Mark springs out of bed, dazed, confused, and assumes a defensive position. After a moment, he realizes where he is.

He looks at his new polished brass cyber servant and commands "Cancel." The robot, which is slightly shorter than Mark, acknowledges and turns off reveille.

"Thanks, Pinocchio," Mark says to his new artificially intelligent companion and helper.

"You're welcome, Gepetto," the robot responds with a mild voice and manner.

Mark sits back down on the side of the bed and runs his fingers through his hair.

"God," Mark mutters, "what a nightmare! That was ridiculous. I'm not afraid of anything." *Too many inconsistencies. Should have known it was a dream. Their cloaking technology isn't that good. No side arm? And those huge sand dunes!* Mark continues to make a mental list of more obvious discrepancies.

He looks down at his legs, rubs them, and bounces them up and down, feeling a sense of relief. As the light in the room slowly grows brighter, he picks up a pill dispenser next to his bed and reads the label in a whisper, "Dream Enhancement Tablets: For Military Training Purposes Only." *Better cut back a little on the narco-training.*

Pinocchio announces "Gepetto, you have two new messages. Number two is from headquarters, priority orange."

"Play number one."

An eerie, blurred light appears in the still somewhat shadowy room and gradually becomes more vivid.

After rubbing his eyes and stretching, he looks up at the hologram as it becomes more clearly defined. When he sees that it's Angela, he falls back on to his bed.

"Play." At this command, the hologram begins to move and speak. Of course, it isn't really Angela; it's her image, her voice, and her Italian accent.

"I'm sorry, Marco. I feel this deeply," she begins in a lifeless sort of way. "I could wish that things were working out. We're just not going in the same direction. I think that I have taken everything that belongs to me, and I have removed my image from the library." Now she becomes animated. "But Marco, I will still want that you may come to the *Lumena* meeting next Thursday night. You're never going to believe it except that you see it with your own eyes."

Mark recalls, "Angela's English deteriorates when she gets upset or excited."

"The things that this man, Seren, teaches. The things that he does. And as I have told you, he looks a lot like you! Come and say to me that I am wrong! Don't be a turd about it. Decide for yourself. I am telling you that it will change your whole life." Angela's face-image suddenly becomes intensely dramatic, "It's going to change the world." Then, her face falls, and her voice trails off *"Ciao,* Marco."

"Freeze!" Mark commands.

The image fades.

"Freeze!" he repeats.

But he has only slowed the image-delete function, which Angela has apparently programmed. She has left. Nothing can reverse that. Shortly her image will vanish and only memories will remain, memories of another time, of another Angela, if he cared to remember.

"Like I want to go to another whacko meeting," he mumbles.

Mark rubs his fingers up and down on his chin as he studies Angela's image. Stunningly beautiful, like a Greek goddess, in exceptional physical shape, large, clear blue eyes that often gleam with tears, long blond hair parted in the middle and flowing over her shoulders.

But as expected, Angela's form continues to fade. Her eyes lose their sparkle, her lips, their redness, and her cheeks, their blush, and her blond hair slowly grays.

"*Carpe diem,*" Mark whispers. "You bombed it, *bambolina.*"

Angela and her image are gone, now and for good, from Mark's apartment. He lies there for a while and stares at the ceiling, thinking.

Pinocchio reminds him, "Gepetto, please remember that the second message is from headquarters."

He responds, "Whatever it is, let it wait. It's only orange." Mark draws in a deep breath and sighs. After he gets up, Pinocchio makes his bed and turns it into a couch.

Mark puts on the running gear that Pinocchio has laid out for him. He stretches while moving over to the treadmill section of the room. As he steps on and begins walking, the floor moves with him.

Mark is also in superb physical shape. When he met Angela for the first time, she said with her heavy accent, "Hey, tall, dark, and buff." Mark is an American, mostly of German extraction, but is also part Cherokee and fiercely proud of it.

Pinocchio brings him a small tray with a bottle of an energy drink and a large protein square, which he consumes just before he accelerates to a brisk run.

"*HoloVision.*"

A soothing female voice responds: "System ready to obey your every command, to fulfill your every wish, and to realize your every dream." Mark has been enjoying his recent upgrade to HoloVision 500. The increase in voxels has significantly improved the quality of 360-D images.

"Sunrise." At this, five hundred microprojectors, all from slightly different angles around the entertainment section of the room, light up, and the stark, bare area before Mark takes on an ethereal light. Everything definitely looks different, even though nothing has changed substantially.

"Light clouds, jogging trail by a lake, assorted trees, flowers, some dogs, and a few people. Peer Gynt, Morning Mood."

With each command, the system magically splashes form and color in the otherwise blank and lifeless section of the apartment. A flute begins to play, followed by an oboe.

Mark runs faster than usual down the jogging trail, even though in reality he is going nowhere.

"Insert program 'Romance One' on the water."

This is Mark's favorite. Ten years earlier, before Haze levels became toxic, he and Angela had met on a jogging trail like this one, and later, he had proposed to her in a rowboat on a lake not far from Rome. An image of Mark—his avatar—appears in the scene, sitting in a small boat with oars but apparently talking to himself. He has forgotten. Angela's image is no longer available.

"Insert tall female with long blond hair wearing blue shorts, a red top, a straw hat, and sunglasses. Seat her across from Mark-1." At this order, a comparable woman fills the space previously occupied by Angela.

Mark continues to run around the lake, watching the goings-on in the rowboat, trying to relive the pleasure of that moment but not quite succeeding.

"Exit program. Save with new female as 'Romance Two.'" The entertainment section of the room returns to a normal blank.

HoloVision. Any image is possible. The number of possible images is infinite.

Mark stops the treadmill. "New scene. Gaming mode. Desert. Extremely high dunes. Thirty human figures in a circle, wearing white robes." And they all appear in 360-D at his command. He grabs his game controller gloves, which hang on the wall next to the treadmill section.

"Keep figures at twenty-five meters." This command moves the group to the prescribed distance.

"Insert Mark-1 in flight gear and armed, running toward the group." Mark's 360-D gaming avatar appears and begins running as Mark stands and watches.

"Create North African chieftain, purple robe and headpiece with only a slit for his eyes, gold chain and medallion around his neck, with large, ornate scimitar to oppose Mark-1.... Action."

A figure similar to the one in his dream appears, and the rematch begins. The chieftain draws his blade and tries to slash at Mark-1. But Mark has control and causes Mark-1 to pull out his flash-plasma side arm. He focuses his first blast and blows the scimitar out of the chieftain's hands. He then disables him, melting his legs, then his arms, and then he kills him, burning out his heart. Mark-1 turns to massacre the rest of his thirty attackers, who are desperately trying to flee. He is able to pick off at least a dozen of them. Mark looks forward to practicing the program in the future so he can finish them all off in one round. "Good combat training," he reasons as he takes off his gaming gloves.

"Mark-1. Behead the chieftain," orders real Mark, at which command the avatar snatches the scimitar and cuts off chieftain's imaginary head. Bright-red virtual blood flows but does not stain the carpet, only the system's simulation of sand.

HoloVision's female voice declares: "Congratulations, Mark, you have won the match. You are awesome!"

Mark looks on, only temporarily satisfied by the mock carnage. He hates losing.

"Save as 'Death in the Desert.' Pinocchio, play message number two." The desert quickly dissolves, and the room goes blank again.

The second message is priority orange from the EuroSecure airbase in Naples. Sand dunes are replaced by the vivid 360-D image of a woman that Mark does not know. She is sitting at a desk and is reading in Italian from a screen lying flat before her. *I've never seen this one before. She must be the new communications assistant for the base.* Mark stops running and whispers. "Excellent choice!" He activates Universal Translator.

"All fighter pilots from Delta-Wing will report immediately to EFHQ Naples to initiate emergency protocols. This is an Orange Alert. If you are not already in the Naples area, you will be briefed en route on the secure channel."

"Pinocchio, acknowledge transmission and freeze."

As he puts on his uniform, Mark studies this new heavenly messenger carefully. She is an arresting beauty. Her shiny black hair is pinned up. Her dark eyebrows arch over milky brown eyes, the kind of eyes that make a man wobbly. She has certain sweetness about her, an innocent glow that reminds him of Audrey Hepburn or maybe Ciora. To Mark, she looks like she has just stepped out of a classical painting. The desk hides half of her from view, but what is visible is more than enough to fill Mark's thoughts for some time to come.

"Save image of female and file under 'Birth of Venus.'" Not exactly like Botticelli's, but far more inspiring.

After checking the pop-out control panel to make sure that the communication has been acknowledged and that the new image has been saved, Mark sweeps Venus into his portapack, which he fastens to his belt.

He looks at the robot, "Do you have my breakfast ready, Pinocchio?"

"Yes, Gepetto. All your nutritional needs will be met until noon. Have a nice day, Father."

"Secure the apartment, and don't take any wooden nickels."

Pinocchio processes this statement. "Gepetto, wooden nickels never—"

"Cancel! And put yourself into security mode."

"Acknowledged, Gepetto."

Mark takes a small container from Pinocchio and steps into his personal elevator pod. The door closes, and he drops a hundred fifty-six floors to the lobby of his apartment building.

—3—

DEFENDING THE DREAM

"Beware the Ides of March."
Shakespeare, *Julius Caesar*

Rome, the Eternal City, reborn, far exceeds its former glory. Thanks to unrivaled Roman technology and the renowned skill of her engineers, the architectural restoration of ancient Rome is in progress. The radiant metropolis is crowned with the *Bolla*, the "Bubble," a plasma energy dome that not only protects the city's classical core but also enhances her heavenly appearance. The dome is created by a fusion-generated blanket of energy flowing to a central tower eight-hundred meters high from a series of mainstays on a perimeter fourteen kilometers in diameter. The Bolla's color and transparency can be adjusted according to Haze levels outside. During the day, if pollution is high, the tint is altered to a rich blue, and flying drones generate puffy white clouds. At night the drones create the illusion of a field of stars and even a full moon. Well placed underground fans and temperature control units create a balmy, gentle breeze. It's always spring in the Eternal City.

Inside the cupola, every effort has been made to restore the beauty and grandeur of the ancient capital. Repairs and renovations have permitted the Coliseum to recover its former festive face and its capabilities for mass entertainment. The Curia Julia, the new meeting place of the senate, has been completely restored for official use. The Circus Maximus has been renovated and is hosting MAXIMUM shows in 360-D. All religious structures have been razed, even the Pantheon. Rome is completely secular; religion is banned, although a free exchange of other ideas is encouraged. The senate remains committed to the idea of creating a new humanist realm, a second Renaissance for humanity.

Inside the Bolla, the *Pax Romana*, the Roman Peace, prevails. Rome, the city set on seven hills, majestic in its splendor, boasts thousands of years of varied engineering and architectural achievements interspersed with ultra-modern megabuildings, some over two hundred stories high. Rome is now greater even than in the "Golden Age" of Augustus. It is the crown jewel of Italy and indeed of the entire European Federation. The casual observer would suggest that it is a city worthy to be the seat of a royal empire and that it lacks only an emperor, a new Caesar, but most of the Roman Senate has fiercely disagreed in public debate.

The Coliseum, the Theater of Pompeii and the Theater of Marcellus continue to host shows, games, extravagant spectacles, 360-D movies, and gladiatorial contests. The restoration of other landmarks and monuments is in progress.

The Tiber is filtered and diverted under the Bolla, as are trains and other forms of transportation. Only Roman Citizens, approved Italian citizens, and Eurocitizens with an appropriate security clearance are allowed within her gates.

Outside the boundaries of the Bolla is a different world, no sunny days, puffy white clouds, or blue skies. The atmosphere is usually toxic, sometimes deadly, the result of decades of world-wide pollution, volcanic eruptions, dirty bombs, and assorted environmental disasters. Outside, one sees no megabuildings or restored classical edifices. Eight years ago, Vatican City, left outside the Bolla, was leveled by waves of terrorist bombings, leaving it in ruins. The Papacy has since returned to Avignon, France, where it is not actively supported by the French government but is tolerated with no overt hostility. Outside the Bolla lie ghettos, a succession of neighborhoods populated by peoples from old Italy and by immigrants from all over the world.

Some accuse the senate of focusing only on Rome and of acting as if the rest of the peninsula did not exist. To their credit, Roman administrators have been diligently overseeing the slow yet progressive expansion of the Bolla covering Rome and of the smaller energy domes over other large cities. Their benign plan is to make room for more restoration, more citizens, and a more universal sharing of the neo-Roman lifestyle, *La Dolce Vita*.

Elsewhere in the Federation, similar renovation projects are underway: Paris, the City of Light and Love; London, affectionately or perhaps contemptuously called Babylondon, but newly named the Regal City; Prague, the Golden City; and Vienna, the Imperial City. Other major capitals of the European Federation are likewise committed to this rebirth plan, however, Rome has regenerated faster than any of the others, and her dome is larger and far more sophisticated. Progress has been impeded by ruthless terrorist attacks from numerous groups outside the dome, but since the Bolla was first generated ten years ago, the city proper has known only prosperity and peace. Unrelenting assaults on Rome's supply lines both on land and at sea also hinder the noble project.

Mark enters a secure compartment on the hypertrain to Naples. He locks the door, sits down, and takes a deep breath. After the train starts, he stares out the window as Rome passes by in slow motion, like a movie he has seen countless times.

The hypertrain enters a tunnel, passing under the Bolla and through the security curtain. The trip will not take long now. Mark blacks out the window and plugs his portapack into the compartment's system; he tunes to the secure channel, and sits back for the briefing as the hypertrain speeds away from the domed city.

Mark tunes in and is now looking at the large assembly hall used for briefings. The director of EuroSecure, unfortunately not his glamorous communications assistant, appears before the group. Mark looks around and spots several pilots he knows but has never really connected with. He thinks about trying to get together with some of his old buddies from the Praetorian Guard after today's patrol runs; maybe they could go to one of the shows.

The big boss is predictably solemn and dull as he explains the current potential "crisis" to an audience of hundreds and a cyber-audience of hundreds more. Mark activates Universal Translator. The chief does seem a little more animated than usual, so maybe there really will be some real action soon.

The director clears his throat and then begins: "A major build-up of North African pirates has been detected in several sectors. We've seen such activity before, but intelligence is picking up rumors of a formidable offensive in the works. We've seen growing evidence that this assault will be backed up by some kind of new jamming technology. We're not sure exactly what that means."

He again clears his throat and takes a drink of water. He then scratches his bald head.

"At this point, the Federation is not concerned about a full-scale invasion. The hostiles potentially have sufficient fire-power to cause some confusion or minor disruptions, but our technology will prevail, of this we are confident. We call on you to serve Rome, to be alert, to defend the dream. Remember, you are protecting our way of life and are in no small way a part of Rome's destiny. Rome is destined for greatness, but Rome is under attack. We must be vigilant sentinels—"

As the director drones on into patriotic rhetoric, Mark finds his mind wandering. He will receive his specific assignment in a matter of just a few minutes, just before he takes off. The rest of the briefing will just be hot air.

"HoloVision."

The silvery voice again answers: "System ready to obey your every command, to fulfill your every wish, and to realize your every dream."

"Shrink secure transmission. Zoom in on speaker in the center." At this, the assembly disappears, and the director immediately becomes a less imposing figure, less authoritative, and ironically, less boring, about the size of a small dog.

With his portapack controller module, Mark moves the director all around the compartment, bounces him up and down, runs him in circles and squares, and impels movement creating other geometric patterns.

But to no avail, he is still dull.

Let's try the Paint'n'Sculpt program. And let's see if we can make the chief a little more exciting, more handsome.

Mark first gives the director a moustache and a beard, grows it, shrinks it, and experiments with various colors. Since the director is bald, Mark graciously restores his hair but then decides that he looks better without hair. To compensate, he gives him earrings, a few tattoos, and a nose ring to give him a more macho air.

The director is concluding his remarks. "Sorry, sir," Mark mutters to his boss, "No improvement. Maybe I just need to practice more with this program."

Finally Mark abandons his project and begins to think about how to get Angela back, or at least her image. How can he talk her into another marriage contract? Does he really want her back? At the start, they seemed to have lots of things in common: they worked out together, they partied, they traveled, and they liked the shows.

But Angela had changed. She had become ever more obsessed with causes, spirituality, fringe ideologies, moving from one flakey group to another. First, she got hooked up with that Enviro-Vegan-something-or-other bunch. Then there were the Stargazers, the UniMonde, the Purifiers, and now the Lumena. Early on, Mark went along with her, but then the meetings, the practices, and the rituals required began to invade and consume both their lives. He had hoped that she would eventually become disillusioned with them all, since none of what they were teaching ever appeared to work or have any practical value. He had never quite figured out how to wean her from their influence. There was no real hope of a happy relationship until she had her eyes opened. Maybe he should go to the meeting and see if he could find something that would discredit the group and somehow convince Angela, and...

His thoughts then turn to the communications assistant, Birth of Venus. He pushes the droning director's image off to the side.

"HoloVision."

The female voice again answers: "System ready to obey your every command, to fulfill your every wish, and to realize your every dream."

"'Romance Two.' Replace blond female in boat with 'Birth of Venus.'" Mark has tied his portapack into the compartment's system of microprojectors to enhance the voxel quality of the holographic scene.

Mark instantly views the park with a lake. And sitting across from Mark-1 the new communications assistant, like a new Eve, freshly placed in the Garden of Delights. She is in the boat, that is, the half of her visible in the original image; the bottom half has been created by the program based on physical probability forecasting.

Nice, but the program needs a few fresh touches. He looks forward to working with this new material. "Save as 'Romance Two. Venus on the water,'" he commands and then closes the program.

The audio speaker announces: "Naples in ten minutes!" The director's image is still off to the side, muted. Now he is waving his arms slightly as he speaks.

Okay, time to see what's happening in the world.

He commands: "News in English." Six 360-D icons appear floating before him with labels and previews. An enthusiastic voice announces "News and Views of Rome from inside the Bolla, from on the street, and from around the world. Please select."

Marks studies the icon labels. "Entertainment for Feast Days." "Actions by the Senate." "World News," "European Federation in Talks for Greater Unity." "The United States Sees Hopeful Progress in Drug Wars." "Weather Inside and Out."

Mark selects "Weather."

Scenes of Rome parade before him, and an enthusiastic weatherman appears and declares: "The weather is perfect in the Eternal City, the land of perpetual springtime. Outside the dome, no Rogue Storms are in the forecast. Toxic levels in the Haze will be high through Wednesday, and a 20% chance of mild volcanic activity."

"World News."

"Russia and China have entered their second week of talks to try to resolve ongoing border disputes. Israel has expressed confidence in its new defensive energy shield, although the military build-up around its borders has increased significantly in recent days. And a fragile cease fire between Iran and Iraq ended this morning when—"

"Entertainment."

The entertainment icon displays options with 360-D previews. Playing at the Coliseum, *Thermopylae*. At the Circus Maximus, "Gladiators Galore, Guts, Gore, and More!" At the Theater of Pompeii, "Love Quadrangles," and the Theater of Marcellus, "Trilogy of Tears."

Mark watches a few previews of *Thermopylae, the* war, and then some scenes of the gladiators in action but thinks, *I've already seen the holomovie twice. Plus, I'd rather do real combat or at least play a hologame myself, but watching someone else fight? Waste of time!* And "Trilogy of Tears?" Emotional slop. Finally he selects "Love Quadrangles" and watches previews, only to shut it off after a few minutes. *Same deal. I prefer the real thing. I don't want to watch someone else.* Still, he might check with Paolo, Massi, or Gilberto to see if they would want to go see a show or go bar-hopping later in the week. Time to seize the day. Time to spread his wings and fly. Time to check out the new communications assistant.

—4—

ROGUE SANDSTORM

For every new technology, there exists a counter technology that will disrupt it, block it, jam it, or render it partially ineffective. The Federation is not engaged in a traditional arms race but in a contest between magnetic signatures, a tech race, and the leader is defined in terms of microseconds and microbytes in cyberspace. For now, Rome's superior tech-power is faster and creative, and its opponents' capabilities are only destructive.

Mark arrives in Naples and proceeds to the base. The city also has an energy dome, but it covers far less area and is much less spectacular. Like many other smaller European cities, much of Naples's population has relocated to underground dwellings and passageways or air-tight units on the surface, many resembling large independent compounds that provide a fair degree of security for residents.

Deep under the former NATO airbase near the city, hundreds of Prochain Mirage fighters prepare for take-off to relieve Alpha-Wing, which has been patrolling for twelve hours due to the Orange Alert. The titanium ceiling retracts slowly, and dim sunlight shines down into the massive caverns. Mark is finishing a routine systems check of the mother craft and daughter drone. He looks out his cockpit window at a sea of aircraft about to lift off vertically and ascend to different altitudes.

At the green light, a controlled explosion of engines lifts all the planes skyward, as if Vesuvius had erupted, and thundering fighters ascend only seconds apart with digital precision to preprogrammed altitudes and then blast off to their patrol routes.

Mark and his two warplanes have been assigned a path dangerously close to the northern border of the African continent. The flying armada of aircraft spreads out at blinding speed, forming a seemingly impenetrable blockade, like monstrous spiders spinning a massive web, scanning, looking for prey.

Mark makes an initial run westward, eventually passing southern Spain before turning back eastward. "*No cowboy antics this time,*" he thinks. "*This is not a drill.*" He remembers this ominous reminder broadcast through BattleNet just before take-off. He whispers, "And this is not a dream.... I hope."

Mark flies on for several more hours, detecting no suspicious activity. He is listening to Tchaikovsky, first to Swan Lake, which makes him think of Angela, who danced ballet for a few years. A bit later, he switches to The 1812 Overture. Mark enjoys hearing the sound of cannons booming suggested by the big drums. *Perfect prelude to combat.* The music becomes steadily more intense as it builds up to the measures with bells that sound like a victory celebration.

As the overture nears completion, the ride becomes unexpectedly rough, and Mark hears a high-pitched sound. He looks at his sensors, but they are registering nothing unusual. He decides to switch to manual control and sets the drone daughter craft on "mirror."

Mark struggles with the stick, but systems all read normal, except that both planes are descending and changing course to the south. His heartbeat and breathing accelerate. "Tractor beam? They surely don't have that yet."

He looks out his cockpit windows, left, right, up...nothing. His fighters have turned, or have been turned, toward the African continent and are continuing to descend. Mark fights with the controls and starts giving verbal commands to the systems. No response.

Mark realizes he is coming in for a landing in the middle of nowhere.

After several minutes of losing altitude, the planes drop abruptly and violently hit the desert sand. They skid, and eventually come to a complete halt, leaving Mark bewildered. He looks out, trying to assess the situation and to understand what has just happened. He has indeed landed in the desert and is surrounded by dunes.

"This can't be!!!" he shouts out to no one. "A nightmare can't become real! It was just a dream!" He looks again to the right, and then to the left, expecting to see someone or something. Not a soul, nothing but sand piled high on every side. His compass is spinning, and his GPS is blank, as are the instruments on his panel.

From a transponder inside his flight suit, Mark sends out a distress signal, but he receives no reply. He tunes his radio receiver to see if other pilots have run into trouble. He picks up a transmission from HQ to all combatants.

"Several units have engaged the enemy. Their disruptors are mostly ineffective, but they may have developed some sort of barrier ray projector that could be used more effectively if they find a more effective power source. However, no aircraft are missing. All are accounted for. Details to follow." The emergency receiver then unexplainably shuts down. His plane has no power. He cannot transmit further.

What? I'm not missing? He switches on the homing beacon, but it doesn't appear to be working either.

Mark looks over at his drone daughter craft, which has maintained the prescribed distance from his plane, but it seems dark and powerless as well. He pulls the manual release for the cockpit cover, grabs his desert survival kit, and climbs out, dropping to the sand.

The wind is picking up. He halfway expects to turn and be confronted with something or someone. He feels like Neil Armstrong, just landed on the moon. Mark looks down and presses his boot into the sand, leaving a slight impression, which is quickly erased by a gust of hot wind. He withdraws his flash-plasma side arm and points it to a nearby dune. He squeezes, and much to his relief, the weapon discharges and liquefies the sand on contact.

While dragging his survival kit, Mark begins trying to climb a sandbank close to him, which he does with some difficulty. As he reaches the top, he turns in a circle gazing in every direction. Then he looks back down at his two warplanes, which are lifeless and defenseless, of no help at all. The wind is picking up even more. If it gets any worse, the planes might be completely buried within an hour or less. And he might, too—.

Again, he looks in all directions, but he sees only a sea of dunes made restless by the wind.

Wait.

To the east, he sees a front. Could be a Rogue Storm approaching. Mark identifies a relatively level area, descends to it, and pulls his tent out of his survival pack. Again much to his relief, it opens and quickly assumes a ball shape large enough for him and possibly one other person. He slips inside, sealing the entrance. The kit's small mobile power pack appears to be functioning. He will have sufficient food, water and energy to endure any storm for at least twenty-four hours, and maybe longer. The tent is programmed to stay upright and to keep him from being buried, but the wind still might toss him around, depending on how bad it gets.

Mark looks out the neoplastic porthole and observes that the storm has picked up speed and is moving his direction, boiling like a bizarre hurricane of dust, reshaping the face of the desert. He sits, watches, and waits. It looks like it might be a Rogue Storm, the worst kind. This is going to be bad.

As the winds become more intense, Mark sees what looks like a faint fire inside the central cloud and bolts of lightning all around the surface. Strange. Maybe it's just a mirage. He hopes it's only a mirage. It's certainly not a dream. Well, probably not.

The raging sand is becoming increasingly denser, intermittently obstructing his view.

Suddenly Mark thinks he hears a shrill voice, someone crying out. He can't make out what the voice is saying. He looks out the portholes on each side and squints his eyes. On one side, he sees what might be a small human form about fifteen meters from his pod. *It's probably the wind howling, but it sounds like a child. That's impossible. Out here?*

Mark continues to watch and listen. The cries are louder and more frequent. The storm's power is increasing.

Then, the cries abruptly stop. Now he has to investigate.

Mark opens the pod, crawls out, and staggers out in the general direction of the voice, struggling to drag the tent behind him. He is still wearing his helmet. The visor is starting to fog up a little, but he can't take it off.

"Hello!" he shouts into a built-in mike. His voice is amplified by a speaker in his helmet. "Is anyone out there?"

No response.

Mark thinks he sees a dark shadow about five meters ahead. It's a bulk that seems to be moving and sinking into the sand. He leaps ahead and as he does his hand slips from the handle for the tent, which is quickly blown away by the wind and disappears. Forget finding it. He has to reach the shadow, which is still sinking. He lunges but grabs...only sand. In a panic, he begins trying to dig with his hands.

Nothing.

"Where are you?" Mark yells. He turns, looking back for his tent. He then gets up and starts running, only to be blown over by a strong gust of hot wind; he tumbles down the side of a newly formed dune. Once he is stable, he begins fighting the fury of the wind, trying to get to his feet. He falls again and again. It's no use. He finally lies down in the sand, resigned, as if awaiting his own inevitable burial. He has long hoped to die in combat, but this? This isn't even a good hologame ending.

As Mark meditates on his coming demise, he hears another sound that doesn't belong in the desert. He tries to sit up and wipe off the visor on his helmet. He squints, and thinks he sees a faint light. "Another mirage?" he wonders. But the sand is rapidly covering him.

The sandstorm moves relentlessly, billowing and shooting clouds of dust a hundred stories high, an all-consuming desert monster driven by warring air currents, rolling along as if alive.

But he sees a light shining through the thick, moving veil of sand—no, several lights. After just a few moments, Mark can discern a hemispherical shape, a craft, four blue flames from engines on its perimeter and numerous floodlights all around.

He hears an amplified voice: "I've got you, Captain Knutson!!!"

The ship hovers over Mark and descends closer to him. Its underbelly opens, and two arms appear, grabbing Mark and pulling him inside. A blower initiates a quick clean-up of Mark and the sand inside the small ship, which is probably only about four to five meters in diameter and three meters high. It is shaped like an impossible ladybug. The underbelly closes and seals itself with a loud pop. The wind outside continues to rock the small craft.

The pilot helps Mark remove his helmet. He is a large man with wavy blond hair, burly and jovial; he is about a half-head taller than Mark.

"Master Sergeant Mikhail Mikhailovich Drevnerussky, Search and Rescue, at your service, sir!"

"Thanks! Are you really Russian?"

"*Da!*" He laughs. "Did you not catch the 'russky' part?"

"Yeah, but all the Russians I know who speak English have at least a slight accent."

"Ah! Russian father, American mother. I think you are going to be okay now," he reassures Mark. "I am glad to see you alive!"

"I'm happy to see you as well! I wasn't sure my homing beacon was working. I lost all power."

"Well," the sergeant responds, "the signal was weak, and the storm didn't help, but at least there was no jamming from the pirate coalition. This is an unusually powerful storm, and I think even they have taken cover."

"Thanks for hanging in there and finding me in all this. I thought it was all over!"

"Oh, captain, have faith! I have never yet failed to recover a pilot. You will be no exception. I bring them back alive and well, always."

"Okay, thanks again. But before I lost power, I heard a communication that all warplanes had returned safely."

"I'm not sure I heard that one. With your permission, I'll secure the craft. This is a bad storm, and it's getting worse." Mikhail moves to the pilot section and busies himself at the controls, studying readouts, sensor stability, and programming functions. The windshield is thick and small. Mikhail shuts down the exterior lights, so the glass portal goes black.

"The storm will probably bury us, at least for a time, but we will escape. We will rise!" he exclaims, "As from the dead, eh, captain?" He laughs boisterously.

"If you say so, sergeant. For a while there, I really thought I was going to die."

"Perhaps you are hungry? Here, have something to eat." The sergeant pulls out several containers of rations. "What would you like to drink?"

"Do you have Coca-Cola?"

"Done!"

Outside, the fury of the storm is unabated, but the small ship remains relatively stable.

"Captain, if you have anything that needs to be recharged, feel free."

"How about my side arm and portapack? With all this energy loss, I'd feel better with them fully charged."

"Should be no problem. Right there, on the bulkhead." Mark pulls them from his flight suit and plugs them in.

"Would you like a little music to pass the time, captain? Maybe some Tchaikovsky?"

"Actually I was just listening to several of his pieces."

"Good choice."

"But no offense, how about something else, or even something else that's Russian?"

"Do you like Rimsky-Korsakov? Perhaps Scheherazade?"

"Okay, that's relaxing. I just hope we aren't here for a thousand and one nights."

"Ha! Done."

The hemispherical pod fills with the sounds of a symphony orchestra intoning the mystery and beauty of the mellifluous female story teller.

"A time to dream, is it not?" asks Mikhail with some seriousness.

"God, I hope not," Mark says.

"Eh?"

"Sorry, it's very nice. I actually love it, and I love classical music in general."

"So, the warrior has a heart?"

Mark does not reply.

The sergeant thinks for a moment and then remarks, "I don't know how long the storm will last. We'll just have to ride it out. Then, I can get you back to headquarters in Naples safe and sound. I've already notified them that I've found you."

"Do you have any holographic programs or games on this ship?" Mark asks.

"Yes, several, but just for a moment perhaps we can chat and get to know each other. Tell war stories maybe? I usually don't get to spend much time with those I rescue, and sometimes they're unconscious for a good while."

"Sure, I think I'm conscious." Mark laughs for the first time. "So how long have you been with Search and Rescue?"

"A little over four years. I love to save lives. I suppose I prefer that over taking them. No offense."

"None taken. I love being a pilot. And I am just doing what has to be done." Suddenly Mark remembers, "By the way, as you approached, did your sensors pick up any life forms nearby?"

"Of course not!" Mikhail responded, "I would have rescued them along with you! Why do you ask?"

"I just thought I saw someone out there as the sandstorm was picking up. Thought I heard a cry for help."

"The desert sun creates illusions, sometimes an oasis, or sometimes an invading army. The wind and sand can make shadows come alive. They both play deceptive tricks. Even more so when there's a storm approaching and the wind is violent, like with this one. I saw only you on infrared."

"I'm just relieved that I didn't miss anyone out there."

"I think no one would be out here, except us, the soldier and his angel, so to speak."

"So to speak, but a pretty good angel. I like your success rate."

They both lean back in their chairs at the rear of the craft.

"So you're from Russia, but your mom is...?"

"Actually my family lived in Moscow until I was fourteen. We then moved to Israel. Later, I spent a few years in California as a medic before the situation deteriorated there. Then I came to Rome because my family lives there, and I wanted to join the cause of saving lives for EuroSecure. How about you?"

"I'm from Oklahoma originally. Mostly German and part Cherokee, actually one fourth. I always wanted to be a pilot. I made some runs with the U.S. Border Patrol in the war against the cartels and even stuck it out through the big reorganization. They needed more helicopter pilots. Ultimately it seemed a losing proposition."

"Do you think defending Rome is a 'losing proposition' perhaps?"

"I like the life there."

"Worth fighting for?"

"I'm here, aren't I?"

"Of course."

"Hey, off subject, but how about that new communications assistant? Have you seen her?"

"I'm not sure. What is the name of this new communications assistant? Is she just for your wing or for the airbase? I think our section is structured differently. We have a different mission and receive different orders. Our assistant is a man."

"Honestly, I don't know. There has been a lot of administrative shuffling around recently, but I have her image stored in my portapack. If we have enough juice, I'll show you."

Mark connects to the ship's system and then activates the portapack with his fingers over the pack and orders, "Show 'Birth of Venus.'"

She is quickly projected into the craft, her top half in 360-D. Oddly, Mark is glad to see her.

"Why, yes, I actually do know her."

"Really!" Mark acts excited for the first time. "Tell me, who is she? What do you know?"

"Her name is Dominique Lécuyer. I'm sorry. I don't know her terribly well. I was not aware that she is now a communications assistant. She must have been promoted fairly recently. You are interested in her..., romantically perhaps?"

"Uh, yes! I mean, look at her! *Bella, bella!*"

Mikhail laughs, "She is certainly beautiful, so perhaps we should listen to Beethoven, Für Elise, or something similar for those in love?"

"Okay, can you tell me anything else about her?"

"I don't know a whole lot more, captain. When we get back to headquarters, perhaps I can show you where her office is."

"That will do nicely. Thanks!"

Mother and daughter lie buried in the sand. If they are not also rescued, pirate predators will come and find them. The storm unleashes its power unhindered. Eventually it will reach the sea and create maritime mirages and aquatic sculptures.

—5—

SLEEPING BEAUTY – INFINITY VERSION

"Captain, this storm could last more than an hour. It seems to be stalled. Can I offer you some entertainment, beyond great music? You asked about games?"

"Sure! What do you have?"

"Perhaps you know the hologame, *Sleeping Beauty*?"

"Version 24? I've played it many times."

"That's the game, but this particular version is just out. *Sleeping Beauty - Infinity Version.*"

"Infinity Version? What does that mean?

"Let me show you." Mikhail hands him a helmet along with transparent gloves, boots, and a waistband. They both don their instruments of virtual war.

Mikhail turns on the power, and Mark finds himself with his new friend in the middle of a desert. He is wearing armor, but Mikhail is not.

"So you just ejected us outside, right?"

"No," Mikhail laughs, "you are still in the rescue craft. This is just the first level."

"Okay, how does it work?"

"This is the easiest level on the road to saving the sleeping princess. However, even here we can adjust the level of difficulty, number and type of opponents, and various other elements."

"How hard can the levels get, and how many opponents can you face?"

"That's just it. No limit. That's the 'infinity' part."

"I've played at level twelve. I'm not sure how it could be more difficult. You can only take on so many opponents."

"The game has no real limit to difficulty or opponents or types of scenarios, and there's the challenge. No matter how good you get, there's always room for improvement."

"Bring it on."

"I choose a sword and a chain, one with special properties." Mikhail stretches out his hands, and the weapons appear. "And you?"

"Give me a flash-plasma blaster or two."

"Sorry, this game is lower tech, more traditional warrior-style fighting. Perhaps a sword and a shield to start?"

"Flash saber?"

"No, just a sturdy sword and shield. You can use the shield effectively, as you will see."

Mark nods in assent, and the sword and shield appear in his hands.

"I don't care for these low-tech weapons, but I have to say, this new version is amazingly realistic. Incredible graphics and effects!"

"This particular game goes well beyond the current usage of avatars or even 360-D visual. It creates an interface between the AI and your neurons, creating a dream-like effect."

"Wow! I didn't know the technology was that far along. AI interface with neurons is still a little sketchy. How is it dream-like?"

"When you play an ordinary game, you are mostly conscious that it is a game and that you are wearing a helmet and gloves or in more advanced games, a waistband and boots. But when you dream, you believe everything you see is real, even though it's only a dream. Similar principle here."

Mark continues to look around. "It certainly looks real. It's hard to imagine that I am actually just wearing a helmet and the other gear." Mark is a little apprehensive about being in anything dream-like, especially in the middle of a desert, but this is a dream he can control himself, more like when he toasted that chieftain in his apartment.

"Now let's look at one of our opponents. This will give you a good idea of how it works and what the possibilities are." Mikhail takes off his right glove and adjusts the game controls; a small scorpion appears on the sand about five meters in front of them, at which Mark bursts out laughing.

"Whoa! I'm scared already!"

"Patience. Let me ramp this thing up." He makes an adjustment, and the scorpion instantly grows to three meters in height.

"Okaaaaaay!"

"I haven't started it, not to worry...yet. How about another level or two of difficulty? Say, acid coming from its legs, its claws, and its stinger? Of course, it presents no real danger to you. It will only seem to eat away at your armor. And by the way, you can jump up to six meters in the air, but remember, it can jump as well."

"Okay, sure. I've done things similar to this in other games."

"And just another little touch." Mikhail makes an adjustment and transforms the black emperor scorpion into what looks like a jeweled brooch with emeralds set in gold, dazzling rubies for eyes, and claws and legs of sterling silver."

"Nice. Surreal, beautiful, and deadly," Mark responds, somewhat in awe.

"Of course, it's not real. You will want to remember that as we begin the game. To start, I'll let you take the lead."

"I think I'll remember. Bring it."

At this, Mikhail commands, "Activate."

The emperor scorpion comes to life. It immediately spots its prey and begins its advance toward them. Mark begins running without hesitation toward the impossible bejeweled monster vermin. Mark moves quickly to meet his challenger. He is confident; he is skilled at this type of game.

First, he catapults himself over the insect, which repeatedly snaps at him in the air, trying to bring him down. He thinks that he will have a brief advantage out of its range of vision, but he quickly realizes it has four eyes, two rubies in the front and two in the back, and it lunges its stinger at him.

Diabolical, he thinks as he lands. He leaps again and while in the air takes out one of the eyes with a slash of his sword. A stinger barely misses him. He lands on its left side and severs one of its claws as he does. But the scorpion is incredibly, perhaps unnaturally fast and spins around to catch him with the other claw, which it does. It grabs part of Mark's leg armor, and he falls to the sand.

"*I needed that*," Mark thinks. He cuts off the claw and jumps again, this time toward the head, ramming his sword into the insect's brain. He mounts its back and repeatedly runs it through. It finally drops to the sand, dead.

Mikhail claps. "Very impressive, captain! I commend you."

As Mark climbs down off the mammoth dead bug, he comments, "Thanks, but I've done a scenario fairly similar to this one before. I assume you've mastered this level?"

"Oh, I've practiced it countless times, but I still come back to it. Always good to drill the basics. Here, let me show you."

Mikhail resets the scene. "Okay, let's increases the size of the scorpion by five, restore its missing parts, and ratchet up its speed by ten. Let's let it breath fire, and have acid shooting out of it claws and stinger."

Mark quips, "Uh, good luck. Let me know if I can help. You know, you have no shield or armor."

"I never use them."

Mikhail stands motionless as the megamonster bug attacks at seemingly lightning speed, but Mikhail seems to move faster than lightning. He jumps, and the insect attempts to snag him and blows acid toward him. It also tries several times to roast him with its fiery breath.

It's all almost a blur to Mark. Then, Mikhail jumps and lands on the beast's left side in between its stinger and its claw. As it turns and faces its human opponent, Mikhail is spinning his chain over his head. When he releases it, the chain flies through the air and, like a power saw, severs the claws, the legs, and the stinger in a series of blindingly fast yet precisely calculated movements. The monster is rendered impotent.

Mikhail looks at Mark. "Practice makes perfect. It's all in the wrists, captain."

Mark just stands there, in shock.

"Are you sure you should still be in Search and Rescue?"

"Ha! This is only a game, Captain Knutson. Real combat is far more challenging, as you know. Shall we move to the next level? It's just over that ridge."

As they cross over, the landscape begins to look like a central African plain, with the same type of trees Mark had seen there when he had hunted in Tanzania years before.

"Let me guess: lions? I've faced off with real lions, you know."

"Not exactly, but you are almost right. These are partly lions, and some of them are armed."

"Really. Partly lions? Armed lions? How does that work?"

Mikhail calls the new foes into existence. Four warriors are in the distance running toward them.

"Only four opponents?" Mark asks.

"We can raise the number of opponents to the power of infinity. You can just pick your number. But before you think about taking on more, watch and see."

Mark looks up and notices four large birds flying over the heads of the four warriors, maybe eagles. They fan out and begin circling like vultures, but wait, coming from yet another direction are four additional creatures that run like lions. A total of twelve opponents. As they close in, Mark begins to see the truth: they are all hybrids, different combinations of man, eagle, bull, and lion. He will be facing flying lions with eagle's wings, lions with the face and horns of a bull, and men with lion heads.

Mikhail freezes the action. "For this level, you may choose two more weapons."

"How can I manipulate all four of them?"

"Simple, here are two more arms." And two arms sprout out of Mark's middle torso. "Also, you can jump twice as high."

"Outstanding! I'll take another sword and a mace covered with spikes." The weapons appear, and Mark briefly warms up, swinging his mace and swords in synchronous rhythm without allowing them to collide with each other. He keeps the shield in front of him.

"I'll let you start. By the way, these are more challenging than the scorpion. There are twelve of them, and each group has a sort of specialty, plus the man-lions carry weapons."

Mikhail reactivates the program. Mark begins running away from all three groups, and all three turn in pursuit. Now and then, he stops and turns around to assess his enemies. He watches how they move and respond to him. The eagle-lions have caught up first and begin their attack, extending their talons—no, they are large claws. These are lions with wings, jaws, and claws.

Mark turns back and runs toward the flying felines; he leaps high into the air to meet them. With two rapid sweeps of his sword, he decapitates one and clips the right wing of another. Both bodies fall to the ground.

Mark jumps again. He lands and is ready to take on the bull-faced lions with horns, who meet his challenge and come running at him at full charge. He leaps toward them.

As Mark comes down swinging his mace and his swords, he narrowly misses the horns of one; he plants one sword deep into its heart but cannot retrieve it. With the mace, he bashes in the head of another. He spins and smashes the bull-face of the third lion with his shield. The fourth charges him and attempts to gore him, but he leaps aside and brings his sword around, cutting off its front two legs.

The four men with lion heads are catching up, and the remaining two eagle-lions are behind him. Six opponents left.

"The odds are better now," Mark thinks. Mikhail is observing the contest from a fair distance. "The odds are better now!" he shouts.

As the four lion-headed men warriors approach, Mark sees that they each have two weapons, swords and another object that Mark cannot identify. They have lion heads and teeth, and they roar. Initially, they circle him. He is down to one sword but he still has his mace and shield. Overhead, the remaining two eagle-lions are descending rapidly.

Mark begins swinging the mace over his head. All the creatures slow their advance, watching for his next move. Suddenly he does a cartwheel to his left, using the force of the mace and brings it down on one of the warriors, smashing his lion head and then jumping up high enough to take out another of the descending eagle-lions.

Four opponents left. *No challenge here.*

Back on the ground, he regains his footing, and he is ready. But the creatures begin to act oddly. The lion-faced men roar and simultaneously hurl something at Mark.

Magnetized bolas incoming. The remaining lion-eagle swoops down and blocks Mark's attempt at an evasive maneuver. Two of the bolas wrap themselves around his legs, and their magnets fasten tightly to his armor. He can't raise the mace fast enough, and two of the lion-faced men are suddenly behind him.

Mark falls to the ground.

Mikhail appears out of nowhere. He raises his right hand and the remaining creatures disappear. Everything goes dark.

Mark pulls off his helmet.

"What happened?"

"Sorry, captain, the craft sensors have just notified me that the sandstorm is waning. We'd best be making preparations to get underway. Are you all right?"

"Of course. Just a little frustrated! I was really close to winning. You can't send me back?"

"I'll save it, captain. We can't tell HQ that we were delayed because we were playing hologames in the desert, can we? Such activities are good for training and in rescue operations can be therapeutic, but my orders are to take you to safety as soon as possible."

"So how did you make those creatures disappear? Is there some disintegrator weapon?"

"No, sir, just the game genie. It's only a hologame, captain. Remember, it's not real."

Mikhail returns to the pilot seat. External light is showing through the small windshield. He studies the sensors.

"We are only partially buried now. It should be an easy lift-off. Go ahead and fasten yourself in."

At length Mikhail fires up the four engines, and the small craft begins to rise slowly. After a few minutes, he sets a course and blasts off toward the Mediterranean.

Mark leans back and breathes a sigh of relief. He feels frustrated again. He has lost his planes and lost at the game. But as consolation, the mystery of Dominique is still sweetly on his mind.

The ladybug ship begins picking up speed to two hundred kilometers per hour. Within minutes, it is cloaked and is flying at low altitude over the waves.

Hermes, invisible to mortal eyes, wearing his golden sandals, skimming over the sea like a low-flying gull, gliding over the whitecaps like a powerful gust of wind.

Mark feels drowsy as he listens to Beethoven's Sonata Quasi una fantasia (Moonlight). Maybe he can grab a power nap. Maybe he will have a better dream this time...

—6—

RENAISSANCE IN ROME

"Wake up, captain. We're approaching Naples."

Mark begins to stir. He feels exhausted.

Mikhail makes the craft transparent using exterior cameras and interior projectors as they near the harbor. Mark looks all around. He feels a sense of relief in seeing something familiar.

"Dive," commands Mikhail, and the ship submerges and descends to the security gates, which upon identifying the craft, open, allowing them entrance. They pass through various scans, and after a short time, emerge in an underground harbor with an enormous open area where other vessels are moored. Mikhail docks and shuts down power, and they both emerge from a hatch on the starboard side.

"Captain Knutson," says Mikhail as they approach the security portal, "I have enjoyed our time together. I hope to see you again sometime."

"I'm going to beat that game," vows Mark with a smile.

"I have no doubt."

"And don't forget. Tell me how I can meet Dominique...uh..."

"Lécuyer."

"Right. How can I contact you? What's your i-connect code?"

"I'll find you, captain. I promise. Remember, I'm good at finding people!"

"Point taken!" They both laugh and part company. Mark begins the check-in process.

He passes through another scan, and the guards look him over. One of them says, "Captain Knutson, your presence is requested in the office of the wing commander."

"Have they retrieved my warplanes?"

"I am not sure, sir. He may be able to clarify."

Back in the desert, a large hulking airship hovers over the sand at a low altitude. Its belly opens and a violent rush of wind comes out, blowing up a cloud of sand all around. The airstream continues until the ship finds its buried treasure: two Prochain Mirage fighters. A large hatch opens and long mechanical arms drop from inside the ship and fasten themselves on the mother. They quickly pick her up and ingest her. They again emerge to lift the daughter craft and swallow her. The hatch closes.

Saturn, devouring his children.

Mark enters the office of the wing commander and salutes.

Commander Murillo remains seated. "At ease, captain. Please take a seat."

Mark sits down but remains attentive. Murillo is a stern man but fair. Mark has great respect for him. He speaks fairly good English with a slight Spanish accent.

"We have retrieved your two warplanes. Initial reports are that they sustained no damage and seem to be working perfectly. What happened, captain? You're the only pilot who did not return back." The commander looks at him intently.

"Sir, I ran into some kind of energy field or tractor beam. It felt like an overwhelmingly strong wind, strong enough to force me to land. My stick was not responsive. I kept fighting with the controls and somehow set down. Eventually I had no power at all. I'm sorry, sir, I can't explain it."

"Very well, captain. You're a good pilot and officer with an excellent record, but I'm putting you on temporary reassignment while all this is being investigated. It's quite unusual. We have to be sure that there were no security leaks. And if what you say is true, the enemy may be experimenting with some new technology, which is what we have suspected."

"Commander, I was rescued by—"

"I know who rescued you. I don't know him personally, but he has a good record. We will make questions to him."

Murillo stands up, and Mark stands as well.

"Take a few days off, Captain. Then, on Wednesday, report to Roman Security Headquarters. I believe you spent a number of years with them in the Praetorian Guard."

"Sir, I feel I am ready to get back in the air."

"You have your orders, captain. You'll be notified when and if you are to return to aviation patrol. I understand that the Roman security office has some concerns right now. Rome can use your experience. Your reassignment should be easy to explain to those who may need to know, since you have spent previous time with the guard and given those heightened security issues. Dismissed."

"Yes, sir." Mark stands, salutes, and exits the room in sharp military fashion. Once he is well down the hall, he strikes the wall with his fist. He enters the elevator to go up to the surface, and he strikes his fist against the elevator wall. What is he going home to? He has been twice defeated, once by an invisible enemy he could never see, and a second time by a hologame. And all that with Angela's desertion. He hits the wall of the elevator several more times.

As Mark enters the station to catch the hypertrain home, he hears someone call his name in a sea of people.

"Captain Knutson!" Mark turns and sees Mikhail.

"Sergeant." He is glad to see a friendlier, more supportive face.

"How fortunate that we should run into each other so quickly! You are headed to Rome, yes? So am I. I have just been given a few days off."

"The wing commander told me you would be questioned about what you saw in the desert."

"I've filed a preliminary report. They told me they would contact me when they are ready for further questions. I'm not typically furloughed after a rescue. I guess they have special concerns because of the unusual circumstances. Anyway, they know where to find us, do they not?"

"Right."

The two board the train and search for a seat.

Mikhail whispers in Mark's ear: "Captain, it is again your lucky day! Let's sit here."

Mark looks at the seats. Across from them is...Venus.

Mark is dumbfounded. Unexpectedly ecstatic, but stunned. He looks at Mikhail a little suspiciously.

"Dominique! *Quelle surprise!*"

"Mikhail! *Comment ça va?*" She smiles. It is a far more beautiful smile than he had previously imagined. *No woman could be this beautiful. It's impossible!*

"Dominique, permit me to introduce to you Captain Mark Knutson."

Mark stretches out his hand nervously, and the train jerks, causing him to fall back clumsily into a seat facing Dominique. Mikhail sits down next to him.

Trying to recover, he rambles, "You're the new communications assistant? I believe you did the security alert briefing as I was coming to Naples just this morning..., or was that yesterday? What is today? Sorry, I guess I've just had a long day. Mikhail here rescued me in the desert." Mark hoped she would find his disorientation amusing, but instead he thinks it has had the opposite effect. Trying to recover, he repeats his question, "You are the new communications assistant?"

"I am." Dominique smiles briefly and then looks out the window. Mark likewise looks out and tries to discreetly activate the camera on his portapack.

"So how long have you been a communications assistant?"

Dominique looks at Mark and smiles wryly. "That's classified, captain." She then looks out the window again.

Mikhail breaks the ice. "Dominique, it seems we have not spoken in some time. We should get together with those friends we have in common. Perhaps Captain Knutson could join us?"

"Perhaps."

In person, Dominique is way beyond Venus. Mark hopes that terrorists are not currently jamming signals or anything. He hopes that his portapack camera is working perfectly and aimed correctly.

Dominique seems distracted, still staring out the window. Mark is dying to study her full face. He notices a slight reflection in the window, which he tries to observe without being observed.

Dominique's hair is jet-black but glossy and smooth, and her skin is milky white. She has crossed her legs and is leaning on her right palm as she watches the landscape pass by. She is wearing a bracelet of tiny cockle shells. Mark can see only her profile, part of her lips, her long eyelashes, and almost sculpted black eyebrows that set off those eyes...those big eyes that he could get lost and very confused in. She looks like a professional model, even in military garb. Mark will study her images more closely when he returns to the apartment.

Trying not to stare, he reels out his pad from his portapack and begins sending texts to various friends, inviting them to hang out around Rome with him over the next few days.

He looks up again. Her lips are like fruit, a glossy red apple that he would like to... *"I'm writing a poem,"* Mark thinks. *"No,"* he muses, *"I'm looking at a poem."* Mark has never before cared much for poetry.

As they arrive at Rome's perimeter, they pass under the Bolla and through two security scans.

"I've given Mikhail my i-connect code. Let him know if you all would like to take in a show or something."

"Thank you, captain," Dominque replies politely. "I'm afraid that I don't do shows." She stands up. "Mikhail, good to see you. Captain, *enchantée.*" She turns and begins her exit.

"I'll be in touch," Mikhail assures Mark as he stands and leaves him.

Mark departs the hypertrain station and takes an aerocab to his own building. Inside the Bolla, the sky is filled with vehicles of all sizes. Everywhere you look, there are walkways, crossovers, and stairs, plus aerobikes, aerocabs, and aerocars, all flying every which way with never a collision. Rome is a beehive of activity night and day. The transport synchronization program is flawless and actually creates a distinctive kind of beauty, a harmonious symphony of moving lights and vehicles of many shapes and sizes.

In minutes, Mark arrives at his building and enters his personal pod which he has previously called down. He rockets up one hundred fifty-six floors. As he enters his room, he almost runs to Pinocchio. Mark stops and plugs his portapack into him.

"Welcome home, Gepetto."

"Access and play last recording!" He orders with a certain excitement. Pinocchio complies and channels it to HoloVision. "System ready to obey your every command, to fulfill your every wish, and to realize your every dream."

Mark blurts out, "You got that right, lady!"

As the lights come up, the image is forming. Venus will be born again right before his eyes. But wait, the initial image is of her legs, unfortunately covered by her uniform pants. Mark struggles to adjust the angle.

Finally he sees that he had eventually moved correctly, and there she is, in full and glorious view, in 360-D, living color, looking out the window. "Come on, I know you looked at me, even oh so briefly." Eventually Dominique did glance toward him while he was texting.

"Capture now and extrapolate."

Like a sculptor fashioning a statue, a hi-tech Pygmalion, Mark reshapes the holoimage and gives it new life. He raises two chairs from the floor in the entertainment area, sits down in one, and seats Venus across from him, freezing the image. She is now looking at him without looking away, smiling at him without refraining from smiling.

The voxels are of extremely high resolution. The recorder camera has captured the indescribable beauty of her dark eyes, their sparkle, and their mysterious quality. He feels himself melting as he is gazing on her beauty, not thinking of unrequited love, or of Angela, or of his recent defeats, not even about the cool treatment he received from her. Mark is dreaming again. *Carpe diem*.

"Pinocchio or somebody. Play Ravel, Boléro."

The faint, distant sound of light percussion and a flute begins the magic of music to echo the enchantment of Dominique's countenance. As Mark meditates on the image, a piccolo, a harp, an oboe d'amore, and other woodwinds begin to do their work in rhythmic sequence.

"HoloVision."

"System ready to obey your every command, to fulfill your every wish, and to realize your every dream," again announces the familiar female voice.

"Replay all audio on this portapack image sequence. Track. Analyze voice."

The French Aphrodite speaks: "Mikhail! *Comment ça va?*"

Mark loves this only moment of enthusiasm as the words come from her lips. And in French. She lights up.

The audio sequence continues its work in ingesting and re-sculpting Dominique's voice. "Replicate and insert voice with words 'Mark, *je t'aime!*'"

As ordered, the hologram professes love for Mark. "Mark, *je t'aime.*" Mark leans forward.

"Again."

"Mark, *je t'aime.*"

He sits back. "Female clothing selection. Expensive dresses." To his right an array of attractive dresses appears. He sees a red one he likes, snatches it from thin air, and hurls it at Dominique's image. It is long and silky, one she might wear to the opera, one that Angela would have never worn. Dominique has style and class that Angela lacks. Plus a certain enigmatic quality.

As Boléro intensifies, Mark again leans forward to touch her face, to try to imagine kissing her. He closes his eyes and kisses the air. His hand reaches for empty space and blocks one small section of projectors, temporarily disintegrating part of her face.

Mark sighs, leans back, and thinks to himself, *"You've got it bad, boy."* Boléro reaches its frenetic climax and ends. Mark closes his eyes.

"Tchaikovsky, Dance of the Sugarplum Fairy."

Mark is tired, but he opens his eyes irregularly to look at Dominique, who is frozen.... Venus de Milo never looked so hot. He closes his eyes again.

Mark is swimming in crystal clear water. As he comes up for air, he notices that Dominique is swimming beside him synchronously. He glances ahead and sees that they are approaching a waterfall. He sees a brilliant light behind the falling stream. They both reach the base and get out. Dominique runs under the cascade. Mark tries to speak to her, but he is unable. She is laughing and smoothing her hair back with her hands. The tumbling water runs down her face and arms and legs and glistens. She is more beautiful than he had ever imagined.

"I love you, Mark," the dream Dominique confesses. "I love you with all my heart."

Mark feels that he cannot breathe. He reaches out to embrace her. "I love you, Dominique! *Je t'aime!*"

As he lunges forward, he falls headlong down a sand dune. He raises himself and looks around in disbelief. He is awake now and on the floor. He yells, "I hate dreams!"

Mark notices that he has an incoming call. It's not Dominique but rather, Massimo Sansone.

"Hey, Knutson! Are you there?"

Mark remembers that he had sent Massi a message while on the train and that he had given Massi his special i-connect code last week. He looks up not at gorgeous Dominique but at Massimo, who is a sort of ugly hulk with a big chest and a loud mouth. Massi went to college in Florida.

He connects and answers, "Hey, Massi."

"Party time, Buddy! Get yourself in gear and meet us at the Coliseum about seven o'clock. We all chipped in and got a semi-private box with private room privileges. Bring Angela."

"Uh, we just split up."

"Oops! Sorry, man, my extremely bad."

"No prob. What's playing?"

"*Thermopylae.* Plus there's some live gladiatorial action before the main show. But hey, first I have to do an hour at the Curia

Julia. The senate is doing some business, and they are needing as many Praetorian Guard members as possible in the audience, even a former PG like you would be welcome. Bring your operations belt and oracle glasses if you still have them."

"Are they worried about uninvited visitors in cloak?"

"I think that's what the meeting's about."

After Massi disconnects, Mark looks at Pinocchio.

"You heard him! Get my belt and oracle glasses and other gear, and send a request for reactivation and connection to the security network."

In seconds, Pinocchio replies, "You are approved, upgraded, and connected, Gepetto."

"Outstanding, my son, maybe someday we'll get you upgraded, and you'll become a real boy."

"Thank you, my father," replies Pinocchio.

—7—

LA DOLCE VITA

Mark drops one hundred fifty-six stories down to ground level and steps out on to the street. Rome is ablaze with artificial lighting. Megabuildings, some over two hundred stories high, transform into larger-than-life ads every few minutes. It is a shifting rainbow of colors, a constant stream of images and marketing messages.

NIKE. A colossal runner in motion, but stationary.

Mark looks to his right. An old-style Coca-Cola bottle about fifteen stories high.

Looking to his left, he flags an aerocab from a line of them in front of his building. The cab stops, he gets in and scans his face to pay.

"Curia Julia."

The senate meets in the ancient stone structure, which has been refurbished and restored to be as close as possible to the original, and it is seemingly "no-tech." Only security personnel use advanced technology. Some architectural changes have been made to allow an audience of about one hundred in the gallery above. Cameras record the proceedings, but none is visible. Below is a forum with no microphones or sound system. Marble columns and three rows of stone benches on either side overlook an ornately tiled and colorful floor. Up front, an engraved stone podium oversees the assembly from a raised platform. High on the wall, over the podium, Mark sees a large engraving:

SPQR
Senātus Populusque Rōmānus

Mark took Latin in high school and understands the sign, but he is wearing his oracle glasses, and they automatically translate: "SPQR. The Senate and People of Rome." In the gallery above, there is standing room only, and Mark, Massimo, and other PGs maintain vigilance. Oracle glasses allow them to see into an unseen hi-tech world as well as empowering them to analyze everything in their field of vision.

All fifty senators are in attendance. Ninety some visitors fill the gallery; all were scanned thoroughly before entering.

The senators, both male and female, wear identical togas. They do not use their real names while in session but classical Roman names as honorary titles. Some names are those of historical members of the senate.

Lucius Aurelius Laurentius is president of the senate; he is anti-fascist and anti-religion.

The vice-president is Julia Severus, who is moderate in most issues.

Others in the leadership include Quintus Fabius Maximus, senatorial overseer of the Praetorian Guard, and Cultural Affairs Director Scholastica Mercator, both of whom are sympathetic to the idea of Rome welcoming a new Caesar.

Sextus Marcellus Fabricius is the secretary of state and is a moderate.

Finally Romanus Santori, overseer of the Roman justice system, who is anti-fascist and anti-religion.

The honorary Latin names are used in debates and are written in the record, although all senate business and discussions are conducted in Italian.

Magnus Clericus, the senate clerk, stands up and calls the meeting to order. Mark's Italian is fairly good, but he listens with Universal Translator.

"The City of Rome: Ruled by the will of the people of Rome, overseen by the people's representatives in the senate. Fifty senators assembled to protect the sweet life. Long live the dream. Long live Rome. Long live the Roman senate."

Applause.

Laurentius, the president, stands up to address the assembly. He wears a laurel wreath as a modest sign of his office. Laurentius is elderly and somewhat frail, but he still has a magnificent voice and rhetorical skills admired by all who hear him.

"Fellow senators and people of Rome, we meet today to continue an ongoing discussion about the proper governance of our beloved city at this time in her history. We have had a healthy debate thus far, for we all love Rome, the sweet life, and want only the best for Rome and its citizens. Long live the Roman dream!"

Applause.

"However, as we know, there exist elements outside the bubble that are bent on destroying Rome."

Mark is leaning against a wall and is already bored. He does not really feel needed. Massimo whispers in his ear: "Relax, Knutson. I appreciate your coming, but you're just here for back-up."

President Laurentius continues: "Rumors abound and intelligence reports are unclear as to the specific identity of some of these enemies of our city. A small number of groups have the ability to jam and disrupt our scans, sometimes our communications and a few of our weapons. But whatever their name or ideology, make no mistake, they are committed to the end of life as we know it, the good life, the sweet life."

The senator pauses for just a moment to cough. He takes a drink of water.

"Our principal concern is with a group we have called the Neo-Fascists, for want of a better term. They are well hidden from our technology and our operatives. Some believe they do not exist at all, at least that we are not aware of an organized group with fascist ideological designs on Rome. Others say they hide their troops and their armor in caves in the mountains on the peninsula and shield themselves from detection using technology they have stolen from us: Roman technology! All such claims and rumors are under constant investigation."

Laurentius does not elaborate on how the Neo-Fascists can have Roman technology unless certain Roman technology experts have leaked it to them.

President Laurentius goes on: "The question before us today is what actions the senate should take in order to be prepared for an appropriate response or perhaps a preemptory strike on such a group, if indeed such a group exists?"

Laurentius steps away from the podium and raises his voice slightly.

"Many issues have arisen. Do we expand the powers of the state? Of the Praetorian Guard? Of the senate? Or dare I suggest, those of your humble servant, the president of the senate? We know that some situations may require a swift, decisive response and that the senate is not known for its swiftness or efficiency, but do we dare take even a baby step and turn a free society into a police state in which certain fundamental civil rights would be surrendered? All our citizens surely have the right to pursue the sweet life as they see fit and in private!"

Laurentius paces to the right and then to the left, looking at the floor. He then turns to the assembly and concludes:

"Such conversations must be held. So much is at stake. I yield the podium to Senator Sextus Marcellus Fabricius, who will speak for those in favor of increasing certain executive powers."

Applause.

Fabricius is young and handsome. He has a classical Roman haircut but is wearing glasses, probably oracle glasses.

"Mr. President, distinguished senators, and noble people of Rome. It seems obvious to some of us that these perilous times require a more radical response. Special executive powers must be granted. These would include a greater latitude with regard to abridging selected civil rights in this war on terrorism and tracking possible suspects, yes, right here in Rome. We must respect all traditional judicial guarantees, but flexibility is required. Our president is clearly anti-Caesarian, however, we know him to be a trustworthy man who always consults with key leaders before making any important decision. I would suggest that we invest such powers into an executive committee that would include the president, Colonel Valenza, head of the Praetorian Guard and—"

Mark is still bored. Massi again whispers in his ear: "Hey, Knutson, hang in there. Relax. Would you believe that all the senators below are holographed? I just found out."

Mark rears back and looks at Massi, then looks at the senate, then looks again at Massi.

"Whaaa..? I thought there was no technology here. Where are the projectors?"

"All over. They're blended into the artistic designs and the carvings on the stone. The senate has the latest of everything."

That settles it. Mark leans back against the wall and accesses his operations belt controls. He connects it and his portapack with his oracle glasses and switches to "view cinema." He decides to watch *Lord of the Rings* and scrolls to his favorite scene in the movie. He especially likes the siege of Minas Tirith, during which the Riders of Rohan charge down the hillside and wade into a sea of Orcs. "And the sun rises!!!" Mark has imagined himself galloping down the hillside with that army since he was only a boy.

Later, after Legolas jumps off the Mûmakil's tusks, Mark pauses the movie to check what is going on. Senator Romanus Santori has taken the floor. He is young and fiery. He speaks with confidence, one could even say, with authority.

"And so, my esteemed colleagues, I can scarcely believe what I am hearing here. On the basis of rumors and no real evidence of sedition, we are contemplating a prostitution of the Roman dream? What next? Will we in addition choose an official religion or two? Do we need 'The Duke,' Lord Mussolini, to return from the dead? I ask you, what elements in Rome's past have prevented her from fulfilling her destiny? What factors have eroded at the dream, and which ones have almost destroyed it? You know the answer! Caesars, emperors, and Christianity! One or more of these has been responsible for a long series of declines and falls, and its ultimate, catastrophic decline and fall was because of Constantine, who combined all three."

Many senators murmur their approval.

"But you may point to Rome's many achievements fostered by the Caesars who were benign. I would say to you, give praise to Rome's engineers, artists, soldiers, and scholars, not to a line of mad tyrants who led us to the ultimate insanity! I tell you that Rome has risen again and not by some miracle from heaven or the schemes of a despot! We must learn the lessons of our history and stay committed not to repeat them."

Santori stops and seems to be thinking for a moment, as if carefully formulating his proposal.

"I would suggest that the senate meet as often as necessary to conduct Rome's business and maintain her security. We must as a governing body consult with Colonel Valenza and members of the intelligence community so that we may make the best decisions possible. We must preserve our freedom from tyranny and guard fundamental civil rights! Rome is our pride! Rome is our goal! Have done with lesser things! We serve the City set on Seven Hills founded by the great Aeneas, the Eternal City. Rome has fallen in past times. She must not fall now! We must not fail her! Long live Rome! Long live the Roman senate! Long live the Roman dream!"

Thundering applause.

Mark thinks, *Santori would make a good Caesar.* Frodo and Sam make their way toward the Cracks of Doom.

When the meeting is over, Massimo tells Mark, "Go ahead, Entrance 26. I told the others you're coming. I'll be along shortly." Mark leaves the Curia Julia.

Rome by night. Mark hits "cab call" on his portapack, and an aerotaxi arrives in seconds. The cab cuts the blue flame of its four engines and lands gently on a cushion of air created by its pressurized braking system.

After he scans his face and is approved, he commands, "*Il Colosseo.*"

"*Tre minuti,*" the robot driver responds. The cab lifts off, and Mark stares out the window at the splendor of Rome. Modern megabuildings dwarf those of earlier eras. It's a busy night. Traffic is visible at almost every altitude, moving every possible direction.

Sony: *La Migliore HoloVision!*

The cab arrives, and Mark gets off. The Coliseum is lit up, especially around the multiple statues that populate each level. The restoration has been perfect; the theater is clean and polished, always ready to entertain. Mark moves toward Entrance 26. As he approaches, he sees Angelo talking loudly in Italian, telling jokes to the group, and laughing uproariously.

Mark sees that they all have dates. Angelo spots him.

"Knutson! Where's Massi? Where's your date? Are you going to rent one?"

Mark whispers to Angelo, "Looks like you already have." Angelo punches him in the arm and laughs. Mark clarifies, "Massi's on his way."

Mark is among old friends. All of the men and one of the women, Corrie, are probably still active members of the Praetorian Guard.

"So what news from the front, Captain Fighter Pilot?" Vincenzo slaps Mark on the back. Everyone else stops to listen for the reply.

"I actually got shot down...sort of. Anyway, I'm being temporarily reassigned, probably within the next day or so, back with the PG."

The group reacts with great surprise.

"Just until they do a security sweep and investigation. They're not sure what kind of technology brought me down. So what's new with the guard?"

Gregorio replies, "The same. A new jamming technique every day, or so it seems to be. At least they make some kind of try. It's all outside the Bolla. But so far, everything is okay on the inside."

Demetrios adds, "Here in Rome, things are fine. The PG is on the job. I do not know why they're sending you here. I doubt you'll see any action."

Corrie interrupts, "Hey, no shop talk here. Only fun and pleasure tonight!" All agree, and even Mark assents, though he feels like a fifth wheel. No date. No Angela. No Dominique. Happily no one asks him about Angela. Finally Massi arrives.

STARBUCKS. Cappuccino, per piacere!

As the groups enters the Coliseum, they are scanned and given the green light.

"Our box is at Gate 32, B Level, box 14."

The Coliseum is radiant, dressed and laced in lights, filled with statues of warriors and murals of classic battles. It can comfortably hold 80,000 spectators, and tonight's show is a sell-out.

"You know, Massi, I've seen this one before, and I could have watched it at home."

"Oh, sure," Massi replies, "with those mini-holograms. Come on, Marco, nothing like the real thing! This is an epic battle. Life-size everything, plus the real-life gladiators before the main show."

"Right."

On their way to their box, they encounter vendors shouting in Italian and a number of different languages.

"Enhancements this evening, ladies and gentlemen? Enrich your experience! Heighten your sexual pleasure! Expand your mind!"

Massi and others buy drinks and chemical boosts. He announces, "Hey, nothing but fun tonight, guys! Remember that we've even rented a private room in case you want to take an intermession!!! But remember, you have to take a number!!!"

He laughs uproariously, and everyone laughs with him. He then turns and whispers to Mark, "You want a partner? Look over there! Any sex or any color you want, man!"

"No, thanks, remember? Angela? Uh…"

"Oh, right, sorry, *amico.*"

McDonald's…ed anche un Big Mac!

The group settles into their seats as the show begins with a preview of *Salamis*, the great naval battle between the Greeks and the Persians. The latter's enormous ships lumber into the narrow strait. Behind them sail a row of Greek triremes, swift, narrow assault ships built to ram. Visual effects look good. Reading about it is one thing, but seeing it, as if you were there, that's something far better. Mark likes military history. *"I need to see this one again."*

The first show begins. The lights come up, and a life-size beached whale lays in the center of a hundred or so gladiators, who are armed with swords but no shields or armor.

Massimo turns to Mark, "Tonight's special! I love watching these condemned criminals from the provinces get slaughtered. At least they give them a fighting chance. Two-to-one."

The enormous whale on the stage opens its mouth and about fifty bears emerge roaring. The bears disperse and charge at the gladiators, who have nowhere to go. They must stand and fight. Many try to engage a bear face-on while their partner attacks from behind. Sometimes it works. Sometimes it doesn't.

After a short time, Mark looks up at the scoreboard to check the number of survivors: HUOMINI 86, ORSI 47. The elimination of the human beings is slow. Many don't appear to know what they are doing.

"Massi, do they ever give these guys any training?"

"Nah, they're just good at killing defenseless people! Morons! Serves them right! I feel sorry for the bears. They don't feed them for like a day before these contests. Ha! Man, I would love to go out there and take on a few myself. I killed maybe a hundred bears last month in my *Ultimate Hunter* hologame at Level Twenty!"

Some of the ravenous bears have begun to dine on human corpses while the others continue the fight and maul their victims. Blood is spilled and smeared everywhere. Many in the audience are cheering for the bears. Mark is uninterested. He saw a similar show last month with wolves.

After the bears win, the huge stage sinks, and a different platform glides into place. The theater goes dark for a brief time. When the lights come up again, new gladiators are posed, ready to fight. This time, one-half the players are human but not criminals; these are professional entertainers. The other half, their opponents, are holographically enhanced robots. The robots are programmed to fight convincingly but not to harm or kill. It is impossible to tell the difference between the two until the end. The humans always slay the machines, or they seem to. In the interim, the battles are realistic, complete with holographically generated blood and guts, and the fast-action fight sequences are choreographed like a violent ballet.

As the drums beat and trumpets call to battle, about a hundred pairs of combatants begin the contests. They have different combinations of weapons, but all are made of enhanced titanium. The Coliseum is filled the roar of the crowd and with sounds of clashing metal and fast action that is sometimes hard to follow with the naked eye.

Mark's group watches only occasionally. They are busy drinking, laughing, and eating. Several couples have taken a number and in turn have gone to use the private room. Mark is bored again. *This is not combat. There's nothing at stake. It's just all for show.* But he tries to distract himself by focusing on select pairs of fighters, studying their moves, and pondering what he would do. He watches one particular pair close to their box. The two are circling, jabbing, probing, and each is striking the shield of the other.

Mark mutters, "Quit screwing around. Attack!"

One lunges forward and as he does, he misses, but his opponent seems abruptly stunned and quickly vanishes, disappearing from top to bottom.

The remaining warrior is frozen, which is what the robots do when the contest is over or when their human opponent steps off the platform.

Mark leans forward. "Massi! Look at that! What's going on?"

Massi turns and looks. "What? Which pair?"

"To the right corner, nearest to us. Look! That one fighter standing motionless. The other one has just disappeared!"

Massi studies the single frozen warrior and squints a little. "Hmm. So what? Maybe the human left?"

"Massi, I was watching! The human just disappeared! The one frozen is a robot. That's what robots do when the match is over."

"Yeah, I know. I used to practice with robots. Awesome training! Don't worry about it, Marco! Hey, man, you're tired! Think about what you've been through in the last couple of days. You probably blinked or nodded off. Watch some other pairs." He takes a swig of his beer and goes back to talking to the group.

Mark looks intensely at the spot where the warrior had vanished. Nothing. Maybe he did fall asleep.

When the battles are concluded, the huge stage begins to sink, and the lights on the arena floor go out for several minutes. When they come back up, *Thermopylae* begins, a timeless tale of victory against overwhelming odds. Greek warriors will again fight and die bravely, but this time, all will be holograms.

It's hard for Mark to concentrate. He's seen *Thermopylae* before, and he's trying to wrap his mind around what he knows that he just saw. A human warrior participant in the contest disappeared; the invisibility started with his head and proceeded quickly down, as if he had been paralyzed and a cloaking sack had been slipped over him.

When the show is over, the group of friends leaves the Coliseum along with rivers of satisfied spectators, all talking and laughing loudly and making their way to the exits.

Outside, as they are saying their goodbyes for the evening, an attractive woman strolls by the group. What little she is wearing is bright red. Many follow her with their eyes, but Mark tries not to. Some of the dates yank or punch their companions.

She walks past the crowd toward a park not far away. Massi leans over and whispers something to Mark as they both enjoy the view. But suddenly she seems jolted, and her head vanishes, and then the rest of her body. Within only another second, she has disappeared completely.

"*Cosaaa?*" exclaims Massi in disbelief, squinting his eyes.

Vincenzo tries to explain, "Probably an ad for a magic show. Or maybe she was a hologram. You can't tell the difference. Just wait a second."

Massi is not satisfied. This evening, he has brought his PG operations belt; he snaps on his oracle glasses and scans carefully. The glasses pick up fleeing ghostly shadows that appear to be carrying the now invisible woman in a cloaking sack.

Massi immediately pulls out his side arm and broadcasts a warning directly toward them through his operations belt speaker. "*Alt!!! Guardia Pretoriana!!! Alt!!!*" This command has the exact opposite effect on the startled crowd of exiting spectators, who when they see that Massi seems ready to fire, run in a panic, screaming and moving in every direction.

No response. As he fires a tracking drone from one of his wristbands, the remaining members of the PG begin running in pursuit. None of the others has brought their operations belt or any equipment except Mark. No one thought to bring lightning boots.

Massi and Mark take the lead in the chase, but the crowds impede them. Massi is watching the readout from the drone when the display abruptly goes blank. The kidnappers have disappeared into the trees and crowds in the park. He sends an alert to PG headquarters.

They finally stop running and gather to discuss the incident.

"They were cloaked," Angelo observes.

"Impossible! Only PGs can cloak." Massi retorts.

"Terrorists?" Mark asks.

"Impossible! They don't have the technology to do that, and terrorist cannot be in Rome."

Mark wonders out loud, "Unless we have moles…"

"That's impossible, too."

—8—

THE LIGHT WITHIN

Mark reports to PG headquarters the next morning. He knocks on the door of his old boss, Colonel Valenza.

"Sir?"

"Knutson, yes, come in. At ease. Please, have a seat."

Valenza is an imposing figure, large, intense, and articulate. His English is excellent.

"I am pleased to have you reassigned to me, captain. EuroSecure informs me that the investigation into your warplanes going down in the desert is proceeding as planned. No problems forecast."

"That's good to hear, colonel."

"The fact is that we need you here in Rome. The situation has changed. You were at the Coliseum last night with some other PGs?"

"Yes, sir."

"And you observed some suspicious activity."

"Yes, sir, we saw—"

"The Coliseum has already reported the unexplained disappearance of the one gladiator. The other victim was a young lady, whom your group watched disappear. Sergeant Sansone filed a report. He claims you spotted two cloaked figures in flight carrying her in a cloaking sack. Both bodies were later found in an abandoned building and were apparently used in some kind of bizarre ritual involving human sacrifice. Their hearts were cut completely out. And all this inside the Bolla. That we find disturbing for many obvious reasons."

Mark is stunned. "Sir, how could this happen?"

The colonel replies, "We're not sure. To our knowledge, no single group has access to technology that would permit hostile agents to enter Rome and give them cloaking capabilities. Something has changed, captain, something essential."

"But how does human sacrifice fit with any of those groups?"

"I have no idea, but we need to get to the bottom of this. We must be vigilant inside the Bolla and outside. That's where you come in."

"I'm ready, sir. What will be my assignment?"

"You'll be supervising a squad. Your executive officer will be Lt. Lorenzo Pavoni. Yours is one of many task forces outside the Bolla, surveying the NE-12 quadrant, about six square kilometers. You should work in teams of at least three and separate only when absolutely necessary. You should be in plain clothes, in whatever can effectively hide your operations belt and other equipment."

"Yes, sir."

"Go out and mix with the people, but be on your guard. These areas are rife with fanatics and crazies of all kinds, plus numerous fringe religious groups. In some cases, the two are the same. Neo-Nazis, Neo-Fascists, and Neo-everything else."

"What about the pirate coalition?"

"They have been behind some of the terrorism in the past, but they have more recently concentrated on attacking our shipping, at least for now; plus, their technology is not that well developed."

"I'm not so sure, given my recent experience in the desert. What about the jihadists?"

"For the moment they seem obsessed with killing each other off and with the destruction of Israel. No indication they have any interest in Rome per se. Maybe all these groups will just annihilate each other. We believe that most inhabitants outside the Bolla are harmless, but we need security teams to gather intel, maybe even infiltrate groups here and there."

"What's in the operations belt now? About the same items? And the wristbands and lightning boots?"

"Mostly the same, however, almost everything has been upgraded, improved. You'll carry an additional side arm, of the old but reliable gunpowder and lead variety. So far, they can't block bullets, at least not this caliber. With that, you should be able to outgun everything we know about. Most of these people are not so advanced technologically, but as you know, those that are advanced are quite good at jamming our signal technology. That's the card they have been playing most of the time...well...until that attack by the cloaked kidnappers."

"I've just seen a glimpse of the pirates' recent technology in North Africa."

"It would seem now that some group has found a way to get inside the Bolla and use cloaking equipment."

"Why did they kidnap and kill those two people?"

"Probably just to prove to us that they can, right in front of our noses. I don't get the human sacrifice connection there, though. That doesn't sound like the neo-Fascists. In any case, they likely made your group as off-duty PGs and decided they would put on a little show."

"They definitely got our attention. One was a gladiator, the other a beautiful woman, sort of a 'Beauty and the Beast' pair-up? Is there any significance in that?"

"That has been discussed, but otherwise we see no obvious connection. But keep thinking. We all need to be sharp and stay ahead of the enemy in every way. You have your work cut out for you, captain. Dismissed."

Mark stands and snaps a salute. The colonel returns one.

"*Buona fortuna.*"

They shake hands, and Mark leaves the building and walks back into the street.

Whereas in ancient times, Rome conquered the world, now the world has come to Rome's doorstep. Outside the Bolla, most wear old, dirty masks that are only slightly better than breathing in the Haze. It is hard to make out and identify specific facial features as most inhabitants also wear protective goggles. Their garments are from many countries, stained, worn versions of cultural garb in most cases. The seething masses populate make-shift slums and buildings that are collapsing from neglect or have been ravaged by terrorist explosions for many kilometers all around the Bolla. In Rome, citizens enjoy perfection, perfect order, and a perfect world, but outside, inhabitants experience only unrest, chaos and danger, an incubator for revolution. Any possible revolt is held at bay by the power of the Bolla and agents of the Praetorian Guard.

Thursday arrives. Mark puts on his oracle glasses, operations belt, utility wristbands, and lightning boots. He cinches his belt with the two side arms. Ready for anything now. He will begin his first patrol tonight. He remembers the Lumena meeting and decides it could be part of the job. Angela said they would meet in the old Luce Theater, not too far from his assigned sector. *It's worth checking out.*

He meets up with his executive officer and his team of five at the northeast exit. After brief introductions, Mark gives them their assignments.

"Lieutenant Pavoni, I believe you have already been working in our assigned sector."

"Yes, sir. You are familiar with changes in technology for the operations belt and your other gear?"

"I believe so, lieutenant."

"I understand that it has been a while since you were on the job here."

Mark looks at him, thinking that Pavoni probably wanted to be in charge again, as he had been before.

Mark explains, "To start, I'll take only two of the team with me. I have a lead on a small group that is just outside our sector. Just an intelligence run, no fireworks anticipated. I'll trust you to do the tough job of checking out our sector. I'm counting on your experience, lieutenant."

"Yes, sir." Pavoni seems satisfied for the moment.

The tunnel is crowded this evening. Many Romans regularly exit the Bolla to visit the various unregulated businesses and indulge in what they have to offer. Some of them own the businesses. Mark's team exits the Bolla, and all are scanned. Security is tight. They separate and disperse into the dark labyrinth.

Mark and two guards proceed to the old, dusty theater, which seats about five hundred, but when they get there, they see that only about one hundred have shown up. Most of the audience appears to be from inside the Bolla. Mark has instructed his two men to sit in different parts of the theater and to turn on the cameras in their oracle glasses.

Mark tries to remain inconspicuous, but Angela spots him and comes to sit with him.

"Marco! I'm so excited that you are come!" she exclaims.

"Right."

"You will not be able to believe what you will see!"

"Right."

Soon the auditorium quiets as a robed figure enters, followed by a dozen others. He has a hood pulled up over his head that is partially covering his face.

Well, well. What do we have here?

The figure moves to a crude wooden podium. He is carrying something which he deposits on a small table next to the stand. It looks like a planter of some sort. He pulls back his hood and takes off his robe and tosses it on a nearby chair as he surveys the audience.

"Well, so this is Seren?" Mark whispers to himself. Angela hears him and affirms, "Yes! It's him!"

Seren is tall, olive-skinned with thick, shiny black hair and well-trimmed beard but in Mark's opinion does not resemble him in any way. Nonetheless, Angela punches his side, "*Hai visto?* Just like I said. You two could be twins! You should grow a beard!"

Seren is wearing a black double-breasted suit; the coat is bordered in a glossy silver. Mark thinks, "*He definitely has good taste in clothes.*"

Seren has presence. As he pulls an old-style microphone toward him, the audience falls silent. He pauses for several seconds as he surveys the crowd.

He begins in English, "Friends, Romans, and countrymen. Lend me your ears...." He allows the audience a few moments to digest what he has just said, and then he quips, "I thought a Shakespeare quote would make a nice opening."

Murmurs of laughter from the crowd. Mark is not amused. Seren then switches to Italian. Mark listens via Universal Translator.

"I have come here tonight with several goals, simple objectives. I come with a mission, a purpose driven solely by transforming truths that can be proven and cannot be denied."

Pause for effect.

"I am aware that members of the Praetorian Guard are in attendance this evening."

That got Mark's attention. *How could he know? Even Angela couldn't have known that he has been reassigned!*

"Correction," he smiles, "I *assume* that members of the PG are here tonight in their diligent quest to protect Rome and her destiny. If I were ruling Rome, I would expect them to do no less. But look, one and all! My assistants and I are unarmed." He opens his coat. His assistants follow suit and open their robes.

"You can search us if you doubt. We come with no weapons, unless you consider the truth a weapon, and indeed, the truth can be a powerful one, a threat to those who do not understand it or who refuse to receive it."

Mark leans forward, puts his chin on his fists, and listens intently. Seren begins pacing back and forth. His commanding voice fills the theater; he doesn't seem to need the microphone. The theater lights darken slightly, and a single light focuses on Seren.

"Therefore, I wish to affirm my belief in the destiny of Rome. I support the Roman senate completely. What I have to say in no way criticizes or contravenes any of Rome's noble ideals. I have nothing to hide."

He moves over to the table and places his left hand over the top of the planter and presses it firmly into the soil.

He then continues speaking. "I believe that those ideals will in time be achieved and that more and more people will be able to enjoy the benefits of Roman citizenship and residence in prosperous cities like Rome and Paris and London. I have only something to add, to help fuel the dream of the sweet life and make it a reality."

Seren looks down at the planter, as if studying it. He seems to be massaging the dirt.

"Rome eats well, but the great capital must import most of its food. Rome nobly desires to include more in its dream of the good life, but progress is perhaps too slow. Think about humanity at large. Most of the world is hungry, scratching for food each day, and many are literally dying of starvation. This terrible problem has faced us since time immemorial. And who has offered the final solution?"

Seren's hand is still in the soil. He withdraws it, and as he does, a small vine appears. Mark keeps a careful eye on the plant.

"No, my vision differs only in Rome's unhealthy reliance on technology alone. Please hear me. I am not against technology. And unlike many groups outside the Bolla, I have no religious purpose either. That would go against the most basic precepts of the eternal city and the humanistic vision of her rulers."

Mark notices that the vine is now at least a foot longer after only a minute or two. *Just a magic trick or hologram. Nothing dangerous here.* He signals his team members to leave, and they do, along with several other spectators who are apparently not impressed.

"It is not my plan to start a new religion, a fanciful dream about a god out there in the universe somewhere. I am here to help all of you discover the 'light within.' If we can do this together, we will solve all the world's problems, one by one."

Mark rolls his eyes and runs his right hand through his hair.

"No, there is no god, and we are not gods, but we are not without a certain godlikeness, so to speak. We all have life energy within us. Perhaps you have heard this called the 'aura.' Let us begin our reasoning with the most obvious facts. We change, grow, reproduce, and evolve. Rocks do not. We have within us power, a mysterious life force. Every living thing has this light, this force, yet we, obviously the most intelligent, still don't know how to use it."

Standing in front of the table and blocking view of the plant, Seren adds, "You will inevitably be thinking about some science fiction movie, I'm sure." He laughs, and most of the audience laughs with him. "Such films are all pure fantasy. But that we are evolving as life forms is scientific fact. The question is, into what? Are we smart enough to understand the next step and how we might steer ourselves on a course of power that can turn this warring planet into a paradise for all? You have a light within. Its power is dormant, untapped, but it can develop and grow. If you listen, believe, and put my teachings into practice, you will feel it. I will show you how to use it. Follow me."

He steps aside, and the theater lights come up. Mark sees that the vine has grown and is quite large! It is covered with clusters of grapes, dozens of them! The vine now extends from the table to the floor. The audience buzzes with surprise. Mark squints his eyes, and his mouth is open slightly.

"Marco, did you see that? Didn't I tell you?"

"See what?" he responds under his breath. "Cheap trick."

Seren continues, "Friends, there is no magic here, no technology. In your presence and before your very eyes, I have transferred a little of my inner light, my life force, into this humble plant. No sunlight needed. No water. The 'formula' is quite simple: Life transferred to life."

The crowd is murmuring approval and amazement.

"Come, all you who doubt, and eat of the fruit. And if you like it, you are welcome to sample a complimentary cup of wine, made from grapes grown only with the help of the light within, my inner light."

Mark jumps up and moves toward the front, and Angela follows him. He has to check this out more closely. About half the audience has come up to sample the strangely cultivated fruit. Mark stands in line and watches Seren as he carefully studies each person who comes to take grapes. When it is their turn, Mark picks two, but Angela takes five. Mark glances at Seren, who smiles at him briefly, which gives Mark the creeps.

As they move away, Angela begins eating the grapes. She turns and looks at Seren, and he smiles at her and nods her direction. She smiles back at him nervously and keeps walking, stumbling slightly and bumping into Mark's back.

Mark eats the two grapes. They are sweet, not like any he has ever tasted. Angela has eaten all five of hers. *"Che uva formidabile, meravigliosa!"*

"Yeah?" Mark grumbles, "It was a trick, a scam. There are so many ways he could have done that!"

"Marco," Angela responds defensively, "these are not a hologram. They are not growing anywhere except right here. You saw them growing. You were watching the miracle! Can't you just accept that perhaps he has something..., something important to teach us?"

"Nothing I want to learn."

"He's having another teaching session in a few weeks. Come back. Sit more closer next time. Watch him more carefully if you doubt. He seems so open, so honest."

"I'll think about it." Without saying good-bye to Angela, Mark leaves the building and meets up with his team of two in the street.

Corporal Lagorio bursts out, "That was so much comedy! He teach us how to become good farmers? Thanks, *capitano*, for permissioning us leave. I was having hard time trying not to laugh. What a strange person! And a boring one, too. What happened after we are left?"

Mark replies, "More of the same. Send me your holorecords. I'll submit them with my report. We'll let HQ evaluate."

Sergeant Ricci jokes, "Wow! I would love to catch that assignment! Watching and reading such reports! I could recover some sleep! *Capitano*, what is the next assignment? Something it is more dangerous, yes?"

Everyone, including Mark, laughs. "Sorry, *signori*, I was acting on a tip. Let's proceed to our zone. Maybe we'll gather some more interesting intel."

—9—

CHERCHEZ LA FEMME

Mark transmits his report and goes with his team to their assigned sector. On Friday evening he decides to go to his favorite outdoor coffee bar and spend some time relaxing before his shift begins at midnight. He chooses to walk instead of taking an aerocab. He is wearing his operations belt and utility wristbands under his clothes and his lightning boots, which look like ordinary boots until activated. He now puts on his oracle glasses every time he leaves his apartment.

It's a beautiful evening in the Bolla. The scant sunlight that filters through it is dimming, and the artificial lights are coming up to compensate, a vast assortment of colors and sizes. Mark particularly enjoys watching one megabuilding that portrays a cowboy blasting his six-shooters. Another is a forty-story Marilyn Monroe making a weak attempt to prevent her skirt from rising up due to a sudden gust of air beneath her. Still another is an ad for a vacation package in Paris, scenes from the City of Light in the midst of the Eternal City. At one point, the building holographs into a gigantic Eiffel Tower, culturally incongruous but effective.

A lot of people are on the street. Mark receives a text update from PGHQ. "The suspects in the kidnap-murder that were in custody have now been released. Insufficient evidence. No new kidnappings reported. Stay on the alert."

Mark reaches the café and sits at an unoccupied table. He orders a Coca-Cola and then switches on the small speaker in his oracle glasses and scans various music selections displayed on his lenses; he lands on a Led Zeppelin song, Stairway to Heaven, which he plays. He leans back and sips on his Coke, content to relax and watch people pass by for several hours. He listens to song after song, which gives him peace.

At length, Mark orders *spaghetti alla carbonara, pane di Lariano,* and a glass of *chianti classico.* He is thinking about Seren and his phony grape-growing demo and about Dominique. May the two never meet. As he meditates on his experience in the desert, trying to understand it, to recall more details, and then he thinks about Mikhail.

Mark surveys the crowds passing by and notices one figure almost a head taller than the rest. Can it be?

"Mikhail!" he shouts, trying to get his attention.

Mikhail sees him and moves toward his table. "Captain Knutson, I am so delighted to see you! All is well, I hope?"

"Couldn't be better! It looks like I found you this time."

Mikhail laughs. "That is true."

"Do you live near here?"

"No, captain, but I do enjoy walking along this street with all the cafés. It's obviously a popular area."

"It is. Please, do you have a few minutes? Have a seat. Funny, I was just thinking about you and remembering our brief time together. Are you still searching and rescuing?"

"Yes, I am, but no pilots for the moment. We've had only a few random attacks on our shipping. They sank one, and I was part of a rescue squadron that went to search for survivors. I believe we got them all home safely."

"No time to play *Sleeping Beauty* with them?"

Mikhail laughs, "No, no time for that."

"Well, I am eager to play it again and beat it. I hate losing. It leaves a nasty taste in my mouth."

"Yes, well, perhaps we can get together and give you some more practice. Give me your i-connect code."

"Okay, but give me yours as well, and I'll send a message to you."

The two continue chatting for some time. Mikhail receives a call.

"Excuse me, captain…. 'Yes?'" Mikhail gets up and steps away. Mark can hear him say, "Yes, I'll be there soon."

When he returns after a few minutes, Mark asks, "Anything important? Not an emergency alert, I hope."

"Oh, no, just getting together with some friends. I seem to be a little late. Would you like to join us?"

"No, thanks, I'm going to work outside the Bolla soon."

"You have not been returned to service? Are you not a pilot anymore?"

"I'm still a pilot, but I'm on a temporary assignment while the incident in the desert is being investigated. Have they asked you any more questions?"

"No, nothing further. I'm sure you will be flying again soon. I know that is your love."

"It is that."

"I should be going now, captain. Please, let's be in touch. We can soon return to the glorious combat of *Sleeping Beauty*?"

"Definitely, sergeant." They shake hands. Mikhail turns and walks away. Once he is about ten meters from him, Mark raises his right arm discreetly and fires a tracking microbyte from his wristband at the back of Mikhail's jacket. He initiates a display on his oracle glasses that shows Mikhail's movements as a small flashing red arrow that points to his trail.

Mark begins to follow him from a distance. He likes Mikhail, but he is just wondering about him. His new Russian friend seemed a little secretive today, maybe slightly nervous, which was not like him, but then, he doesn't really know him all that well. Mark still has a little time to kill before he has to report for work.

Mikhail is moving toward the edge of the Bolla, toward an exit, or so it appears. Mark launches a mosquito drone from his left wristband for an aerial view.

The camera projects the view on to a small area on his oracle glasses. Mikhail is walking purposefully. He is joined by four others.

Then two more meet the group, followed by five others. They all shake hands or hug. It seems like a group of friends going out on the town or maybe out of town completely for God knows what. It could be harmless. Okay, it happens. Many Romans exit the Bolla for a variety of reasons.

Wait. Mark lowers the drone for a better horizontal view. He sees a familiar face.

It's Dominique! She is with Mikhail and the group. Mark begins running. What the...? Did he miss something? So Mikhail maybe has a thing for Dominique? They were just pretending to barely know each other?

The group is about two blocks from the exit, and Mark is closing fast. He's not sure what he's going to do when he catches them. He can't arrest them, so he tries to think of ways to observe them without being noticed.

He keeps the back of Mikhail's head in view. Mark sees a big crowd moving toward the exit, which seems a little more congested than usual. Mark is watching his readout and glancing at Mikhail.

Suddenly an explosion rocks the area. No one was ready for that. What is this? A freak accident? A malfunctioning system? Terrorism? In the Bolla? Impossible! Mark runs quickly to the site. The death radius appears to be about forty meters from the side of a building, and the shock wave has taken out his mosquito drone.

Many are dead, and the panicked crowd is running away from the bodies. Mark wonders if it is an isolated attack. The emergency channel is only reporting this incident and calling for help. He sees Mikhail, who is fighting the mob apparently trying to reach the injured. That's his job.

Mark then looks for Dominique. He is close enough to begin pursuing a woman that he thinks is her. The terrified crowd has separated her from her companions and is pushing her down a nearby street. She seems to be struggling to get to the side of a building away from the relentless flow of the frightened, swarming horde.

Mark perseveres and pushes his way forward. There she is, standing next to the wall, her hands covering her face. He is within twenty meters of her when she unexpectedly faints.... Her head disappears first, then the rest of her, a cloaking sack!

Mark activates the *specter* function of his oracle glasses and spots two men in cloak. They are dragging Dominique down an alley, and Mark pushes his way toward them. The kidnappers press on into the dark, unaware that anyone can see them.

Once Mark is in the alley, he shouts: *"Alt!!! Guardia Pretoriana!!!"* The two startled figures look up and open fire. Mark's force shield activates automatically and protects him. He withdraws his flash-plasma side arm. How to stop them without harming Dominique? Even "stun" could be risky since she's already unconscious.

Things begin happening fast. They continue dragging her hastily down the alleyway and firing. They finally drop her on the pavement in an effort to hasten their escape, but Mark has activated his lightning boots and has overtaken them. He jumps, knocks one off his feet with a kick and lands his fists on to the back of the other. The fall has damaged their cloaking devices; both suspects instantly become visible along with the bag that is covering Dominique, who is lying just a few meters away. He notices that they are wearing filter masks and goggles.

The two jump to their feet to confront Mark. He wants to vaporize them, but he needs them as witnesses. He tries the stun function, but they are shielded against that. As he reaches for his other gun with metal bullets, one of them pulls out a long knife. The other likewise pulls out a blade, and they both come at him. It's a new game.

Mark assumes a defensive position. "Ex-cel-lent," he mutters slowly as he takes a knife from his operations belt. It is dark and with their masks and goggles, he can't quite make out their facial features. He is taking a holorecord of them both as he studies their moves.

The two circle him slowly. He faces one, who lunges at him. The one behind him spins his left leg and knocks Mark off his feet, but Mark quickly regains his balance and looks at them defiantly. His oracle glasses are still securely in place. Then Mark spins and again knocks one off his feet. The second one will be easy.

But suddenly two additional cloaked figures appear on the periphery of his visual field. He again reaches for his side arm as he runs back to protect Dominique, who is lying half conscious and moaning. As he tries to get near her, one of the newly arrived combatants slashes him in the side with the knife. He falls, but immediately recovers and squats in front of Dominique's body. He fires a stun at his assailants, but with no visible effect. He quickly checks to see if she is injured.

When Mark looks up again, he sees that two of the figures have vanished, either into a nearby building or down another alleyway; the other two are running fast. He withdraws his other side arm and fires a spray of bullets at them; he thinks he may have hit one.

Using a special power saw attachment for his knife, Mark cuts open the thin, metallic fabric of the cloaking sack. It is like gauze, permitting the victim to breathe, but it is strong, preventing escape. As Dominique comes to, Mark remembers the pain of the knife wound. He crumples.

"What is happened?" asks Dominique, confused as she tries to sit up. "Are you okay?"

"Captain Mark Knutson, at your service, *mademoiselle*," answers Mark with a weak smile. He rolls over on to his other side.

As Dominique continues pushing aside the cloaking sack, eventually removing it, she sees blood on his shirt. "Captain! You're hurt! Please tell me what has happened."

"*Mademoiselle*, you were kidnapped by unidentified individuals. They somehow had the technology to put you in cloak with that sack, and then they carried you to this alley. I followed and confronted them. You see the result."

Dominique immediately sends Mikhail a message: "Come! Your friend Captain Knutson is seriously injured!"

Mikhail has been tending many who were wounded in the explosion. Medical kits and an army of medical personnel have arrived, and injured victims have been evacuated. Mikhail grabs an extra kit and begins running toward Dominique's signal.

When he arrives, he finds Dominique hovering over Mark.

"What's happened?" he asks. "Are you injured?"

"I'm okay, but the captain is not."

"Knife wound here," Mark tells him with some difficulty raising his bloodied shirt tail revealing a gash just above his operations belt. Mikhail opens the kit and unfolds a pad, which he places on the wound and links to a small screen for analysis. After that, he activates a larger unit, which begins its healing work, relieving the pain, stopping the bleeding, and sealing the wound.

"This will take about five minutes. Looks like they missed major internal organs. You should be feeling better soon, captain, but please lie still."

"It's just a flesh wound!" Mark protests.

Mark is feeling miraculously better. He is looking up at the face of Venus, who is hovering over him with profound concern on her face. A delightful experience in a kind of bizarre way.

Mikhail asks, "Dominique, what happened? How did you end up here?"

"I don't remember. I thought I had freed myself from the crowd and was catching my breath when...well, nothing...I must have fainted. When I woke up, I realized I was covered in that sack there. The captain tells me that I was kidnapped. He apparently confronted my abductors and was wounded."

Mark looks at Mikhail, "It was sort of like that hologame we played. I guess I lost again. I was doing well with two of them, but then two more showed up in cloak...okay, I mean, they didn't literally show up. Get it?" He laughs faintly, wincing slightly from pain.

"You did not lose, captain, I think that you were vastly outnumbered and that in protecting Dominique you were one hundred percent successful!"

"Being outnumbered has never been a problem for me before," Mark muses, "except in that hologame."

Dominique, relieved to hear their banter, interjects, "Do you two spend all your time playing hologames? Or does real life interest you?"

Mikhail and Mark both laugh, although Mark winces again.

Dominique apologizes, "Actually, Captain Knutson, I'm so sorry for my rudeness. I must thank you for rescuing me."

Mikhail adds, "He saved your life."

"Yes, I'm sure of it. How can I thank you enough?"

Mark thinks, "*I'm sure we can work something out.*" But he responds professionally, "All in a day's work, *mademoiselle.*"

Mark is now able to sit up. "Which reminds me, I need to be thinking about getting to work, which is where I was headed when I saw the trouble. Am I cleared, doc?"

"It's your call, but please, go easy for a time. Perhaps you can let someone else do the martial arts?"

"Roger that."

"And we need to meet up with our group. They have messaged me that they are okay. Captain, the invitation is always open if you would like to join us. We are going outside the Bolla to help in a project with some other friends."

"Is it safe to go outside? We really don't know what will happen next. And are you sure they won't be needing you here in the Bolla?"

"I'm not officially a part of Rome's medical corps. But they know I'll help if needed. And not to worry. We're a fairly large group and well-armed. It's extremely important that we go help those friends tonight. We'll be watchful."

"How can you watch for cloaked assailants?"

"Actually several in our number are PGs and have oracle glasses. And again, you are welcome to meet our group and hang out with us."

Dominique adds with some enthusiasm, "Yes, please join us some time!"

That seemed pretty open and honest. Maybe there's nothing more to their relationships than what meets the eye.

Mark is somewhat relieved but also feels uneasy inside. He knows that he must report to HQ about the incident and his involvement, that he must await instructions about a possible reassignment, given what has just happened. Maybe the pirates will be stepping it up to the south, and he can get back in the air.

"I'm sorry I can't tonight. Work, you know. Maybe some other time."

Dominique shakes his hand with both her hands. "Another night, then, captain. Please. And take good care of yourself." He looks into her eyes and sees her genuine concern for him. Something inside him is burning.

"Of course. I would like that," he responds with considerable restraint.

Mikhail adds, "I'll contact you, captain."

They all return to the main street and separate.

Mark begins transmitting his initial report about the incident and how he intervened. He awaits instructions. He thinks about how this may change life in Rome and his job. The bomb was surely a terrorist attack. And the incident with the cloaked figures is a repeat and is just a little too coincidental to not be related to the blast.

He receives instructions, "Assemble team and continue to your assigned sector, but follow up on any tips. The perpetrators are likely based outside the Bolla. Reserve units have been called up to gather information from survivors and to do a discreet sweep of Rome."

Mark updates his team and assigns Lt. Pavoni to take charge while he pursues a lead alone.

Pavoni notes, "That is not the standard procedure, captain. Regulations state that we are to move in groups of three." He stares at him.

"This is a special case, lieutenant. I don't want anyone to make me as a PG leading a team."

Mark can't tell if his explanation satisfied Pavoni.

"You're in charge until I contact you."

That seemed to go over better.

He activates his display on his oracle glasses and searches for Mikhail's location. The microbyte is still lodged in Mikhail's garment and is sending out telemetry. Mikhail and the group are in fact approaching the exit. Why? Where are they going outside the

Bolla? Who are these friends they have to help tonight? Are they all crazy? And with this new danger.

Mark moves along toward the exit tunnel. This is part of the job, he reasons, but something is bothering him. How is he going to give a full report about the activities of the EuroSecure com assistant, a couple of PGs, and a member of a Search and Rescue team? He couldn't think about that now.

Mark steps on the motorized stairway going down. He is scanned. He continues down to a moving walkway under the Bolla and is scanned again. He sees *Carabinieri* everywhere in uniform. It looks like security has been tightened but ever so subtly; they probably are trying to contain the panic.

The scans approve him and display SICUREZZA ROMANA identifying him as a security agent without reference to his rank or affiliation. No one challenges him. For the moment, he doesn't need to tell Mikhail or Dominique exactly what his temp assignment is. They probably left the city without a problem because of their credentials.

Mark exits Rome. As he does, he moves from order to disorder, from ultra-sanitized to never-sanitized, from prosperity to poverty, from serenity to struggle. He watches Mikhail's signal and stays out of sight, about a block or more behind him.

Mark passes people without really looking at them. Better not to. Keep a low profile. He puts on a filter mask, rubbing just a little dirt on it. He is wearing casual clothes, but just in case, he steps into an alley momentarily and rubs himself against a filthy wall. He finds an old garbage dumpster and completes the reverse metamorphosis.

Mark exits the alley, now better able to blend. He must make up for lost time and close the gap on Mikhail. Still in range. Interference seems minimal tonight.

After a few minutes, though, the signal seems suddenly weaker. They appear to have taken off on a side street or an alley. Mark begins running. He watches the status. They are zigzagging through the streets. What are they up to? Where are they going?

Mark is closing in. He is getting close. Just around the next corner. But the signal fades almost completely.

He's wise to me!

He turns the corner and adjusts his oracle glasses. Their footprints are recent. With a special app on his glasses, he can read the recent heat signature. All prints lead to the side of a stone building with no windows or doors and come to an end. The street is empty, but he looks all around him for possible hostiles in cloak.

Mark pulls out a spy-pin from his operations belt. He activates it and inserts it into the wall. The pin tip becomes white hot as he pushes it in. When a small light flashes green, he withdraws the pin and inserts a telescoping microcamera snake with a lens at one end and a projector at the other, presses a small button, and the wall becomes transparent.

Just as he thought. A portal to a hall and then a stairwell going downward. He can see the mechanism for opening and where he has to push to open it. He does so, enters, and begins descending.

The air is damp and musty. The tunnel gets colder as he moves down the stairs. The heat signature is now somewhat blurred but is still the only way to track them at this point.

Mark descends into the subterranean labyrinth, the catacombs, the abode where Death and Sleep intermingle, a forgotten, gloomy realm of worn stone and ancestors' weary bones. Mark is guided by the light on his operations belt. His oracle glasses show him which turns they took, which stairways.

Finally he comes to a wall; the heat signatures veer to the right, but the infrared function on his oracle glasses shows him a small crowd in the room behind the wall facing him. He decides not to locate the entrance but to investigate without entering. Mark again pulls out his spy-pin and activates it, inserting it into the wall and then the microcamera snake once the hole has been opened.

After just a moment, the wall becomes transparent as the camera emerges on the other side and begins transmitting imagery to the projector. The stone seems to dissolve before him.

Mark studies the scene. It is a gathering of some sort. He can see about forty people, all from behind, except for the speaker or leader, who is on a platform and is facing the camera. Everyone else is standing. What kind of "project" is this?

Mark tries to adjust for sound but for some reason the quality is poor. He hears a lot of static. It's like a worn record on an old record player, like the one his great-grandmother used to listen to.

Finally he pulls out the camera snake and puts his ear up to the small hole. He listens. What? Wait, they seem to be...singing? What the...?

Mark reinserts the camera snake and stares at the group, his mouth slightly open. He recognizes the song they are singing and blurts out a whisper in astonishment: "Christians?"

He imagines his report: "Yes, sir, I tracked a not particularly subversive religious group to a dungeon full of rotting corpses where they clandestinely meet to...uh...sing.... And by the way, the group includes at least two EuroSecure employees and a couple of PGs..."

Wait. A guy on the back row is turning around. He's looking right at Mark. It's Mikhail, but he's not smiling. Mark becomes uncomfortable, and he moves to the left, and Mikhail's eyes seem to follow him. Mark wrinkles his forehead and squints his eyes.

Mikhail raises his right hand toward the back wall, and the entire image blanks out. The transparent wall returns to stone. Mark begins jiggling the camera snake and trying to recover the image.

Then, Mark passes out.

When he wakes up, he realizes that he is on the floor. He opens his eyes and hears a rustling sound. The passageway is pitch black, so he puts on his oracle glasses and looks both ways. He sees a faint light to his left, and some people down the hall wearing white garments, moving away from him. They seem to be talking. The light is not strong, but it is bright enough for him to make his way toward it. The oracle glasses do not reveal anything unusual, no one in cloak.

He reaches for his operations belt, to add more sensory capabilities, but then he realizes that the glasses are not working.

He looks down at his belt. It's dead. Nothing is working. He is completely without power. It's becoming a familiar scenario.

Mark moves along the dark tunnel toward the faint light ahead, and the light is moving. No choice but to follow the light and the group, whoever they are. He makes his way along carefully. He hears no talking now, only the sound of dripping water.

Mark is trying not to make any noise. He reaches for his side arm, which should activate at his touch. It's dead. He withdraws his gun that shoots bullets—Old Reliable when technology fails. He tries to visualize martial arts in the dark passageway. Here's hoping that won't be necessary. The light keeps moving and turning and ascending.

More voices again, murmurs, but no footsteps. He wonders if they are aware of his presence.

At length, the lights vanish, and the tunnel becomes quiet, but he sees a faint glow ahead. He is on a staircase that he recognizes. He has returned to the entrance, and the stone has not been pushed back completely over the opening. Some light is filtering in.

Mark emerges and looks every direction. Nothing. No one. He feels his operations belt rebooting, and his oracle glasses are working again. He begins moving back toward the entrance to the Bolla. He wonders what time it is and looks at his belt. "Impossible!" he exclaims. He was apparently out cold for several hours.

As he enters the Bolla, he is feeling tired. He passes through the first two scans. It occurs to him that he needs to contact his team for a report. Just before he passes through a second scan, several *Carabinieri* approach him.

"*Capitano* Knutson, please come with us."

He protests, "Is there a problem? You do know that I am with the *Guardia Pretoriana*?"

"*Sì, capitano.* It is precisely your headquarters that desires a secure communication with you."

They escort him to a small room and leave him. Mark notices that they have locked the door.

Marks sits. As he does, Colonel Valenza appears in hologram across the table from him.

"Captain Knutson, I see you're okay. Where have you been? You literally dropped off the radar. Your team sent a report, but they were uncertain of your location."

"Sir, I was following a lead, as you—"

"You can explain that in a moment. But first, my staff has reviewed your recent reports and has studied your movements in the last day or so, those they could track. In their summary they have suggested some irregularities I would like for you to explain."

"Of course, sir."

"You were at the *Colosseo* and witnessed two incidents of cloaking and kidnapping. Later, you were near the explosion after which four more citizens were kidnapped. I'm glad you were there to provide some eyewitness testimony and to save a life in the one case."

"Sir, that is correct. What was irregular? Did I leave something out of the report?" Mark did not mention Dominique by name. He now worries about implicating her somehow.

"Let me continue. I haven't viewed all the reports, just a summary prepared by my staff. That first situation at the *Colosseo* has been contained and explained to the people who saw it. No need to start a panic. You later attended some sort of meeting outside the Bolla and outside your assigned zone with two of your team?"

"Yes, sir, I was acting on a tip, as you instructed."

"No problem there. I did watch that holoreport. Seren is one of dozens of preposterous prophets we've been following. No weapons were detected. We'll keep that file active. Anything else we should know?"

Mark now worries about implicating Angela. "I think the speech was the most important part, and as you say, we've heard a lot of that before. But I would like to keep track of that cell."

"Use your own judgment, captain. Then, we have the bomb. My staff summarized the reports of all agents on the scene: twenty-five people dead, four kidnappings. These were sure to result in four corpses to be ritually sacrificed, but you saved one of them from that. As before, we located bodies a few kilometers away, as I said, sacrificed barbarically. The official word is that they died in the explosion and were mutilated beyond recognition."

Valenza pauses for a moment and shakes his head.

"We've explained the bomb to the people of Rome as an old gas pipe with a leak that somehow met with a spark. That has happened before. The explanation seems to have calmed things down a bit, but I'm not comfortable with all these explanations that are not 100% true. On the other hand, we can't have widespread panic."

"Sir, the explosion scene was horrific. I'm glad I was able to do something."

"My staff has expressed the concern that you just happened to be in the area and that you were without your team. Can you explain this, captain? Rome is a big city, and they point out that you have been present or very close by when two separate assaults occurred."

"Sir, in the first case, I was at the Coliseum, a public place, with other off-duty PGs. In this more recent case, I was moving toward the exit, toward my assigned patrol sector. When I heard the blast, I was several blocks away, but because I was wearing lightning boots, I quickly got close enough to the explosion scene to spot two of the perpetrators, who were cloaked. I pursued and engaged and was wounded in an altercation when two more cloaked suspects showed up."

"Yes, my staff has briefed me on the report of a Search and Rescue agent who treated you and others."

Mark again becomes nervous. Colonel Valenza apparently hasn't made the connection to Mikhail, the same Search and Rescue agent who rescued him from the desert. He doesn't want to have to explain anything else.

But Mark elaborates, "I was on my way to begin my shift. Rome is large, but there are a limited number of exits. Once I had been treated, I contacted my team that I was in the process of—"

"Following another tip?"

"Yes, sir. I didn't think it would take so long."

"And what was the result?"

"Sir, nothing of any consequence. Another of the...as you say... countless bizarre groups that populate the zones outside the Bolla. Interference levels were high. Some of my equipment was not working."

"Okay, file a report. But exactly why did it take you so long?"

"Sir, I tracked possible suspects through buildings and underground tunnels. Frankly, sir, without technology I got lost in the dark passageways. As I said, my instruments weren't much good down there."

"Very well, captain. In the future, take at least some in your team with you when doing surveillance. A minimum of three on each one. That's standard procedure. Submit your report. My staff will brief me."

"Yes, sir. And who are these bombers? Do we know?"

"No more than the last time we discussed the kidnappings. My current guess is still the Neo-Fascists. They remain high on my list."

"But the kidnappings and the ritual sacrifice of the victims?"

"Well, again, that doesn't seem to fit their M.O., but we must continue our investigations and try to make some kind of sense of it. We will find these bombers and cloakers whoever they are, wherever they are!"

"Do you think they have chosen specific victims for some reason? Or is it all just random?"

"They may be related, of course. My staff has not been able to find any connection yet. They even considered your 'Beauty and the Beast' theory, but with no apparent link. Meanwhile we need more intel from our agents in the field, agents like you."

"Colonel, I will redouble my efforts to protect Rome. By the way, has EuroSecure finished their analysis of the incident in North Africa?"

"Not a word from them, captain. We all have our hands full right now. This bombing may signal an escalation of some sort. Carry on."

Colonel Valenza disappears.

—10—

VENUS REBORN

Rome is slightly unnerved. Somewhat fewer people populate the streets, fewer vehicles in the air and on the roads, yet as the days pass, the signs of *La Dolce Vita* and progress continue. Whole buildings advertise products and reflect the Good Life, the privilege of being a Roman.

Mark sits alone on the floor of his apartment. For the moment, the room is void of images; he has raised no furniture and has created no holograms.

He is thinking, trying to take in the last week or so. First, Angela leaves him. He has an eerie dream. Even for a drug-induced dream, it's weird. His warplanes go down in the North African desert almost like what happened in his dream, and then he meets Mikhail, his rescuer, who introduces him to Venus, who all but ignores him until he saves her life and follows them to some pointless underground religious sing fest, at which point his technology blanks out and so does he, after which he is detained and questioned by Colonel Valenza.

And then there was the creepy freak show where he saw Angela.

"Pinocchio. Play 'Greensleeves.' Guitar." The soothing sounds of sixteenth-century London fill the bare room.

"HoloVision"

"System ready to obey your every command, to fulfill your every wish, and to realize your every dream."

"Restore 'Romance Two—Venus on the water.'" And the lake scene reappears. Mark-1 is in the boat with Dominique.

Mark scrolls through his file of Dominique images on his portapack. He finds Venus on the train, who is more up close and personal. Fortunately he did record Dominique hovering over him in the alley with compassion and concern on her face.

Mark hurls this last image toward the boat, and Venus takes her place across from him, or at least across from his alter-ego, Mark-1.

A green light begins flashing. Incoming call. It's Mikhail.

"Exit 'Romance Two—Venus on the water' and save."

Mikhail's image is seated, so Mark drops a chair from the ceiling and seats him, activating the holovisit function.

"Sergeant?"

"Captain! I am delighted to see you again! You are well?"

Mark thinks, *"Which 'again' do you mean? Again since the alley or again since that underground tomb?"* Best to play dumb.

"I am well, yes, completely healed, thanks to your expert intervention." He wonders if Mikhail will bring it up. But why should he?

"Just part of the job, Captain." We have been quite busy, but things seem to be calming down. I heard the explosion was an old gas line?"

"Yes, among the risks of reclaiming an ancient city. At least that's the official word."

"We have had similar explosions before, and so it makes some sense, unless you know about the kidnappings, which few people do."

"I think HQ is still investigating. I haven't heard anything new."

"We were indeed fortunate that you happened along."

"Well, yes, I was on my way to the exit...uh...to do some work outside the Bolla. I wonder if maybe Dominique was targeted specifically. Do you think it was random? She is a communications assistant for EuroSecure, and her image is out there more than the average person's."

"I hope not, but far more important people could have been targeted. I haven't heard that they have seen any pattern. I'm sure that things are under control for now; however, we must be vigilant. That's the word coming down from above."

"Right, but she is beautiful, and the victim at the Coliseum was a beauty as well."

"That is true, but I know of no proven connection. Captain, speaking of Dominique, I wonder if you are free this evening? She would like to thank you more personally for saving her life. I wondered if we three might go out together."

Mark suddenly feels much more energetic. "I'm free. Just name the time and place!"

"The newly upgraded park, Il Parco Centrale, near the north shore of the lake, seems like an excellent place. I go there often to relax and meditate."

"Do they have boating set up yet?" Mark smiles at the possible irony.

"I believe they have it ready. You are wanting to rent one?"

"Maybe. Just an idea." It could be a little early for him to presume that he could take Dominique out for a romantic boat ride.

"Mikhail, she is single, isn't she?"

"Yes, she is."

How is that possible?

Mikhail suggests, "How about we meet at four o'clock? Maybe we can have dinner together. Perhaps afterward, you and I can play more levels of *Sleeping Beauty?*"

"Sounds terrific to me!" Mark's mind is on fire.

"Your place or mine?" asks Mikhail.

"We can come to my place. I'm sure the program is compatible with my system. Or yours would be okay. Let's finalize later."

"See you at four o'clock by the lake?"

"Check."

Mikhail disappears.

"Pinocchio, initiate a search for a hologame, *Sleeping Beauty – Infinity Version.*"

"Gepetto, I can only find *Sleeping Beauty 25*, just out."

"Hmm."

Mark arrives at the park early, but he sees that Mikhail and Dominique have arrived even earlier. He is wearing his oracle glasses as sunglasses. All in all, it's another beautiful spring day in the Eternal City.

Mikhail sees him and comes up to him, shaking his hand vigorously.

"Captain! So good to see you!"

"Likewise."

Dominque is carrying a basket. She sets it down and approaches Mark. She takes both of his hands in hers, leans forward, and kisses him on the cheek.

"*Merci bien*, Captain Mark. I thank you so much for saving my life." She looks at him and smiles warmly.

The smile is so warm that Mark feels like he is melting inside, but he tries to retain his composure.

"It was my job and my honor," he replies, not quite sure where that well-expressed reply came from but glad it came from somewhere. He smiles in return.

They all three go to sit on a bench in the shade. Mark is watching carefully all around them and has set his oracle glasses to detect anyone or anything in cloak. He is a little nervous.

"Let's hope for a less eventful meeting this time," jokes Mikhail.

Mark replies, "I still haven't processed the incident fully."

"Nor have I," agrees Dominique. "Hey, I've brought some sandwiches and soft drinks. Do you like Coca-Cola?"

"As a matter of fact..."

The three eat and chat for an hour about everything but the incident. Mark does not bring up what he was doing there, nor does he mention how he followed them to the catacombs outside the Bolla. Unlike their first few meetings, Dominique is paying much more attention to him. She is wearing a bright yellow sun dress that reveals her flower-like beauty and freshness. He is trying not to stare at her, but her eyes, her laugh, and her allure are all nearly impossible for him to ignore. Mark discreetly taps the stem of his oracle glasses to activate his recorder.

Mikhail suggests, "How about a boat ride? They've just started renting them here."

Mark falters nervously, "Well...uh..."

Dominique interjects, "That sounds like fun."

They rent a boat, but Mikhail announces, "I need to go back to my apartment, captain, to do a few things. You are coming over later, yes?"

"Yes, of course, I—"

"Then you two have fun and get acquainted."

This can't be real. I'm in heaven. But he continues to survey all around; he must remain vigilant, undistracted.

Mark and Dominique climb into the small boat, and he rows it out to the center of the lake. They see other boats around them, also with couples on board. A slight breeze, artificially generated, is blowing in from the north.

Dominique is wearing a large straw hat that is fastened to her hair with a yellow ribbon. He cannot help but compare the current view with his memory of Angela on the rowboat ten years earlier.

Dominique remarks, "Everything seems so quiet. It's been calm since the incident. Even the patrols to the south and east report only a little activity, minimal actually. You knew this?"

"I hadn't heard anything, but I guess I'm not in the loop."

"I can tell you because you are a EuroSecure pilot. Everything is unusually peaceful. It's uncanny."

"The quiet before the storm?"

"Perhaps."

"Surely there's no coordination of the groups? They didn't all decide to just calm down and make peace?"

"It seems unlikely."

They pause for a moment and enjoy the natural beauty of the park.

Dominique finally changes the subject. "Tell me about yourself, captain. Where are you from?"

"Oklahoma originally."

"Oklahoma. That sounds so romantic."

"Not really."

"And you are single, yes?"

"Yes, I recently ended a contract that had been on the skids for some time."

They again sit and look at the lake without saying anything for several minutes.

"Tell me more, Mark," which she calls him for the first time without adding 'captain,' "What do you like to do, other than flying planes, martial arts, playing hologames, and saving princesses?"

This had better be good, thinks Mark. He finally replies, "I love music, especially classical music. My mother was a music teacher in a public school. My dad was…uh…sort of a cowboy."

"Opposites attract?"

"Apparently. I can't think of two people more different from one another. And you, Dominique? Where are you from? You are French, right?"

"Yes, I'm from Paris. That's where my father lives. I'll be taking some leave there soon. My mother is passed on seven years ago, and *Papa* is not currently in good health." Her face looks sad for the first time.

"No brothers or sisters?"

"No, I am an only child."

Mark suggests, "How about some music? Swan Lake Suite, or would that be too corny since we are on a lake?"

"Oh, yes!" Dominique laughs, "That would be perfect."

Yes! He initiates the music on his portapack, and Dominique closes her eyes and leans back, taking it all in. She seems to be moving her legs and arms slightly in rhythm with the rolling and swaying of the great masterpiece.

"I used to dance to this, in Paris."

"You were a ballerina?"

"Yes, for several years. My degree is in the performing arts with a specialization in piano, but I also have danced, have done acting, and have painted."

"And now, communications assistant for EuroSecure. How did that happen?"

"I loved my life in Paris, but I wanted to do something to help the effort. My father is a retired general in EuroSecure."

Mark instantly makes the connection and is astonished.

"General Lécuyer?"

"Yes. You have heard of him?"

"Who hasn't? General Lécuyer's daughter!" Mark struggles to process this new information. "Dominique, do you suppose that the terrorists targeted you specifically for kidnapping?"

"I don't think so. How could they know? Lécuyer is not an uncommon name, and all such personal information is tightly guarded."

"They could know a great deal. In fact, they do know a lot more than we have assumed. But as for your father, he was a hero of many wars, an inspiration to me and so many others, a courageous soldier, and a voice of reason."

"He is a man of peace who hates war, but he always said, 'That which hates you will come looking for you. Be prepared to meet it with courage. It will attack you and those you love. Be ready to defend them with your life.' I'm not a warrior like you, but I felt I could do something. The Federation is under attack. The threat, it is real. *Papa* is no longer an active participant; however, he does still have connections. How do you think I got a position as communications assistant for the EuroSecure base?"

"I'm still not so sure you're out of danger. And I am certain that you got the job on your own merits. I do know the quote from your father. He's a great man. He's not doing well?"

"Not well at all."

"I'm so sorry to hear that."

"*Merci.* Thank you, Mark, for your concern." Dominique smiles but has a far-off look in her eyes as she looks up at Rome's tall buildings and listens to the suite.

"How do you know Mikhail?"

"He's a friend of a friend, actually a friend of several friends."

"You said you don't know him well."

"I don't. Today is probably the most I've ever spoken with him, I mean, one-on-one. He's just around at social gatherings. He doesn't talk to me much."

"Seems like a nice fellow. And he saved my life."

"Then we both owe him something."

"So how did you learn English?"

"Oh, in school. Plus, *Papa* did several tours in the U.S. One year in Texas and two in Virginia. That helped."

"Texas? So you have seen a few cowboys?"

"A few. I wish I had seen some Oklahoma cowboys. Are they different?"

"Do I look different from a Texas cowboy?"

"A little," Dominique replies playfully.

Twenty classical pieces later, Mark and Dominique are getting to know each other, laughing, and relaxing together.

After a time, Dominique announces, "I do have to go now, Mark." Mark acknowledges and begins rowing to shore. He really doesn't want it to end. He ties up at the dock and helps Dominique out of the boat.

"I would like to see you again. Is that possible?"

"How about dinner one day soon? I do know of a good French restaurant."

Dominique scoffs, "Good French cuisine outside France? I don't think so!"

"Okay, maybe a good Italian restaurant?"

"Are there any in Rome?"

"I'll try to find one."

"Be in touch." As they say good-bye, they shake hands.

While Mark stands on the shore, he watches Dominique blend into the crowd and turns off his recorder.

PART II

—11—

SLEEPING BEAUTY REVISTED

Mark goes to Mikhail's apartment.

"Captain! How did things go with Dominique?"

"Outstanding…, I hope."

"She wanted to thank you for what you did."

"I feel thanked, and then some."

"Are you ready for some serious combat?"

"Yes! But don't I need to repeat and beat that level that beat me?"

"Not necessary. Perhaps a preview of what is ahead and some practice runs first, then you can repeat the entire game."

"Okay, what's next?"

"The next level is called 'Serpents in the High Places.'"

"Which means?"

"Mountains and peaks, the haunt of dragons, snakes, and other hybrids that are slithery and don't play fair."

"Ex-cel-lent," Mark mutters under his breath, as he always does when facing a nearly impossible challenge. Mikhail activates his gaming system, and they both don helmets and game gear.

"You want the same weapons with four arms, I assume?"

"Fine."

"Special capabilities. Hmm, you'll need to fly considerably higher and jump farther for this one, which I've already programmed. I will give you the ability to spin your body and your weapons rapidly. You can become like a buzz saw without losing your equilibrium. Your opponents do attack from behind or any direction they choose. And remember that your weapons, primitive as they are, are sufficient to slay any creature in this game, no matter how powerful."

"I'll be unbeatable!"

"Don't be so sure. Your opposition will have special capabilities as well. And they will not spare you or your feelings. You'll see."

"Bring it!"

"Remember, captain, this is only a game, it's not real. The only consequence is seeing the 'GAME OVER' icon and exiting abruptly."

"Thanks, I know it's a just game."

"Yes, but you may forget. That's the power of the illusion. Plus the technology is quite advanced. Remember what I explained to you before; you may believe it to be real, as you do when you're in a dream."

Mikhail starts the game, and the two find themselves standing on a tall peak, surveying the horizon. He sees a distant red light that looks like the sun setting, but it's not.

"That light is near your ultimate goal. To get there, you must fight your way through more levels and then defeat the Emerald-Green Dragon and awaken Sleeping Beauty."

GAME OVER.

Mark and Mikhail take off their helmets. "What happened? We hadn't even started!"

"The serpents have no rules. You must be on the alert. I believe we were killed by stealth from behind. I should have frozen the game until I had explained everything to you. I'll reset."

Again, they are standing on the peak. Mark is vigilant, surveying the landscape all around him. He senses a slight movement, but Mikhail beats him by slashing at the attacking serpent and beheading him.

"We have to watch each other's backs, captain. Two are better than one, as you know, since you fly two warplanes."

"And I see that you're again not carrying a shield or wearing armor?"

"In this game, your partner's vigilance is your best armor and shield."

"Let's fly."

They leap from the mountaintop into the air and land on the next mountain. No resistance so far. Mikhail slashes his sword to the left and slays a dragon that appeared one microsecond before. The beast falls dead instantly and rolls down the side of the mountain.

"You've played this before."

"Experience may help, but you have to be on the alert, ready for anything. I have indeed played it before; however, I need you in this battle, and you need me. You may not see anything, but you will feel something in your gut, like an evil foreboding. Act on instinct. Strike before thinking."

Almost immediately they both begin to sense something, and they lash out ahead of them. More dead snakes and dragons. They jump toward the next mountain. Mikhail switches to buzz saw mode, and Mark follows suit. In that form they take out a whole squadron of flying serpents.

"I could really get into this game!" Mark comments to Mikhail once they land on their feet. "It's so much more advanced than previous versions."

"This level will be good practice for facing the Ultimate Dragon Boss.

More dragons attack and spit out fire toward the two virtual warriors. Mikhail takes an evasive maneuver, but Mark's armor is damaged, and he has lost his mace. He holds up his shield and hurls his sword into the heart of one of the dragons. Mikhail has a boomerang sword device. He slings it and decapitates the other.

They jump up and land on the next mountain. "Quick thinking, captain. Nice move, going right to the heart of the monster. Remember that. It's their most vulnerable spot."

"They have hearts?"

"Yes, in a snaky sort of way." They laugh.

Mark and Mikhail continue making their way across the mountain ranges, slaying various types of serpents and trampling snakes as they go. Mark is gaining confidence in the game.

"We're approaching the dragon boss for this level. Up to this point, they have been easy."

Not far off, Mark can see a dragon perched on the last mountain peak. They both leap toward it.

Up close, it doesn't look all that large. Mark readies his sword and shield. He hurls his sword at its heart, but the sword passes through it.

"It's a hologram," Mikhail remarks. "A hologram created by a holographic program. You can't hurt it, and it can't hurt you."

Mark looks down at a nearby lake. Suddenly a beast with three heads bursts forth out of the otherwise quiet waters. It spews fire from all three mouths and has claws and countless tentacles. It is a fiend twice the size of all the others and with twice the speed. The dragon is in constant motion and on the attack. Mikhail suggests to Mark, "I'll go for its back. You take the front." A tentacle knocks Mark out of the sky and slams him into the side of the mountain.

He rebounds and, flying through the air in buzz saw mode, he begins trimming snake-like tentacles at a high rate of speed, but the tentacles grow back instantly. He tries to penetrate to get a fix on the heart, but seemingly nothing on the creature stays still.

Until it vanishes. Mark sees Mikhail in the distance, who is on the attack apparently against nothing but air. His pattern seems erratic, yet he is finding his marks.

Mark begins the same maneuver and quickly slams into the side of the mountain, pinned by a claw which has now become visible, and—

GAME OVER.

Mark sits motionless for a few moments and removes his helmet. Mikhail has already removed his.

"That was intense. I guess I lost."

"Chalk it up to experience."

"You didn't lose. Why did you stop? Could you have taken him alone? I guess you didn't need a partner."

"I have taken him alone. But it's just a game. We can play more later. Partners need training."

"What's next? Bigger dragons?"

"No, the next level is quite the opposite. It's called 'Smoke and Mirrors. Shadow Warriors and Swamps,' and other surprises."

"What's the challenge?"

"You must be both wise and cunning. Brute force and weapons will not be enough."

"So what's the point of the level?"

"Survival! To persevere and get to the following level alive."

"How can I defeat the Ultimate Dragon Boss if I couldn't beat the boss on this level?"

"You'll need help, and we will arrange some. No one takes on the Ultimate Dragon alone."

—12—

DINNERS WITH DOMINIQUE

"My eyes were liars, then, because I never saw true
beauty before tonight." Romeo

Mark and Dominique have been holophoning and seeing each other
informally for several weeks now. It has been a time of uneasy
peace in Rome, but peace nonetheless.

As previously agreed, Dominique meets Mark at an exclusive
restaurant within walking distance of the Trevi Fountain. Mark
is wearing his EuroSecure uniform. His pants and jacket are dark
blue, his shoes are black patent leather, and he has two gold braids
on his right shoulder indicating that he is a captain. He stands at
the top of the long staircase, waiting for his date.

Dominique finally enters, wearing a full-length black evening
dress that swirls from her shoulders to her feet. Her hair is up,
fastened with a diamond-stetted clip, and she is wearing earrings
that sparkle like falling stars that Mark would like to catch, but
Mark first has to catch his breath when he sees her. His heart is
beating fast.

Love is in the air.

"You look...stunning! *Mademoiselle, tu es incroyablement belle!*"

"*Merci, Mon capitaine.* You speak French? I did not know."

"Not much. I've been reviewing and practicing."

"I like that. I also like men in uniform, you know." She smiles confidently.

Mark extends her his arm, she wraps her hand around it, and they descend into the restaurant, which specializes in French cuisine and boasts a unique atmosphere. Dominique fits it all like a glove, and it fits her like...like...her dress.

Mark's camera in his oracle glasses is ON.

The pianist, or perhaps the virtual pianist, is playing Débussy, Arabesque. The restaurant is called the Galerie des Glaces and is modeled with hints of the palace at Versailles. Behind the pianist is a view of the famous gardens in 360-D. Many radiant chandeliers, like hanging vines of precious stones, illuminate the tables and the dance floor. Classical sculptures set into the walls and statues of gold on the floor contribute to the regal atmosphere. The floors are marble, and on the ceilings, just a hint of Michelangelo, mural paintings of the heavens, clouds, cherubs, and natural wonders. There are roses everywhere, some real, some holographed.

Mark and Dominique are seated at a table for two, which has real flowers at the center and an elegant silk covering with wineglasses and tableware already set.

"What would you like to eat?" asks Dominique.

Mark does not answer. He studies the menu icons and scrolls through them.

"Something without snails in it."

"You have no *escargots* in Oklahoma?"

"Yes, but we don't eat them."

The pianist begins playing Débussy's Claire de lune.

Mark and Dominique order filet mignon, and Mark has prearranged a bottle of Pontelet-Millon, Red Chateaux. The waiter opens the cork and pours the wine.

They raise their glasses. "*Santé*," toasts Dominique. Mark responds: "And to the future...uh...of Rome."

"To the future," Dominique repeats as she tips her glass to touch Mark's. They each take a sip, and Mark says, "I don't want to talk shop, but I have a question and a reason for asking."

Dominique responds, "Ask me whatever you like."

"How are things on the front? My case has been cleared, and I should be reporting again for duty, but they seem to be stalling or delaying or something."

"I don't know much. It's all quiet. There is an anxious peace. It's eerie, given what happened several weeks ago. Orange alert has changed to Yellow, at least for operations in the Mediterranean."

"I heard that. I'm speculating that the situation in Rome is currently considered more critical. I may be here for a while, which is fine with me. I don't want to leave Rome for now."

"Well, I'm leaving Rome on a daily basis! Media has been busy trying to keep the public informed and calm."

"I'm still leaving Rome at night. Graveyard shift. I'm temporarily with the *Guardia Pretoriana*. I think I can tell you that. We have some concerns. Outside the Bolla, we've noted only the usual activity, nothing dangerous so far, and nothing directly related to the kidnappings and murders that we can find."

"No more kidnappings or murders?"

"Nothing quite like what we witnessed. We are aware of crime, of course, outside the Bolla. And we know of a few groups that just meet, but they engage in no visibly subversive activities. They have no discernable purpose, and some of them don't even meet to eat or drink or do drugs. They just talk...and sing. Can you believe that?"

Dominique keeps her cool. "Who can explain human behavior? Especially in these times."

Mark reflects, "It's puzzling. We've seen so many groups that don't seem to have or use technology, certainly not of the kind that could jam ours or enable them to cloak themselves and their victims."

After playing Chopin, Fantaisie Impromptu, the pianist disappears, and a small ensemble takes his place. Mark looks intently at Dominique and asks, "May I have the honor of this dance?" Mark is seeing real value in all the dance lessons his mother forced him to take when he was in high school.

They step out on to the dance floor and begin moving and flowing together as one. It is as if they have danced together many times before. Mark holds his treasure in an intimate embrace, the most intimate thus far. He has never known love until this night.

They dance and dance and dance.

When the music stops, they finish eating. Mark suggests they stroll over to the Trevi Fountain.

"Aren't we overdressed for that?" Dominique asks.

"Probably," Mark replies.

As they walk to the fountain, they talk. Mark remarks, "Legend has it that a young girl led thirsty Roman soldiers to this very spot, where there was a source of fresh, pure water."

When they enter the piazza, they stand and contemplate the majestic beauty and sculptural artistry of the fountain. A violinist is nearby, playing for tips. He is playing Elgar's Salut d'amour. Many people are strolling around the fountain and chatting.

"Tre-vi. Where three roads converge," Mark observes.

"Or where two roads become one," counters Dominique.

They stare at the fountain without saying a word. After a time, Mark reaches out and takes Dominique's hand. She takes hold of his and squeezes it gently. He looks at her, and she smiles. Something strange and wonderful is happening inside him, something he can't control, something he doesn't want to control.

After a time, Dominique sighs. "Mark, I'm sorry, but I'm really quite tired. I guess I'm not used to so much dancing. I have a desk job now."

Mark laughs but is a bit worried that he might have said or done something wrong.

Dominique seems to sense his uneasiness. "Really, I have had a wonderful time, but I should go. Please, walk me home."

Mark doesn't say anything; he just reaches out and takes her hand again, and she grasps his firmly. They begin walking, still saying nothing. They stroll along the streets of Rome. They feel a gentle—if artificially generated—breeze. Mark and Dominique are oblivious to the relentless, extravagant advertising all around, to the noise of the streets and airways, and to conversations of passersby.

A booming voice fills Rome. *Star Wars!!! Guerre Stellari!!! Episodio 27: Il Ritorno al lato oscuro della forza!!!* And the artificially holographed moon image projected on the ceiling of the Bolla turns into a Death Star for just a few moments accompanied by the new imperial theme music. *Prossimamente al Circo Massimo!!!*

Mark and Dominique watch the ad. Mark comments, "Return to the Dark Side of the Force...again?" They both laugh.

The real virtual moon returns, and they finally arrive at her building. Dominique calls down her personal pod.

Just as she is about to step into it, Dominique looks at Mark, "Thank you for a wonderful evening. I think I will never forget it."

"Can I see you again soon?"

Dominique leans forward and again kisses him on the cheek. She turns and enters the pod.

As the hatch closes, she smiles. "Yes. Call me."

Mark stands there long after she has ascended to her apartment. He is dumbfounded. He is happy. He is frustrated. He is confused. He begins thinking about the next date, about her charm and mystery, and about many unanswered questions.

Mark goes out into the street and heads back to his building. Though it is five kilometers away, he decides to walk.

He remembers that he needs to go to the next meeting of the Lumena. He is uncomfortable with the fact that he didn't share the complete content of his holorecord of the first meeting with his superiors.

When Mark arrives at his apartment, he begins replaying images of Dominique on the boat in the lake, of Dominique in her evening dress. He falls asleep, dreaming of Dominique.

The next day, Dominique invites Mark to her apartment for dinner. He can hardly wait.

Mark arrives twenty minutes early. He ascends in the elevator, pre-cleared to enter the building, and rings the bell. Dominique answers the door, wearing an apron over a casual dress. Mark suddenly thinks even more highly of French cuisine.

"Mark! I am not ready, but come in, please." She hugs him briefly, and he enters.

"Make yourself at home. I'm still putting the finishing touches on the dinner."

Mark wanders around the apartment, studying the furnishings, the paintings, the books, and the general décor. He sees a baby grand piano next to a wall covered by a large mirror. It is all colorful, tasteful, and classy, like Dominique herself. He doesn't notice much technology, only a basic home entertainment system and her portapack.

"I had heard that the French were not as much into hi-tech as is Rome. I guess that's true, if I judge by what I see here."

Dominique laughs as she clatters plates, taking them out of the cupboard. "It's true with me and my family. I like the 'Old World' look and feel."

"And no robot?"

"For what possible purpose?"

"You certainly have a lot of books! And it seems that they are all in French!"

"Yes, we French are like that. I do have many in Italian, English, and some other languages. I confess that I prefer things in French."

The home entertainment system is playing Tchaikovsky, Romeo and Juliet.

While Dominique works to get dinner together, Mark looks over some of the books on her shelves. He tries to read the titles and authors out loud, in English-accented French:

"Léon Tolstoï, *La Guerre et la Paix.*"

"Pas mal!" comments Dominique.

He continues: "Victor Hugo, *Notre-Dame de Paris*. Augustin, *La Cité de Dieu*. John Milton, *Le Paradis perdu*. *La Sainte Bible*. Miguel de Cervantès, *Don Quixotte*. Blaise Pascal, *Pensées*. Charles Dickens, *Un Conte de deux villes*. Paul Verlaine, *Sagesse*. I don't know that one."

"It's a book of poetry. '*Bon chevalier masqué qui chevauche en silence...*'."

"Ah!" Mark still doesn't know what it is about but is afraid to admit it.

Dominique asks, "Have you perhaps read any of those books in English?"

"No. I've seen the movie versions of a few. Does that count?"

"Silly! Are you ready to eat? Please come and sit!"

Mark sits and awaits instructions. He feels happy being a slave to Dominique's whims and wishes. The table is set elegantly with a real burning candle in the middle. Dominique lowers the lights. Before him is a bowl of soup, a glass of wine, and a plate of hot *baguette* slices with butter beside them.

After she pours the wine, Dominique sits down. The flitting candle flame is reflected in her eyes.

"This looks delicious! May I ask what it is? And may I ask if this is the whole meal?"

"This is but the first course! *C'est la soupe à l'oignon*, onion soup, *avec un petit Beaujolais*; that's the wine. Toast?"

Their glasses clink together, but neither proposes anything to toast to. Dominique even seems uncharacteristically nervous this evening. They eat the soup quietly for a few minutes and listen to Chopin, Polonaise-Fantaisie, op. 61, which Mark identifies.

Dominique laughs, "It is *extraordinaire* that this Oklahoma cowboy-pilot knows so much about classical music! Your mother must have been quite a good teacher."

"That she was. I guess she gave me a love for classical music, for all music really."

"And your father was a cowboy. Do you have brothers and sisters?"

"One brother. I haven't seen him in years. We don't communicate much, never did. My parents passed away eleven years ago. That's partly why I came to Rome and EuroSecure. I did a stint with the Praetorian Guard here, too."

"You were a pilot in the US?"

"I was a policeman for three years. Then I was in the air force and was a fighter pilot before they scaled everything back. The army had a bigger need for chopper pilots to fight the cartels. Helicopters never interested me. How about your family?"

"*Papa*, you know about." Dominique picks up the bowls and serves a salad with *shallots*. "I think I told you that *Maman* passed away seven years ago. *Papa* has not been the same since. She was a devoted wife and mother; she followed him all around the world when she could. *Maman* gave me my love for music and the arts. Her dream as a young woman was to become a concert pianist. Before college, she was my piano teacher. I am an only child. Did I mention that?"

"I believe so." Mark looks over at the piano. "I was hoping I would be treated to a concert. I presumed the baby grand was not just for show."

"*Mais non*! That is tonight's entertainment, unless you are prepared to do some cowboy things for me, maybe some rope tricks?"

Mark laughs. Mark is blown away. They continue chatting.

Finally Dominique announces, "Time for the main course, *hachis parmentier*. I think you call it 'shepherd pie?'"

As she serves the food to Mark, Dominique asks, "You went to college, I assume?"

The system is playing Ravel, Gaspard de la nuit.

"Yeah. I didn't major in music. I did Aerospace Engineering, standard for future pilots. How about you?"

"I attended the Sorbonne for a few years but ended up in the Conservatoire de Paris."

"A piano-playing communications assistant?"

Dominique laughs, "It's a long story. I wanted to fulfill *Maman*'s dream, but life...and war tend to get in the way."

They continue to talk but experience long comfortable moments of silence in which they simply enjoy each other's company. Mark can't remember when he's smiled so much.

"Are you ready for dessert? *Voilà, une crêpe Suzette.*"

"I don't see how the food could get any better! The company certainly couldn't!"

Dominique smiles and lowers her eyes. "*Tu es très aimable, monsieur!*"

They finish dessert and have coffee.

Mark feels it's time to define the relationship!!

"Uh, so, I have to ask you something..."

"You have to? I'm intrigued!"

"It's okay if you don't want to talk about it. I just wonder, looking at you, being with you, listening to you, how many boyfriends or serious relationships have you had? I'm sorry if I'm not phrasing it delicately."

"Oh, *pas de problème*. I had several in school, some in college. When I devoted myself to the piano, well, the piano became my boyfriend for a number of years. I was living at home with *Papa* when...*Maman est morte*...she is passed on. I decided to remain there with him for a good while. He needed me."

"And EuroSecure?"

"As you know, I had connections there. Seeing the constant threats against the Federation, I wanted to do something. I'm not a pilot or soldier; however, I am comfortable with communications and media. The pay is good, and I adore Rome. *Papa* was proud that I had taken that step. I worked in the communications department for several years before getting promoted to the official job of communications assistant."

"The face of the base?"

"The voice, only one voice."

They fall silent for a few moments while Mark gathers his thoughts. He knows the question is coming.

"And you, Captain Knutson? The history of your relationships is perhaps more complicated?"

"The only serious relationship I've ever had was the contract I mentioned to you in the park. It lasted ten years. I...we...just broke it off fairly recently." Mark's head drops, and he looks at the floor. "I know what you must be thinking."

"And how would you know that, captain? You have perhaps become an expert on how women think?"

"Psh! My big bad!"

"Let me be frank. No, even better, let me be French! When I first saw you, I found you an attractive man. Mikhail spoke highly of you, even though he had only known you for a short time. I understand you did some male bonding?"

"A hologame in a rescue pod in the desert."

"Yes, male bonding. And then, what can I say, you heroically and gallantly came to my rescue, my knight in shining armor. You put your life on the line for me!"

"It's what I do."

"Mikhail told me more about you, but most importantly, your heroic conduct has told me a lot of what I wanted to know. Last evening, you looked incredibly dashing in your uniform, and you dance divinely."

"There's my mom to thank for the dance skills. I resisted taking lessons."

"I know you are a big tough pilot and soldier, Mark, but I see something in your heart that attracts me the most."

Mark is mystified. "My heart?"

"Yes, I see wounds. I see the recent wound from..."

"Angela."

"Wounds are possible only in a tender heart. That, together with your selfless courage, show to me that your heart is also noble. Both recommend you to me."

"Dominique, I would like to call you my girlfriend. I hope that's not moving too fast for you. Please tell me if it is."

"Is it too fast for you?"

"No!"

"Perhaps it is a little fast. I'll say this: we are dating. I'm dating no one except you. And I don't want to date anyone but you. We're friends, good friends. *Ça va?*"

Mark is relieved. "I like the sound of that!"

Dominique smiles and moves toward the piano. "And now for some entertainment. Bring your wine and make yourself comfortable on the couch."

"May I record this?"

"Of course! But it is only for you! No showing it to friends or sharing it on other media."

"*D'accord!*"

Dominique sits on the piano bench and opens the keyboard cover. Mark sits on the couch as she readies herself. He is enjoying looking at her and at her reflection in the large mirror on the wall next to the piano. Two Dominiques for the price of one.

"I would like to perform for you Mozart, Sonata No. 6, just the first few movements." Mark applauds. He loves classical music, but he is expecting to reach new heights of appreciation tonight. She looks over at him, smiles, and bows her head slightly.

As Dominique begins, her mastery of the keyboard is evident. Mark remembers his mother playing the piano like that.

Mark leans back and allows the music to carry him to thoughts and imaginations that words could never express. Dominique seems one with the piano. It is literally her instrument on which she expresses her passion. She communicates with the keys, and they respond with a sublime beauty that fills the apartment. As she plays, Dominique becomes more elegant, and graceful, and beautiful, if that is even possible.

She continues with other pieces by Mendelssohn and Bach, plus a more recent work by a twenty-first-century composer, Michel Érgal, Tribute. Mark is captivated.

Dominique pauses. "And now, something incredibly close to my heart, some special entertainment, the *pièce de résistance.*"

Mark can only wonder.

Dominique walks over to the screen of her entertainment system and scrolls. She initiates a program and returns to her bench.

"Do you know 'The Prayer'?"

"Uh..., 'Livin' on a Prayer'?"

"No, 'The Prayer'! A song from *The Quest for Camelot.*"

"I guess I missed that movie."

"My silly duck, you no doubt have watched the video of Andrea Bocelli and Céline as they perform it together? They do a version of it in English and Italian."

"Ah! Yes, love it! Classic."

"*Maman* loved it, too. She first heard it when she was a young girl. She said, 'This will be my prayer for my children one day.' She taught me how to play the song, and I know she prayed the words for me."

"I'd love to hear it!"

"*Bien, quelque chose de spéciale. Centre, programme 'Maman,' numéro deux!*" And she plays the opening measure to the song.

At this, another baby grand piano and another pianist appear opposite her in a large empty space designated for holographic entertainment. Mark leans forward, surprised. The pianist is a woman who resembles Dominique, just a little older than she.

"Is this *Maman*?"

"Yes, it is, perhaps ten or fifteen years ago. Isn't she beautiful?" *Maman* remains frozen for the moment. She is an elegantly dressed woman, her hair is coiffed perfectly, and she is wearing a sparkling necklace and a sweet smile on her face.

"Okay, sit back. We'll start." Dominique repeats the first measure, and the holoprogram initiates. *Maman* begins playing, and Dominique accompanies her, echoing her with chords and runs.

Mark is recording all this.

Maman begins playing as she sings the prayer in English. Her voice is exquisite. She asks God to watch over her daughter wherever she goes and to guide her with His grace to somewhere that she'll be safe. She sings a petition for her daughter's safety, that she will find the light of God even in the darkness of night.

Maman continues to play and sing with extraordinary feeling; holographed tears stream down her cheeks. Dominique accompanies her and is in tears, as well. Mark is unexpectedly moved and is fighting back tears himself, rubbing his eyes occasionally. Mark does not consider himself an emotional person. He can't remember the last time he cried. He hasn't cried over Angela.

As the program concludes, *Maman* is again frozen. Dominique is still and expressionless. Mark is stunned. They sit in silence for several minutes.

"I wish you could have met her, Mark."

"I feel like I have." Mark is struggling inside to deal with new emotions and with some he hasn't felt since he was a young boy.

—13—

REFLECTIONS IN SEQUENCE

Seren's second public meeting takes place before Mark goes to work, so he decides to attend on a less official basis. He will not need to report what he sees, but if something seems suspicious, he will be in a good position to see and record it. He again puts on old clothes, hoping to blend and not be noticed by anyone, especially by Angela.

When he arrives at the aged theater, he immediately notices that the auditorium is packed. He ascends into the balcony area, where there is standing room only but at least a better view of things. He turns on his camera in the frame of his oracle glasses.

Mark surveys the crowd, looking for Angela's abundant blond hair, which usually stands out. He zooms in on every blond in the audience.

Not there. Strange. Nothing is happening. The crowd is animated. He hears the name "Seren" whispered a lot.

A line of a few dozen robed figures approaches the stage. Everyone falls silent. They are likely Seren's assistants. All form a semi-circle and pull back their hoods. In one case, blond hair flows out.

Angela, an assistant to Seren. "Why am I not surprised?"

As before, another cloaked figure, approaches the podium and does the same. Everyone in the theater who is sitting stands to their feet without being prompted.

It is Seren. He is smiling and raising his left hand in a sort of greeting to the crowd. He then motions for all to be seated, and those who can sit, do. He is speaking in Italian. Mark again activates Universal Translator.

"Welcome to my friends! Welcome to those who are new! Welcome to the curious and to the skeptic! And yes, welcome to the members of the Praetorian Guard who have been sent to keep an eye on me!"

The crowd chuckles, and many look around for likely guard members. Mark initiates a sweep with his oracle glasses, but they do not pick up any cloaked figures or fellow guard members. "Count: 556" displays on his lenses.

"I am here this evening with my assistants, which some of you will note have grown in number."

Mark watches Angela, who is smiling more broadly than any other assistant.

"Please, open your robes." They obey as one. Seren opens his robe as well.

"As you can see, we are unarmed. We pose no threat to you or to Rome. We come in peace, to benefit all humankind. You have heard the rumors, the stories of things that have happened and perhaps have come to see proof or even to see something new?"

He pauses for several moments.

"Tonight, you will see something new and hear something revolutionary, but what you will hear is not so new. It is the same message I have spoken before and quite openly. Humanity is on the brink, not of war, rather, of an astounding breakthrough in our evolution."

Seren pauses again; everyone is in eager anticipation of what he will say and do next.

"The life-forces within all of us are indeed a mystery. How can mere chemicals come alive and reproduce? Who can explain the why? Science cannot. But that is not the real question, is it? Life happened. Life empowers inorganic matter. Life is energy. No, my friends and guests, the real question is 'Who among us can harness life and its power?'"

If a pin dropped...

"I am no different from any of you, except that years ago, I came to an awareness—that's where it begins, with an awareness—, an awareness of the potential of my life forces."

Pause. Seren places his left index finger over his lips for just a moment.

"We all know that the human brain is a treasure chest of information, electrical impulses, synapses, images, and other inexplicable functions. We use only some of it and understand so little of the living algorithms that inhabit it. What a strange and amazing energy field it is, this thing that some call the soul."

Pause for effect.

"If you are alive and breathing and thinking, you have one!"

Mark wonders when he will in fact say something new and interesting.

"Many years ago, I began reflecting on all this, and as I did, I discovered ancient documents, writings that spoke of spiritual disciplines, of meditation, and of the interconnection of our life forces with all the life-power of the universe. We have all felt that, have we not? We have been drawn to the beauty of flowers and plants, we have admired, even envied the strength of certain animals, and we have experienced an unexplainable affinity with all other living things."

Seren paces in silence and then turns to the crowd.

"I submitted myself to the instructions and disciplines contained in the contents of these documents."

A raucous voice from the crowd questions him:

"What documents? From where? Where are they now?"

Seren is not rattled. "All in good time, my friend. All in good time."

Mark thinks that Seren is an impressive speaker. He still wonders where all this is going.

Seren looks over at several assistants standing to his left. One of them is Angela. They bring him two large mirrors and position themselves on either side of him. They then turn the mirrors to the audience.

"My friends, let's begin with lesson number one. Do you see yourselves in these mirrors?"

Mark scoffs, "Is this the trick?"

The audience does not reply but merely watches. "What do you see? Your own image, but in reverse, a mere reflection. We all understand how this works."

He directs the assistants to turn both mirrors toward him, one on each side of him, with him in the middle.

"Now I see what you cannot see. I will describe it to you, and you will understand because you have no doubt also seen it and marveled."

Seren looks in one of the mirrors and then looks in the other.

"I see myself reflected in both mirrors. As they face each other, I view in both countless images of myself that stretch perhaps into infinity. As a child, I was fascinated by this phenomenon. I looked at my other selves and with a child's innocence tried to reach out and touch them, to communicate with them."

Mark scoffs under his breath, "Psh!"

"Of course, this was nonsense. They are only reflections, but they can perhaps serve as a metaphor, reflections in sequence, or representations of what we only see about ourselves when we consider ourselves from a unique perspective. Without that perspective, we would never be aware of this infinity of reflections."

Seren motions for his assistants to take the mirrors off stage.

"Scientists ponder alternate universes, multiverses, perhaps an infinite number. I do not concern myself with theories or illusions. Rather, I wonder how I might multiply myself, my own life forces, for the good of all humanity."

He then repeats his last line with some emphasis, "Yes, for the good of all humanity!"

Seren goes on: "It is no doubt true that Rome and the human race do not now perceive their need for my message, but the time is coming soon, a different time, when Rome, indeed the whole world, will cry out for my help. All will want to share in the power that is about to be displayed. Rome will fulfill her destiny in this metamorphosis. This Roman Renaissance will begin here, just outside Rome, and Rome herself will eventually embrace it. No, my friends, not war or a violent revolution, but a rebirth, a renaissance...salvation!"

Assistants dramatically draw back the curtain behind Seren, showing numerous tables; grapevines are sprawled all over them, even to the floor, and bottles of wine are stacked high.

"This has been our project in preparing for tonight's meeting. Everyone who wishes will receive a free bottle of wine, made from these grapes which have been grown to full fruition by nothing more than my own life force."

Mark watches Seren carefully. He quickly scans the bottles for possible explosives.

"Of course, you are skeptical, but please, take home a bottle anyway. Sample it, share it. It can do you no harm, only good. It will give you a sense of peace that you have never before known."

Mark is shaking his head back and forth incredulously.

"That will be later. No, tonight we have something special. I have asked several of you in the audience to bring metal objects, anything made of ordinary metal, preferably small and not valuable. My assistants are right now placing about a dozen such objects on the stage before me. May I ask the dozen others who have brought such items to simply pass them to the front? This will give many of you the opportunity to examine them, to see that they are in fact quite commonplace."

Some twenty-four objects of all kinds begin piling up on the stage: empty cans, costume jewelry, metal rods, ball bearings, and old mechanical parts. The clanking sound of metal being piled on metal fills the auditorium.

If he pulls a robot rabbit out of this, I'll be convinced.

Seren instructs his assistants to be sure that all pieces of metal are touching one another. They eagerly comply and then withdraw, each showing a sense of excitement about what is about to happen.

"In the last meeting of the Lumena, I caused a grapevine to grow and bear fruit, right before the eyes of all. You are still doubting? I understand. We have all beheld the convincing illusions that technology can create. But my friends, I am happy to inform you that my powers have increased. I see things more clearly now. I have been able to harness more of my life force and perhaps have tapped into the mysterious power that energizes the universe. I don't know anything about the science of this. I don't have to. I have only had to learn how to release the power, and the universe responds. What you will see is not an illusion generated by a machine. It is real, and I will invite you to verify it for yourselves."

Mark focuses his oracle glasses on Seren.

The lights in the theater dim. Seren kneels down and touches only one piece of metal. He closes his eyes and begins chanting something that no one can quite hear. His fingers start to glow, which causes whispering in the crowd. Mark straightens up and tries to zoom in. Everyone in the audience is riveted. It could be a holographic effect. Mark scans for nearby technology. Nothing.

Slowly, contiguous pieces of metal begin to glow. The radiance gradually spreads, and soon all the metal is glowing. The faint light is reflected in the eyes of all onlookers. Seren withdraws his hand and the light fades from his fingers. The glow diminishes around the metal pieces as well.

The audience is in disbelief, and everyone is murmuring loudly. "Please, my friends. Remain calm." Some press their way forward. "Stop where you are," Seren commands. They obey.

The lights come back up. All the metal pieces seem to have been turned into gold; at least they are all reflecting a golden radiance in the light. Seren picks up one larger bar and displays it to the crowd.

"Solid gold. Those of you who wish may come forward, in an orderly manner, please, and examine the evidence. My assistants will hold the objects they have brought. We have enlisted the others who brought metal articles to hold theirs. We will return the items to them," Seren smiles and raises one eyebrow, "in a somewhat improved condition." Most of the audience responds by moving forward.

"My friends, think carefully about what you have seen tonight. These are not weapons I have forged here before you. Take home with you some of the wine we have prepared. You will find it sweet, pleasing to the palate. It will calm you as no pharmaceutical enhancement ever could. Think about a world in which there is only peace and serenity, no hunger and no poverty. And by all means, even think beyond these two simple demonstrations—growing grapes without sun or water and turning ordinary metal into gold—, what other wonders are possible when you learn to access the light within you? Dare we even contemplate a paradise on earth?"

Mark wants a closer look, and he makes his way down to the front. The line is long. He tries to avoid looking at the stage, but when he does, he sees that Angela is scanning the crowd, probably looking for him.

She eventually spots him and begins making her way toward him. He is tempted to leave quickly, but she catches him and pulls him off to one side.

"Marco! I am so excited that you are here to see this! You saw it, didn't you?"

"I saw what appeared to be a better-than-average magic trick. How does he do it?"

"*Ecco.* Look at it for yourself."

Angela holds out a bracelet that Mark recognizes. Early in their relationship, he had bought it for her. He remembers that it was made of pewter and was of one piece with an engraved figure eight, a "forever bracelet."

"Look at it, Marco!"

Mark takes the bracelet. It is heavier and now seems of solid gold, at least from what he can tell. He turns it several directions but then looks inside it at an inscription. "*For Angela. My love always. Marco.*"

Mark is overcome by both the bitter irony of the message and his astonishment at the bracelet's transformation.

"How?" he mumbles.

"Come, ask him." Angela grabs his arm and pulls him around the crowd up on to the stage. Mark is unexplainably nervous.

"*Signor* Seren," she says to him, "This is my ex-partner, the pilot about which I told you. I think that he is an unbeliever, but—"

"Ah! The pilot!" Seren responds in a most attentive way. "Yes, Angela has told me about you! I am ever your humble servant." He leans forward in a sort of bowing gesture.

"Pleased to meet you," Mark blurts out, not quite sure what else to say.

Seren has a penetrating stare. He is smiling and staring and doesn't seem to blink. Mark again becomes uncomfortable.

"You are a pilot with EuroSecure. An officer, I assume?"

"Yes, I'm a captain."

"Thank you, captain, for preserving the Roman peace and defending Rome against those who would destroy her. And please, you should feel no pressure to believe anything you have seen here this evening. I have faith in the evidence. My words are weak, but ultimately the evidence will convince you."

"I'll consider it, thank you."

Seren moves on to other eager seekers who are full of excitement and questions.

"Angela, I have to get to work."

"Marco, you do not think that he looks like you? You could be brothers with him!"

"Not a bit. He seems more Semitic. I'm Cherokee, remember?"

"You have German ancestors, you have told me, and some Spanish. You have some Semitic blood in you, no?"

"Not likely. Look, Angela..."

"Okay, Marco, there is no hard feelings? Please don't let our problems to harden your heart to what is happening here. This, it is a revolution, but not one like the terrorists plan. This is going to change the world, like I have told you before. This thing tonight should give you a glimpse of how."

"Sure, see you around."

"There will be planned another meeting. I'll let you know."

"Sure."

Mark leaves the building and decides to transmit a report with holorecord of the meeting. He then proceeds to his zone to meet up with his team. It is another peaceful night. They are mixing, blending, scanning, and gathering intel, all of which amounts, as usual, to nothing.

From its founding, Rome, the Eternal City, was called to a unique destiny. During the Golden Age of Augustus, the first centuries of the Common Era, Rome was the greatest cultural and military power in the West. Large expanses of Europe, Asia, and Africa all bowed to Caesar. The world subdued, Roman civilization ushered in the *Pax Romana*, an era of peace and prosperity. Roman roads, sea lanes, and trade routes united the vast empire and enterprise.

Rome, Caesar's mistress, enthroned on the seven hills, had been ruling the world for centuries, until Constantine attempted to craft a "New Rome" on the shores of the Bosphorus. This new seat of power would later be called Constantinople, his "capital of Christianity" and fortification against the Turks.

Rome was not built in a day. The empire ascended slowly and declined slowly, as well. The sons of the Tiber, descendants of duty-bound Aeneas, lost sight of their goal, their destiny. They conquered most of the known world, but their own negligence eventually led to their being conquered.

The glory that was Rome was turned to ruin.

Now Rome has risen again, and barbarians again lie at the gate, waiting, biding their time. Some are more cunning and powerful than the Goths, the Turks, or the Huns. The world has returned to Rome, camping patiently at its doorstep. Will Rome learn the lessons of its history? A new Attila is at the door, and he shares none of the new Rome's noble goals—a grand civilization, a majestic city, and a hopeful future for humanity.

A new Attila lives to destroy and to leave a wake of spilled blood. The first Attila ravaged Rome and confronted Leo the Great, who pled for mercy. When Attila saw that Leo was flanked by Peter, Paul, and heavenly armies, he fled. The new Attila will not compromise. He will not be so easily fooled by pleas for mercy or hallucinations. No imagined heavenly armies will put him to flight.

Can the senate save Rome and preserve its destiny?

Can Seren?

—14—

LOVE BY MOONLIGHT

More happy weeks have gone by. It's like a dream.

Mark picks up Dominique at her apartment building near the Appian Way. They've decided to do a holotour together. Mark has purchased one hour, has chosen six locations, and has selected "on horseback."

The effects created by this particular agency are spectacular, the latest in holotechnology with more than ten thousand microprojectors. Mark and Dominique arrive and are assigned a massive room with two horses waiting on a mobile floor. They mount their steeds, which are real, begin trotting, and the show begins.

The room is first converted into the Great Wall of China and surrounding scenery.

"I always wanted to go here," comments Dominique.

"And here you are. And I've always wanted to be with you."

"Always?" She laughs. "We haven't known each other that long."

"Yes, always."

The sound effects seem natural. The horses' hooves are clopping irregularly, as if they were trotting on real stone. Now and then Mark and Dominique stop to look at the vast expanse of the wall before them and how it snakes its way across lush green mountain ranges. They turn around and look behind them. Same vista, a seemingly endless wall.

Mark comments, "Rome could have used such a wall, a fortification to keep out the barbarians. Hadrian should have built one a little closer to home."

"Ah," replies Dominique, "but Rome now has the Bolla, and brave pilots to protect her." Mark slowly shakes his head in assent as he surveys the landscape.

A narrator begins telling the history of the wall.

Mark comments, "I hope this is interesting to you."

Dominique responds, "It is. I took a course in Chinese history in college."

"Chinese history? Why?"

"I'm just interested in many different things."

It is a sunny day, provided by the program, and they enjoy a light breeze, generated by hidden fans. Mark has chosen for them to be alone here, so they do not encounter others while on the wall.

After a time, the scene changes to the Lauterbrunnen Valley Switzerland. The mountains are considerably higher and are capped with snow. The sky is blue with wispy clouds. Mark and Dominique are trotting down a road leading to a small village, which is couched in smaller, rolling hills covered with evergreens. Two majestic waterfalls shower down from the sheer rock mountainsides.

Dominique comments, "Now I have been *here*. I mean, *there*. The representation is *fantastique!*" Mark loves to see her excited and vivacious.

They enter the village and clop down its cobblestone streets. It is a low-tech environment, an image of a simple life with Dominique at his side. Mark thinks that he could learn to love low-tech under the right circumstances and with the right person.

Mark has allowed townspeople in this phase. They are all friendly, smiling and waving. Some speak in French to Dominique and welcome them both, inviting them to sample the locally produced chocolate or to have a glass of wine.

"It's tempting," comments Dominique.

"Don't get too tempted. It's not real."

"Isn't that the best kind of temptation?"

"I suppose." Mark tries to wrap his head around that response.

The next scenario places them in Oahu, Waikiki Beach, but they are alone.

"I've been here," observes Mark.

"It seems a little odd," comments Dominique. "So lonely. And all the hotels. One would expect tourists to come pouring out of them to splash in the water and swim in the ocean."

"Sorry, I chose no company in this case."

They dismount, take off their shoes, and stroll along the beach toward Diamond Head. The water is crystal clear. They hold hands as they stroll along. As the sun sets, they begin to cast long shadows as do the palm trees.

"It's so beautiful, almost surreal. I wish I could get my feet wet," says Dominique. She extends her right foot and agitates the water.

"See? It is still dry."

Mark reaches down and scoops up two handfuls of water and splashes Dominique, who squeals and laughs. It looks amazingly realistic and convincingly wet, but they are both still dry.

> "My bounty is as boundless as the sea,
> My love as deep; the more I give to thee,
> The more I have, for both are infinite." – Juliet

Suddenly the water beneath their feet turns calm and glassy. They are walking on Salar de Uyuni, the shallow lake in the mountains of Bolivia. All around them, they see puffy white clouds reflected perfectly in the water. The sun has begun to set. They look down and see themselves reflected. They look at each other in the liquid mirror, and then they look at each other face-to-face.

"Talk about surreal," Mark quips.

They continue to gaze deeply into each other's eyes. The urge for the first kiss is there. The time is just not right. Not yet.

The sun sets in a blaze, setting the lake on fire, and eventually the stars come out. A million of them in the Milky Way, and another million in the enormous reflecting pool that is the lake. They see the Southern Cross above and below, a bright full moon above and below. They see their horses, now dark shadows, and the horses' dark shadows reflected in the lake. They continue to stroll, and the horses follow.

The sun rises quickly, and water turns back into sand or sandy dirt as they are now in Monument Valley, Arizona, USA. Before them is a vast desert wasteland, gigantic mesas and ruddy rock formations towering over the flatlands. They see an amazing blue sky and wispy clouds. The mesas cast long shadows. Mark and Dominique again mount their horses.

Dominique remarks as they ride along, "No cowboys?"

"No company of any kind. Maybe we can add cowboys next time. Still, it does feel like you're in an old western movie, doesn't it?"

The big sky is deep blue, and they ride forward toward a seemingly endless horizon punctuated by impossible sculptures of sheer rock that rise up from dirt and have no visible purpose.

Their final holodestination is the Seven Sisters Waterfall in Geiranger Fjord, Norway. They find themselves on a grassy hillside looking across the water at the seven waterfalls, seven separate streams, the highest of which starts at two hundred fifty meters up. Dominique breathes a sigh, and they both take it all in.

"Here's what love is: a smoke made out of lovers' sighs.
When the smoke clears, love is a fire burning in
your lover's eyes." – Romeo

"Perhaps," she says, "we will someday be free to visit such places, the real places. If the world is ever at peace again, perhaps it will be easier to travel to them...one day."

"Seems unlikely. And then there's the Haze. No one has been able to solve that problem yet."

"We can hope. We can always hope."

The ride concludes, and they leave the building and walk over toward the Tiber. They are back in Rome, the real Rome, with its lavish architectural beauty.

Mark has arranged a midnight boat tour of the Tiber. He wanted something more real for a possible big moment. The large sightseeing boat contains a small café. The excursion begins from

Ponte Duca d'Aosta. This particular excursion is called "Amore." All the passengers are in love or are hoping to be.

Mark and Dominique sit at a small table, at its center, a red carnation in a bottle. Mark has tipped the pianist—who is real—to play Liebestraum by Franz Liszt.

They eat, talk, and drink wine.

After dinner they walk to the bow and enjoy the white marble banks and tall lime trees, the unique perspective on Rome from the Tiber.

They feel a gentle breeze, artificially produced. On the Bolla is projected a simulated full moon with light clouds and intermittent twinkling stars.

The pianist is playing more Liszt selections, and Mark and Dominique begin to dance slowly. Dominique leans against Mark and lays her head on his chest. Mark feels a trembling deep inside, a weakness, a vulnerability that he has never before felt.

He pushes her back slightly, and the two look longingly into each other's eyes.

"Mark, *je suis en train de tomber amoureuse de toi.*" Her eyes are fixed on his. Her eyes are covered with tears that glisten in the light of the virtual moon. Mark's French isn't quite that good yet, but he gets the message.

Now is the time. He leans his head forward, and they kiss their first. Two souls mix, gently and with more passion as the kiss continues. They hold each other ever more tightly. Real intimacy has begun. Real dreams have come true, with a mix of emotional confusion that translates into poetry and a million metaphors.

> "O! she doth teach the torches to burn bright.
> It seems she hangs upon the cheek of night
> Like a rich jewel in an Ethiop's ear;
> Beauty too rich for use, for earth too dear." –Romeo

"I love you, Dominique. *Je t'aime.*"

"*Je t'aime*, Mark. I love you." Words spoken in the heart language of each establish the reality of everything they have felt up to this point.

In Rome, all is quiet. Within Mark, all is not quiet. He is not free. He is a prisoner of Dominique, her protector, yet her slave.

Dominique giggles. "Captain, do you have a girlfriend?"

"No, I don't. Would you like to apply for the job?"

"What are the qualifications?"

"She must be a charming French pianist who is devastatingly beautiful with a sort of fatal charm, captivating in every way."

Yes, Dominique captivates him.

"*Oh, là là.* She must be *extraordinaire!*"

"Yes, there's only one woman in the world who fits that description."

She smiles and tilts her head to the side. "And that one woman would be?"

"Well, her name would have to be Dominique Lécuyer."

"That would be me!"

"That would be you, *chérie!*"

"*Exactement, mon petit ami!* Mark, you are that one man for me. Do you remember your Tolstoy? It was said of Andrei, '*Il fait à present la pluie et le beau temps.*' In a city where there is no natural rain or real sunny days, you, like Andrei, make rain and the sun, and every good thing that comes down from heaven, both real and vivid to me."

—15—

A ROSE BY ANY OTHER NAME

Mark drops off Dominique at her apartment building. They do not kiss again, but something has unquestionably shifted. He returns to his apartment, unable to sleep for some time. When he does fall asleep, he awakens repeatedly, convinced that it was all a dream.

Finally, Mark projects six separate images of Dominique into his room: the first one from the hypertrain, then one of her in the sundress at the lake, the one at the restaurant, the one on horseback, then on the boat tour of the Tiber, and finally one of her seated at the piano, playing. All are 360-D, all are moving and replaying in sequence, but none is talking. Mark is remembering, trying to re-experience her. It seems to help him cope with missing her.

Weeks go by. He continues to see Dominique during their off hours. They grow more serious by the day, but Mark still has a concern.

"Where has Mikhail been keeping himself?"

"I don't know. I haven't seen him in a while. He last told me he might be reassigned to another location. I haven't heard anything at HQ."

"You two know each other, apart from work. You have mutual friends."

"Yes, that's true, but I haven't seen him recently, and they haven't said anything about him or heard from him."

Mark senses a certain relief. "May I ask you a difficult question?"

"*Bien sûr*, Mark."

"What is your relationship with Mikhail? Did you ever have any feelings for him?"

Dominique bursts out laughing, and then stops, covering her mouth. "Oh! I'm sorry. It's not funny. It's only absurd! Never! He is like a brother to me. You aren't you jealous, are you?"

"He's not married, at least he's never mentioned a wife. He's a charismatic fellow, handsome, rugged. You are smart, charming, talented and so beautiful, so everything a man would want."

"*Merci, mon canard.*" She smiles and looks at him indulgently. "I love you and you alone. You are my hero. Never doubt that. Was that the hard question?"

"No..., uh." How to ask without confessing that he had spied on them previously? "Well, I guess it was. So no other connection? Like a brother?"

Dominique looks at Mark with a serious expression. He hesitates but finally dismisses the topic. "We will speak of it someday..., just not now."

Later, Mark reports to HQ for a debriefing. His examination consists in part of an interview with Colonel Valenza. He enters the colonel's office.

"Sir, reporting as ordered." The colonel looks up.

"Ah, yes, Captain Knutson. At ease. Take a seat."

"Thank you, sir."

"First, I need to update you on your status, then, I would like to ask some questions about your reports and activities since our last meeting."

"Yes, sir."

Valenza leans back in his chair. "The uneasy peace continues. We have been unable to locate any moles or infiltrators or spies or anything. We had some suspects, but we can't prove a thing. In general, stories and alibis check out. Right now everything seems to say, 'situation normal.'"

He takes a drag from a cigar and continues, "Gathering intel has been made difficult by varying Haze levels and the enemy's disruption and blocking of our tracking devices. We suspect certain types of activity here and there, nothing conclusive. You've seen this in your sweeps of your sector. Same everywhere. The pirates are currently attacking our shipping lanes, but just sporadically. They have not directly engaged or provoked our fighters or our destroyers. In fact, as far as we can tell, they have launched no fighters or rockets against us, just boats and small ships. This almost universal silence in the Mediterranean and in Rome might suggest a central command or coordination. It's hard to pin all this on any single group. Maybe one group is preparing..."

"Preparing for something bigger, sir?"

"Perhaps. That's one of several current theories. Another is that these diverse groups are somehow cooperating with each other, hence, the current peace in the Federation and its borders."

"As I understand the groups in question hate each other and have little in common, except the goal to destroy or conquer Rome."

"You've heard the old proverb, 'The enemy of my enemy is my friend'?"

"Right, now that might make some sense."

"That is likewise just a theory, pure speculation. Until we learn the complete truth, we're stuck. On the one hand, we don't want to start a widespread panic, but we're not ready to declare an 'all clear' either. We've accounted for all isolated attacks so far to the satisfaction of the people of Rome. The city seems relatively quiet and most all are enjoying *La Dolce Vita*, including you?"

"Sir?"

"You have been seen with Dominique Lécuyer."

"Sir, I assure you, there is no conflict of—"

"Not to be concerned, captain! An enchanting young lady. I'm a long standing friend of her father, the general. I served with him in several joint EuroSecure missions and knew him before EuroSecure was even formed. No, no conflict at all. Wonderful people."

"Thank you, sir." Apparently Valenza does not know that Mark rescued her after the terrorist bomb. The summary provided by his staff must not have listed specific names.

"Now tell me about these reports you've been submitting. Everything seems routine. No perception of problems or potential problems, just many unanswered questions."

Mark replies, "Sir, my team and I have been thorough. Outside the Bolla, in our particular zone, we've checked up on countless bars and enhancement businesses—drugs and sex shops mostly—that seem to thrive and keep a lot of that population distracted."

"And some of Rome's population apparently. I've been getting similar reports from other patrols."

"Our team has attended various types of meetings; some seem religious and some do not. None appears to have any kind of security set up. We have detected no weapons or technology."

"What about this Seren? My staff recommended that I watch this one."

Valenza initiates a playback of the recording of the second meeting. Seren joins them in the room and repeats his speech, and they listen to him.

"Sir, Seren is worth keeping an eye on, but again, no weapons. He seems to attract numerous curiosity seekers. We've observed at least three other similar groups in our sector."

"The rhetoric is familiar. Typical nutcase visionary, but unarmed. What do you make of the little alchemy trick?"

"Just that, sir, a trick. I grew up fascinated with sleight-of-hand magicians and illusionists. At the county fair, they would perform their wonders. They could make you believe you were seeing anything. And now, with technology and holographing, there's probably no limit to what they can make naïve people believe."

"You noted no technology present."

"No, sir, but by our next meeting, I will learn how to do the trick and perform it for you right here in your office."

Valenza, who rarely laughs, laughs heartily.

"Yes, just so. I have perused your other team reports and scanned through the holoclips. For the foreseeable future, we want you to stay with us. Your wing commander is in agreement since all is quiet in the Mediterranean for now. At present, the greater concern is for Rome herself. You and your team should maintain vigilance with oracle glasses at all times. Cloaked figures could show up at any minute. Dismissed."

Mark stands and snaps a salute. He leaves to return to his apartment. Just as he enters the room, Dominique calls. She appears before him in full flower, but her eyes are sad for the first time in his presence.

"Mark, I have to leave for Paris right away. *Papa* is not doing well."

"Okay, *chérie*, I'll come as soon as I can get leave."

"Meet me at the hypertrain station in an hour. Gate 12."

"I'll be there."

Mark rushes to the station and arrives early. Finally he spots Dominique and almost runs to her, and she to him. They hold each other in a long embrace.

"I'm sorry, my love. I will come as soon as I can. Please know that I'm concerned."

Dominique wipes tears from her eyes. "I know you are, my love. I'll be okay, and so will he. *La foi*. I have faith in God."

Mark isn't sure quite what to say to that, so he just agrees.

"Of course."

"Yes, and we must speak of it, this question of faith. *Papa* will most certainly ask you about it at some point."

"Uh."

"Don't worry. He doesn't give tests." She smiles. "He will love you as surely as I love you."

Dominique's portapack beeps, notifying her that it is close to time to board the hypertrain for Paris.

They kiss long. Finally she pulls herself away and grabs her bags. "*Je t'aime*. Say a prayer for me." And she boards the hypertrain, blowing him a kiss.

"Of course..."

Mark stands there, watching the train depart for Paris, a place where he cannot be right now to protect her. He cannot define what is happening inside him. Fear and love are in a wrestling match, and fear for her safety seems to be winning as the train disappears from sight. He returns to his apartment and finds a message from Angela. "I have something to show you."

He replies, "Call me if you like."

In less than a minute Angela's image appears in the apartment. She seems unusually excited. Seeing her there is an uncomfortable shock since he has just said good-bye to Dominique. Now, he has no desire to save Angela's image.

"Okay, what is it?"

Angela's image produces a small flower, a rose, or so it appears. The rose is quite small.

"Look! I have grown this with my life force." She holds it out for Mark to see more closely. He studies it for a minute.

"What are those purple splotches? It doesn't seem too healthy."

"Only you would notice that! Can't you only one time see the positive things in anything? Of course it's not perfect! You're missing the point as usual!" Angela becomes visibly agitated.

"So what's the point?"

"That I did it at all!!! My life force made that the seed would grow. Of course I am still learning, but Seren is teaching us; he is teaching those who have spent time with him, learning from his wisdom. It's not perfect, but look! It did grow! Marco, why don't you come to the smaller meetings for disciples? He's met you. You would be welcome."

"Oh, I've been busy."

"Liar! I know things are quiet now. How could you be busy? You're not flying! Marco, the world is about to change. A new age is coming, a true *Pax Romana*, and Seren will help us to bring it in. You'll see."

"When's the next big meeting?

"Soon. I'll let you know. They have rented a much larger auditorium. The word is now getting around. The next demonstration will be far beyond your ability to imagine. Seren is growing in power, not the power to destroy. No! The power to heal, to transform, and to create! The power of life! The power of the light within!"

"Okay, let me know. I'll try to come. I'm going to be in Paris for a time."

"It will probably be a while. I'll let you know. *Ciao*, Marco."

She adds sarcastically, "And Marco...wake up."

Angela disappears.

—16—

A MAN FOR ALL SEASONS

Mark is granted two weeks leave and takes the hypertrain to Paris. He will meet Dominique's father and ask for her hand. He will see her again.

When he arrives, he passes under the energy dome, in Paris called the *Bulle*, and is scanned three times. He registers with the *Sûreté*, the French National Police, and makes himself available if needed.

Paris, the City of Lights, the City of Love, now featuring even more light and more love. Covered by the crown of the Bulle, Paris retains its legendary charm, combining the secularism of Rome with a more noticeable hedonism. Love is everywhere, and wine flows like the Seine. One notes fewer megabuildings here than in Rome, but many do tower over the Eiffel Tower. Their ultramodern design contrasts sharply with Notre-Dame, L'Opéra, Les Invalides, and the Sacré-Coeur. Most of the older buildings have been restored to the appearance of yesteryear. The streets closer to the center of the city are still like small canyons that lead from place to place, from plaza to plaza, from métro stop to métro stop. The French have not razed the magnificent cathedrals. *Au contraire*, they have enhanced them and showcased them as a remembrance of things past, examples of the greatness of French architecture. Artists and musicians still thrive here. Paris is alive, more alive than it has ever been.

Outside the city dome are more teaming masses waiting restlessly to be included in the *Sixième-République*, the realm of *Liberté, fraternité, égalité*, "Freedom, brotherhood, and equality." Paris, like Rome, is working diligently to expand that dream. Progress is slowed in all larger cities of the European Federation by acts of terrorism. Those for whom there is living space and with whom there are no security concerns are admitted to share in the Good Life. Out of necessity, Paris has become a seaport, as Jules Verne predicted hundreds of years before. Supplies from other continents where food can be grown are vital to its survival. As in Rome, millions surround the Bulle and are cramped into shabby apartment complexes and slums. As in Rome, everyone outside the Bulle must wear some type of breathing mask, even if soiled.

Inside the bubble one enjoys many pleasant fragrances, including the aromas of French cuisine and the fragrance of expensive perfumes. Outside the energy dome, the air is a foul-smelling bio-hazard guaranteed to shorten one's lifespan.

Mark takes an aerocab to his hotel, La Trémoille, not far from the Champs-Élysees. He has no patience for the métro subway system. He always enjoys seeing Paris from the air and watching the megabuildings transform their appearance.

Those in Paris are unique. On one of the taller buildings is displayed the Playmate of the Month in slow, sensuous motion. And on another, the *Mona Lisa*, fully dressed, flashes her mysterious smile; she is about fifty stories tall. On still another, *Oedipus and the Sphinx*, by Jean-Auguste-Dominique Ingres, which after a few minutes transforms into the *Venus De Milo*, and then shortly thereafter to *La Liberté guidant le peuple*, by Eugène Delacroix. Artists love to portray women's breasts, and French men love to look at them, enlarged on a megabuilding.

Mark arrives at the hotel. It is late, so he sends Dominique a message that he will come to her house in the morning. His room reminds him of Dominique's apartment. It is quaint, very French, very Old World, virtually no-tech. Everything is clean, and nothing is new. He notes heavy curtains with a big window, thick carpet, a large bed with canopy, and various pieces of finely crafted furniture, a love seat, a coffee table, and various paintings on the walls. He notes only one new world touch, a huge screen on which he might watch whatever his heart desires. He laughs to himself. No movie could be better than Dominique Lécuyer. Fortunately he has brought his portapack and extra projectors.

Mark unpacks and settles in for the night. He has now added to the image library of his portapack all their conversations via holophone. He arranges images of Dominique, old and new, along with her different outfits, into a moving slide show, which he watches over and over, always with a sense of wonder. This allows him to scroll through holograms of Dominique as he drifts off to sleep. So in an angelic way, she watches over him through the night.

> Victor Hugo, *Notre Dame de Paris*, Paris in the morning. "As the sun rises, you climb to some high point from which you can see the entire city. You watch heaven descend and the churches awaken and respond with bells. They are faint at first, as if they were slowly warming up, but soon all the sounds swell and rise in harmony. All eventually meld into a single concert as they converse with each other. Bells from churches, from Saint-Eustache, from the Abbey of Saint-Martin, from the Bastille, from the Louvre, from Notre-Dame, from Saint-Germain-des-Prés. If you listen carefully, you can hear a choir of voices singing in each edifice. The concert becomes an opera. Add to this a half-million murmurs, the lament of the Seine, the infinite wind, and the attenuation of the forests on the hills surrounding. There is nothing richer, more joyous, and more dazzling than these voices and bells that have become an orchestra and a symphony."

This Paris is different, many of the same landmarks survive: monuments, the Left Bank, and the cathedrals, but the scene and the symphony are cluttered with traffic, cars on the ground, aerocars in the air with no effective synchronization program, which produces a cacophonous discord everywhere.

Mark awakens early and with a start. Today is the big day. Meet the father-general. Pop the question. Mark first considers wearing his EuroSecure uniform complete with medals and ribbons, but then he changes his mind. Something semi-formal, something not too anything. He finally decides on a simple, maroon shirt with no tie, a navy blue jacket, neutral pants and maroon shoes, nothing too flashy. He will take along his uniform for their date at L'Opéra.

Once ready, he exits the hotel. Various megabuildings transform into images of the Moulin Rouge, "The Thinker," a Coca-Cola bottle, a swan in flight, and Ramses the Pharaoh.

Mark rents a car, and after a drive through the heart of the city arrives at the Lécuyer home in West Paris, just inside the Bulle. The house is stately, almost castle-like in some of its features, not extravagant in appearance, well kept, with a gate in front. He and his car are scanned, and the gate opens. He pulls into the ample driveway and parks.

Dominique comes out to meet him. He is thrilled to see her again. She is wearing a red suit with red shoes. They embrace and kiss at length.

"How is he?"

"Better, *grâce à Dieu*."

"And how are you?"

"Blissful," she says, smiling and looking up into his eyes.

"And you?"

"Ecstatic. I'm having the happiest dream I've ever had. I just don't want to wake up." Mark is surprised that he would use the word "ecstatic" to describe himself.

They each pick up a bag and walk toward the house together, arm in arm. As Mark enters, he sees a grand entrance area with a long, curving staircase. He notices paintings on most of the walls and a chandelier overlooking it all.

"It's beautiful! Forgive my asking, are any of these furnishings and paintings holograms?"

"No, *mon chou*, *Papa* does not like holographic art or holographic anything. *Maman* did all the interior design. It is still exactly as she wanted it to be, just as she left it seven years ago."

"I'm sorry. I'm sure her death was hard on both of you."

"It still is in some ways. It has been most difficult for *Papa*. I love being here. I grew up in this house, well, mostly, when we weren't with *Papa* on assignment. It holds so many memories. It has her touch and reminds me of her. She's always here."

"In her performance, I saw an elegant and beautiful pianist, but she was an artist as well?"

"She painted most of the pictures you see."

Mark admires a painting that attracts his attention. "I like this one." It is a nature scene by a lake that reflects all the colorful trees of fall. Many birds are flying, and geese are swimming in the water. A little girl is swimming with them. "Could that be you?"

"It is..., or it was," answers Dominique, smiling and stopping to look at it again and meditate on it. "She inserted me into many of her paintings."

Beautiful then and now. Mark thinks about the *Birth of Venus.*

Dominique smiles but says nothing.

"When do I meet the general, I mean, your father?"

"Oh, *Papa* is expecting you. There's no rush. He spends most of the day in bed or in his wheelchair. He's not going anywhere."

"Can we go up now? I'm really anxious to meet him."

Mark and Dominique ascend the staircase and walk down the hall to her parents' bedroom. It is decorated as is the rest of the house, with elegance, good taste, and charm. Mark is nervous. He's not used to being nervous, and he's been nervous a lot lately.

The general is a stately man with thick white hair. Even in his sickbed, he has an undefinable dignity that inspires respect. In every way, he looks like a former army commander.

"*Papa, c'est* Mark. Mark, this is my father."

Mark shakes his hand firmly. He does not smile.

"Sir," Mark says, not knowing what else to call him. "I am highly honored."

"You'll forgive me, captain, if I do not rise." His English is good but heavily accented.

"General, I—"

"No, please don't call me that. I haven't been active in years. 'Gérard' will be fine." Mark is not comfortable with calling him by his first name.

"Nevertheless, I am honored to meet you. Dominique has told me so much about you."

Dominique excuses herself. "I'll go down to see about lunch and leave you two to get acquainted."

The general sits up a little straighter in his bed and fluffs his pillow before leaning back on it.

"And, young man, I have heard a great deal about you."

"Dominique is always so generous about everyone."

"Not just from Dominique. Not long ago I had a conversation with an old friend, a Colonel Valenza. I believe you know him?"

"Sir, I'm currently assigned to his command in Rome."

"Yes. He speaks highly of you. He thinks you're a good agent, and he's heard you're a good pilot as well. He is in possession of excellent reports from your wing commander for EuroSecure. You have been decorated for numerous acts of heroism, both as a pilot and in the Guard."

"I'm always glad to hear about good reports." Mark is at a loss for words.

"Of course, it is good for a young man who is serious about my daughter to be a good soldier. You are originally from Oklahoma?"

"Yes, sir."

"I visited there briefly. I did tours at several military installations in the U.S. several decades ago, before all these current problems began. I was impressed by what I saw. They seem to have their hands full right now."

"Yes, sir, they do."

"I am most impressed, however, by how you heroically saved my daughter. Dominique has told me that story many times, always with some extra detail that she claims to have forgotten."

"Sir, I did what had to be done and would do it again without hesitation. But it wasn't just duty that drove me to the fight. I am in love with your daughter." Mark now has a big lump in his throat. That was much harder to say that than he had anticipated.

"Yes, captain, love is a powerful force, and it can drive us to do many good things. It can fill us with the courage to protect those we love, to defend them, as you yourself have experienced. And it moves us to defend what we believe, as well. The world has always been a troubled and dangerous place. These days, perhaps more so. We need capable young soldiers like you to stand in the gap."

"That, too, sir, is an honor."

"I have a question for you, young man." He smiles faintly. "Why are you fighting?"

Mark becomes tense. "Well, sir, I...uh..."

"Not to worry, captain! This is not a test. I ask for your benefit only. Every man must ask and answer such questions. Why do you serve? Why do you fight? What do you stand for? What do you believe in? All good questions that demand answers, answers that you can live with and live for."

"I do stand for Dominique. Sir, I love your daughter fondly, dearly, and devotedly. I would give my life for her. If ever there were true love in the world, I love her truly." Mark worries that his last sentence came out sounding awkward, perhaps too forced.

"You have been previously married?"

"Yes, sir, I've married once. It was more of a contractual partnership that was not renewed. I always—"

"No need to explain, son." The general's eyes are blue. His demeanor is calm. His voice is raspy but strong and reassuring to Mark. "The world is an increasingly perilous place, despite all this... technology. I worry about my daughter. I will feel better, knowing that she has someone who loves her, someone she can trust, and someone who will always protect her. You do want to marry her, do you not?"

This question takes Mark completely by surprise. He had been considering numerous approaches and had practiced several possible declarations of intent.

"My daughter loves you and approves of you. She trusts you. That, *mon capitaine*, is all I need to know. So I therefore give you her hand and entrust her, my daughter, my precious jewel and treasure from heaven, to you." He begins to cough. Mark hands him the glass of water by his bedside.

"I am grateful, sir. And I am humbled."

"You have asked her to marry you, have you not?"

"No, sir. I wanted to ask your permission first."

The general gently laughs. "Very old-fashioned of you."

Dominique is coming down the hall and calls out to them, "Are we ready to eat, gentlemen?" She enters the room. "Have you yet solved the world's problems?"

"We have," answers her father. "Now we must get the world to listen to us!" She helps him into his wheelchair and pushes him to an elevator at the end of the hall.

At lunch, Mark and the general share their combat experiences, stories about their travels, have some laughs, and talk about Dominique in her presence.

"She is amazingly beautiful, is she not, captain?"

"I was awestruck the first time I saw her. And I still am."

Dominique smiles and shakes her head from side to side. "And when did you first see me?"

"Oh, it wasn't you, it was your image, one of those security update bulletins on the situation in North Africa."

"I must have appeared awfully boring, then."

"That's impossible."

They sit down to eat, listening to Berlioz. Mark sees an opportunity to score a point. "I believe that's the Symphonie Fantastique."

"You are correct, captain. Dominique told me that you have a special love for classical music."

"For all music, sir. My mother was a music teacher."

"A good woman, no doubt."

The general wipes his lips with his napkin. "I assume you have plans for this evening?"

Dominique responds quickly, "I'm sure we do, *Papa*, but the captain has not yet revealed them to me." She looks at him with a wry smile.

—17—

THE LAND OF SUGARS

"I suppose now is a good time to reveal the mystery. I imagine you will want to spend some time getting ready. I have bought e-admissions to the *Nutcracker* this evening at L'Opéra."

Dominique's face lights up. She exclaims: "*Casse-noisette, ballet-féerie*! I have so much wanted to see it again!"

The general finishes sipping his wine and adds, "You know, she danced in a production of the *Casse-noisette* while in college."

"*Papa*! That was long ago, and I only had a minor part. I was but one of many dancers."

"But the best, the most beautiful, and the most graceful."

"This is a multinational troupe, mostly Russian," Mark adds.

"*Magnifique*! Mikhail would approve! I saw a ballet in Rome a few years back in which they tried to use some holograms. It was *dégoûtant*..., disgusting. They say you cannot tell the difference. Well, I can!"

The general remarks, "So far, no holograms have been permitted at L'Opéra. Enough, it is enough. One can only stretch art so far into technology." He looks directly at Mark. "Art is about humanity. It is from humanity and for humanity. So may it always be."

"Well said, sir."

After more leisurely conversation and laughter, Mark and Dominique help her father get situated and then ready themselves to go out. Mark is glad he decided to bring his dress uniform, but not to meet the general, rather, for the ballet.

They arrive early. The system has reserved their seats. Dominique looks even more elegant than she did the night they went dancing in Rome. Now she is wearing a full-length light-blue gown with sparklers everywhere. On her head, a princess crown. For Mark she is a vision of heaven, an angel sent to dwell among mortals.

The *Nutcracker*, beauty and harmony, grace and elegance, all without words, and there really aren't any words to describe the experience. Tchaikovsky knew better than anyone how to use the voices of the orchestra to cause us to imagine, to visualize, and to dream. The combination of his genius with professional ballet is moving and ethereal. History reminds us of the atrocities of which human beings are capable. As we watch the performance, "poetry in motion" accompanied by "the music of the spheres," we catch a glimpse of what humanity was created to do. Not that God intended all of us to dance ballet, but that we were meant to create and not destroy, to love and not to hate, to kill rats (and the Rat King) and not to kill each other. We were made "a little lower than the angels" to aspire somehow to a higher calling.

The ballet, a fairy-tale drama with music, is a magnificent expression of the aesthetic power of the fine arts and the magic of Christmas. The production showcases distinctive stagecraft, colorful costuming, and the exquisite, transcendent beauty of Tchaikovsky's polyphonic score. There are no vocals, but there are many voices.

The theater gallery goes dark. Onstage, snow is falling. It's Christmas. As the guests arrive with presents, they admire the splendidly decorated tree. Enter the children, dancing like flowers, and their eagerness causes minutes to dance by like hours. The living room is full of festive guests and is charged with anticipation.

The young boys march around the room sporting their toy rifles. The young girls sit, admiring their dolls. Later, the adults dance. Fritz, Marie-Claire, and the other children stand in awe of the decorated Christmas tree and are excited at the prospect of presents.

"So many memories for me," Dominique whispers to Mark.

The clock strikes eight, and Marie-Claire's godfather comes in dressed as a magician with gifts he has made for the children. To add to the enchantment of Christmas, he puts on a magic show. He has brought four large dolls, which dance gracefully for a time and must be put away.

He then picks up the "nutcracker," which is carved in the shape of a little man-soldier. Marie-Claire is charmed by it, but Fritz wants it and struggles with Marie-Claire to get it; they unintentionally break off its head, after which they try their best to repair it.

Once all have gone to bed, Marie-Claire returns to see about the nutcracker. The clock strikes midnight, and the real magic begins. The nutcracker has grown to the height of a man. Large mice fill the room. The mouse king enters, wearing a red robe. Gingerbread soldiers engage in an epic battle with the mouse king and his mignons, which eat the gingerbread men.

The valiant nutcracker leads the fight and is joined by tin soldiers. As they duel, the mouse king draws ever closer to the nutcracker and finally knocks him to the ground. The soldier loses his grasp on his sword, but Marie-Claire picks it up and stabs King Mouse.

Mark leans over close to Dominique's ear. "I've never seen that touch. So in this version she saves her man?"

"Yes!" she answers.

"Interesting."

The mice are defeated, and the nutcracker is magically transformed into a handsome prince. He takes Marie-Claire to his kingdom through an enchanted forest in which snowflakes dance.

Dominique grasps Mark's hand. "I was a snowflake, one of many," she whispers. He smiles large and looks at her adoringly.

In Act II, they travel to the Land of Sweets, where the Nutcracker-Prince tells the reigning Sugarplum Fairy about how Marie-Claire heroically rescued him from the mouse king. Dancing sweets from all over the world pay homage and entertain them. From

Spain, China, Arabia, and Russia, they all present their jubilant interpretations of celebration. Flowers waltz, and finally the Sugarplum Fairy and her cavalier dance.

Dominique whispers: "Their technique and timing are perfect!" Mark nods his head in agreement, himself unable to evaluate ballet.

She comments, "The prince and Marie-Claire flow together so beautifully. They are in heaven now. No more strife, no more mouse king."

"Looked like a rat king to me," quips Mark.

All the sweets perform a final dance, and Marie-Claire and the nutcracker-prince are crowned to rule over the Kingdom of Sweets.

Dominique is mesmerized by the production, and Mark is mesmerized by Dominique. She is in tears. She follows the music and the movements with her eyes, sometimes moving her lips as if singing, though there are no words.

"The story is so beautiful, like a heavenly dream. He is cursed and wounded, but her love saves her man."

At the close, the conductor takes a bow for the orchestra, and then the cast members come out to take a bow.

"I'll be right back," Mark whispers in her ear and stands up abruptly. Dominique wrinkles her brow, trying not to be annoyed.

The various dancers pass in procession and take their places as the applause continues, shouts of "bravo!" fill the opera house. Last but not least, the Sugarplum Fairy accepts a bouquet of roses; she then moves stage left, extracting a single rose and handing it to a man who has stepped up on the stage. He is in full dress uniform, so that initially many believe he is the nutcracker, except that the nutcracker-actor has already taken a bow on stage. Someone behind Dominique asks, "*Il y en a deux?*"

Dominique is astonished and stands up without thinking. "Mark!" she exclaims under her breath.

Extending the rose and a ring toward Dominique and in the best French he can muster, he calls out, "*Dominique! Me ferais-tu l'honneur de devenir ma femme?*"

With tears in her eyes, Dominique cries out, "*Oui! Oh, oui, mon amour!*"

The audience, both surprised and pleased, thunders its approval. Some even stand to their feet and applaud.

Tears are running down Mark's cheeks. He can scarcely believe her acceptance. Almost trembling, he turns and looks at the Sugarplum Fairy and asks meekly, "Have I caused a *problème?*"

She smiles with her eyes, tilts her head with considerable charm, and says, "*Mais non, monsieur!* You are in France, the Land of the Sweets!"

Mark descends and almost runs to meet Dominique, who has run to him. They embrace, they kiss, and he gives her the rose and the ring, which she accepts with more kisses. The audience continues to clap and express satisfaction with the unorthodox but ingenious proposal.

Mark and Dominique return to the Lécuyer home and share the news with her father. She shows him the ring; the general is visibly pleased.

"I wish you both many long years of happiness." He leans back into his pillow, smiling. Dominique is radiant. Mark is seriously worrying about waking up.

"We are asleep until we fall in love!"
– Tolstoy, *War and Peace*

No, this is life, and life could not be any better. This is the Good Life, the Sweet Life. He has found it, at last, in the arms of Dominique.

Two weeks pass by swiftly. In that time they visit various tourist sites in Paris.

They go to the Eiffel Tower and eat in the restaurant. Dominique is giving Mark a course in French pastries. Mark thinks this school is amazing. He is majoring in Dominique and minoring in chocolate. His French is improving, since few people in Paris speak English, and he enjoys hearing Dominique relate to everyone there in French. He learns more about her Frenchness as he observes her flourishing in her own culture.

All is quiet in Federation cities. Mark receives a message from Colonel Valenza that he may be reassigned to patrol as a pilot, which does not make him happy since it will mean less time in Rome.

On Bastille Day, July 14, Mark and Dominique go to the Champs-Élysees to watch the parade and the procession of military aircraft overhead. General Lécuyer has been invited to occupy his customary seat of honor in the celebrity box. They watch the pomp and circumstance, the celebration of France's sixth republic. In the street, a file of military vehicles and soldiers. In the air, the awesome power of a succession of *Prochain Mirage* fighters, advanced *Foudre* helicopters, and other impressive aircraft. Mark enjoys the airshow. He is in some ways eager to get back into the air, back into the fight, into some kind of fight, but being with Dominique, his fiancée, is a priority for now.

"Were the aircraft real?" He asks Dominique and the general. "You have limited navigational space within the Bulle. And they were traveling at high speeds."

"Of course they were real!" barks the retired general. Dominique is not so sure.

Late that evening, Mark and Dominique get on the métro and ride to the 18th *arrondissment*, hoping to see fireworks. They go walking and find themselves at the bottom of the vast hillside beneath Le Sacré-Cœur, the tall, white, triple-domed cathedral visible from many parts of the city. Its front lawn is a steep incline with stone stairs and a motorized tram.

It's midnight. The hillside is covered with hundreds of people who are sitting or lying on the grass, waiting to see fireworks. An inebriated man carrying two brightly lit torches runs down the slope. He occasionally falls, almost burning some of the spectators, but the crowd laughs and applauds every time he stands up and begins running again. Mark and Dominique find a spot and lie back and look up. A brilliant burst of fireworks suddenly illuminates the night sky.

Mark wonders what they should talk about. What do they need to talk about? *Carpe diem.*

—18—

PARIS IS HIT!

Several days before he is to return to Rome, Mark receives a secure call from an inspector with the Sûreté. From his portapack, Mark projects his image into his hotel room.

"Captain Knutson, we have a grave concern and believe you may be able to help us."

"Inspector, I'll do all that I can."

"Rome has informed us that you witnessed at least two kidnappings, including one attempted abduction. In these, the assailants were cloaked, *n'est-ce pas*?"

"That is correct, sir."

"I have viewed your reports. I wonder if you could join one of our discreet patrols."

"I am available for activation whenever you choose."

"*Parfait*! Now, let me transmit a clip to you. I will be interested in your evaluation."

Mark assents, and he views a Parisian street in 2-D on the screen in his room. He can see the unique row of street lamps on the Alexandre III bridge only a few blocks away.

"This is from a security scanner, last night after midnight, not many people on the streets. There has been no attempt to jam the scanner, at least not for this clip."

Mark watches a scene unfold. Several small groups are walking along the street. Some are looking at the Seine. Nothing out of the ordinary.

"Now, captain, watch carefully *here*." The inspector zooms in and inserts an arrow pointing to a man and a woman, both quite good-looking. They are standing by the riverside. Both suddenly seem stunned and then quickly disappear top-down. Nothing else happens.

"Is that it?"

"Yes, captain. That is it. It is quite subtle, not like an explosion or a crash, which is why we almost missed it."

"Perhaps the two people could have been a holographic projection?"

"That is always possible, except that we later found two dead bodies several kilometers away. Murder still happens in Paris, unfortunately, but the mode here caused us grave concern. By all appearances, the two were later used in some sort of ritual sacrifice. They had been stabbed. We found their bodies in an abandoned room, hearts cut out. No evidence of any anesthetic. There were candles and other strange paraphernalia there. The general physical appearance of their corpses and their clothing are a match for the two individuals in the clip. We have no other visual record of them between where they disappeared and where we found their bodies."

Mark has a sick feeling in his stomach.

"Does this scenario seem familiar to you, captain?"

"All too familiar, inspector."

"What do you think about the brutal sacrifice? I understand something similar happened in the Rome incident."

"Yes, sir, but we have no explanations, only theories."

The inspector observes, "Rome has superior technology. Paris has security cameras everywhere, however, we are somewhat lacking in the technology to detect terrorists in cloak. In general our level of tech sophistication is not as high as yours. Not many of our agents have the advanced version of oracle glasses as you do, and reports indicate that some groups have improved their cloaking abilities."

"I think that is highly likely, inspector."

"We would request that you serve on one of our roving patrols. Colonel Valenza has been briefed and has approved this temporary assignment. You do have your oracle glasses and your operations belt and other gear with you, yes?"

"Yes, sir, I do. I came prepared for a possible assignment."

"We are concerned, as is EuroSecure, that this may be a repeat of what happened in Rome. I am speculating that they are again... how do you say...testing the water and possibly provoking us."

Mark adds, "Showing us that they can."

"*Exactement.*"

"Are there any new theories about who 'they' are?"

"The kidnappers probably belong to only one group, but to which group? That is the question. I am certain that all the Federation's enemies rejoice at any act of sedition. These are distinguished, however, by their use of cloaking along with the bizarre ritual sacrifice. One might say, a strange combination of the technologically advanced and the primitive."

"I'll do what I can to help."

Mark calls Dominique and briefs her.

He cautions her, "*Chérie*, please be careful. Don't go out more than is absolutely necessary. Don't—"

"Mark! *Mon amour!* Not to worry! I'm here with *Papa*, and we have good security. You're the one who needs the lecture, Mr. Cowboy! Don't get in over your head. You'll be out looking for them, and you're not sure what kind of weapons they may have."

"I'm better equipped than the local security forces, that's for sure. I can handle it, but I'll be careful, for your sake."

"I think you will not be so careful," retorts Dominique with a bit of a frown.

Mark is assigned to a patrol squad, a team of eight, near La Gare du Nord train station.

At about two o'clock a.m., a Sûreté operative with oracle glasses spots three cloaked figures and calls Mark's squad for assistance.

The agent is about fifteen blocks away. They kick their two spider bikes into gear and move to intercept, cloaking themselves. These bikes are rarely used in Rome, although Mark used to pilot one regularly in earlier days. They have eight telescoping tentacles, four on each side, that find niches for support as they move down and above streets at a high rate of speed. The bikes have the capability of moving fast on the ground or on the sides or tops of buildings, which is needed for the peculiar configuration of Parisian buildings and boulevards. Each bike carries four passengers, and the dynamic is similar to that of a toboggan.

As they arrive on the scene, Mark sees the shadowy suspects moving toward a small group of people who are apparently en route to catch a train. Mark is the only one on his team with state-of-the-art oracle glasses and is piloting one of the two bikes.

At the last second, the three suspects turn and appear to notice that the invading force is headed straight for them. One of them engages a deflector beam, which disables the spy-flies already shot at them. He then discharges another beam, which momentarily knocks the spider bikes off their intercept course.

The suspects begin running from their pursuers. They are wearing lightning boots that do not enable them to run as fast as the spider bikes move but do allow them to travel more rapidly through crowds, traffic, small passageways between buildings, and to maneuver quickly, making sharp turns at will.

Both suspects and spider bikes pass by a group of pedestrians at a high rate of speed, kicking up a sudden wind. The walkers hold on to their hats and look around, bewildered. They feel the strong gust of wind but see nothing.

The chase continues at a high velocity down streets and between buildings. Agents are reluctant to use deadly force for fear of civilian casualties, but the suspects are trying to fire at them while running, missing their pursuers and hitting the sides of buildings. Mark continues the high-speed pursuit visually and by instinct.

Predictably, the three split up, but they have only two spider bikes, which have to split up. Mark is close on the heels of the one he decides to pursue. Three fellow agents are with him on the bike and continue to try to launch tracking flies and drones without success.

The suspect is moving toward Notre-Dame where there are still crowds that might be used as camouflage or human shields. The runner cannot scale the sides of buildings, as the spider bike can, but he can move at an incredibly fast rate, leaping over cars, people, and even some one-story buildings. Mark would like to give chase by himself with his lightning boots, but he cannot afford to lose even a fraction of a second.

The suspect is running almost effortlessly. His boots give him the extra propulsion he needs. His feet have wings, propelled by springs and microjets in the heels of the boots. He occasionally looks back to check on his pursuers and is weaving erratically.

Mark maintains a slight altitude above the occasional pedestrians, cars, trolleys, and buses and skims along the sides of buildings.

They approach the Seine where, as expected, large crowds are still active and energetic. Both must slow down.

If he tries to jump the Seine, he's mine. And the suspect heads right to the river without turning right or left. He leaps...

Mark accelerates, ready to knock him out of the air, but suddenly Mark, his team, and his bike are blown out of the air by two powerful blasts of water, apparently from high-pressure hoses. The pursuers and the bike all fall into the Seine. When Mark comes up, he sees the hoses still blasting out streams of water; whoever used them has now abandoned them at the river's edge. After he swims to the side and climbs out, several men help him and ask him in French if he is okay. He nods his head affirmatively and looks around for the other agents, who are also swimming to the river bank. *I hate low-tech.*

Mark surveys the area. His oracle glasses are still working. He can see hundreds of people, but no phantoms. They have vanished into the crowd.

Ghosts are loose in Paris tonight. These have escaped the guillotine.

Mark looks in all directions and scans. A ten-story bottle of Möet & Chandon champagne illuminates the area surrounding them. He files a report and contacts the other team. They likewise failed to apprehend their suspects.

Everything is quiet for several hours, so Mark checks himself off duty and returns to his hotel for the night. At four o'clock a.m., he receives an alert that wakes him up. An early morning explosion has rocked east Paris. Mark jumps out of his bed and puts on his gear, sending out a signal for someone to pick him up. By the time he appears in the street below, a spider bike is waiting for him. As they approach the site, they see that residents of nearby apartment buildings are still pouring out into the streets.

There is a hole in the Bulle, about two hundred meters in diameter, and the base seems to be shorting out. One of the plasma fusion mainstays has exploded, and the others cannot compensate adequately. While a crew works to patch the hole and repair the support unit, other personnel are passing out safety filter masks. Haze levels are low, but some contamination is getting in.

Agents from the Sûreté are searching, canvassing, reassuring, and trying to calm the people, gently moving them back into their buildings. Most all seem emotionally stressed, on the verge of panic.

After an hour or so, a news bulletin is broadcast: A short circuit has caused a small explosion in a mainstay of the Bulle. Crews are working to restore permanent plasma flow. It has happened before.

Mark receives a secure communication from Colonel Valenza.

"Captain, return to Rome immediately. Catch the next hypertrain."

"Sir, I'm in east Paris. There's been an incident. I'll have to get my things at the hotel."

"You are wearing your operations belt and other gear?"

"Yes, sir, but—"

"I've been briefed about the incident, but you're needed here now. We'll have your bags picked up and transported later. Until further notice all leaves are cancelled and all PG personnel will work extended shifts. I've communicated with the Sûreté. They are grateful for your assistance; they seem to have the situation contained for the moment. However, the whole Federation is on a state of high alert."

"Yes, sir, I'm on my way."

Mark calls Dominique on the secure line.

"*Chérie*, I'm on my way back to Rome. I'm sorry. Orders."

Dominique is quiet for a moment.

"Mark, *Papa est malade*. He's much more grave."

Now Mark is really upset. He has to leave without seeing Dominique, and he wants to stay with her, especially now.

"Mark, you must do your duty. Return to Rome to protect her. I'll be okay here. Please call me when you have returned safely, just as soon as you can."

Mark sits on the train and stares out the window. After more than two weeks of heavenly happiness, he is now depressed. He didn't think he could ever be depressed again.

—19—

SMOKE AND MIRRORS

All cities of the European Federation are increasing security. Authorities continue to reassure the public, but security forces have stepped up detection efforts and discreet patrols.

Upon arriving in Rome, Mark sends Dominique a message and then reports for duty immediately. He works an extended shift. Agents are combing the city and outside the Bolla, looking for terrorists, for bombs, for clues, for anything suspicious. After sixteen hours, he returns to his apartment, exhausted, and goes to bed.

Ten hours later, Mark awakens with a start. He looks around his apartment. It is blank, as usual, which is a relief. He will have to report to Naples the day after tomorrow and resume aerial patrols. His aircraft have been restored to service, and he has been cleared to return to duty. Apparently, HQ has some concern about certain activities in the Mediterranean Sea, an increased number of attacks on shipping, potential build-ups in forces that EuroSecure's few remaining satellites cannot quite detect through the Haze and jamming.

Mikhail has called and will be coming over soon. He is bringing a friend with him who has extensive experience in playing *Sleeping Beauty – Infinity Version*. Mark is looking forward to the game. At some point, he would like to return to the first level and raise the stakes; he would like to challenge himself with a higher level of difficulty and more opponents.

The visitor alert bell chimes. Mark opens a view of the lobby next to the elevators. It is Mikhail and a rather large black gentleman wearing a white smock and white pants. Mark approves their ascent.

After a few moments, they enter the apartment. Mikhail and Mark give each other a quick hug, and Mikhail introduces his friend.

"Captain Knutson, may I present to you my longtime friend Iqhawe. He is from South Africa." They shake hands. The new guest is courteous but does not smile. Mikhail is half a head taller than Mark, and Iqhawe is half a head taller than Mikhail. He is quite large and powerfully built.

"I am honored to meet you, captain."

"The honor is mine, Iqhawe. You are perhaps with Search and Rescue as well?"

"Yes, sir."

"You are an officer or a master sergeant, like Mikhail?"

"Master sergeant, sir."

"I'm sorry, I didn't catch your last name..."

"You couldn't pronounce it, sir."

Mark laughs awkwardly. "Probably not. And you are from South Africa?"

"Yes, sir, from Kwa-Mashu, KwaZulu-Natal."

"Ah! So you are a Zulu?"

"Yes, sir, a Zulu warrior. My rank is much higher in the Zulu Nation. I chose to serve here because I believe in the cause."

"Which cause is that?"

"The cause of saving lives, sir."

"Well, that is a good cause. Thank you for coming."

Mikhail interjects, "I have brought an upgraded version, which I would like to install in your system here."

"Upgraded?" Mark asks with some surprise. "I can't even find the original game, I mean, nothing that is called *Sleeping Beauty - Infinity Version.* I don't understand how you upgrade infinity!"

Mikhail laughs as he begins the installation. "It is still quite new, but they're adding new features all the time. Today I hoped we could practice 'Smoke and Mirrors, Shadows and Swamps.' It's the level just before you rescue the sleeping princess, that is, after you defeat the Emerald-Green Dragon."

"Why emerald-green?"

"You don't like emerald-green? We can change the color."

"No need. Just wondering. We've already faced dragons, including that lower-level dragon boss. I wasn't so happy about the results of that contest. How can I be ready for the Ultimate Dragon Boss at the top level? Is it different somehow?"

"This dragon is far more elaborately conceived. It has seven heads which spew a variety of deadly torrents. And on each head, it wears a crown."

Mark laughs, "Seven heads with variety? Does it breathe out something other than fire and smoke?"

Mikhail thinks for a minute and finally says, "Yes, it does, fire, smoke, hail, acid, deception, nightmares, and insanity, among other things. Of course it's just a virtual game, so we can make it belch out ice cream if you like. Before we get serious about the last battle, you must make it through this 'Smoke and Mirrors segment.'"

"Is there any doubt?"

"There will be doubt in abundance, but that is why we practice, no? Iqhawe and I are well trained; we just like to stay sharp. At the final level, we will be fighting by your side and will assist you when possible. We are your support team, but you must slay the Ultimate Dragon Boss yourself."

Mark is getting pumped by the prospect.

"The ultimate challenge, eh?"

"You might say that. Just keep your eyes on the prize."

"And what is the prize?"

"What is life's most valuable treasure?"

"Dominique, of course!"

"Then she is the prize. She is the princess who is held under the dragon's curse."

All three don their gloves, boots, waistbands, and helmets. Mikhail initiates the game.

Mark, Mikhail, and Iqhawe are standing on a small plateau. Before them is a long, dark valley with steep mountains on either side.

Mark hears a high-pitched shrieking noise that never ceases and covers his ears. "What's that noise? Is something wrong with the system?" He remembers a similar sound that he heard while on patrol, just before he crash landed.

"No, captain," answers Mikhail. "It's part of the challenge. You'll get used to it..., or it will break you mentally."

Mark looks at Mikhail and Iqhawe. Neither of them is wearing armor. Mikhail is wearing a simple robe. Iqhawe wears the traditional Zulu headband and a loincloth; he carries a small shield, and short spear. His massive chest is bare, unprotected. Mark looks him up and down and almost asks the obvious.

Iqhawe anticipates the question and explains: "I prefer to travel light in the mountains. I have everything I need."

Mark is surprised. "So you two are not going with me?"

"We will be there when you face the dragon, but on this level, we will each ascend a different mountain and face challenges in the higher elevations. As I said, you only need call to us, and we will be there to assist. Remember, you must call to one of us by name, or we will not come."

"No need, I'm sure," says Mark as he examines his armor, shield and sword. "Just the basics, I guess?"

"Only the standard sword, shield and armor. No extra limbs for this one, no technology. To complete this level, you need something more than armor."

"Endurance?"

Mikhail nods. "Just remember, this is a game, and it's much like a dream. A dream cannot harm you, but it will seem real, and you will believe everything you see, so remember, it's only a game that will seem like a dream."

A pole with a green beacon on top rises slowly before them. In the distance, on the horizon, they see a similar beacon appear just beyond the valley, except it is flashing red.

Mikhail explains, "Start line is here at the green light. Finish line is over there at the red light. Remember, just call out one of our names, and we'll be there in an instant to help you."

Mikhail and Iqhawe begin running and quickly leap to begin climbing the sides of the two mountains and vanish from view.

Mark bounces up and down a little and looks over his equipment. "Hmm. No special powers, just a sword and a shield." He moves forward. "Let's see what kind of hand I've been dealt."

Mark enters the swamp and penetrates the dense vegetation and trees. He presses forward for about an hour in the thick, soupy goo but sees no challengers. His legs are becoming tired so he rests for a moment.

Without warning, the bottom gives out, and he is falling down a mountainside, colliding with rocks and ricocheting from boulder to boulder. Finally he lands back in the swamp, under water. He comes up, spitting and wiping his face, trying to see around him and get his bearings. Still, he is alone. He's not sure why he didn't lose his shield and sword, but he still has them. He presses on for about another hour. His sword is drawn, and he struggles to keep his sword and shield out of the murky water.

Mark feels something bump against his leg. He steps back and stabs the water repeatedly. He feels it again, now on both legs, even through his armor. He tries to raise himself out of the water by partially scaling a nearby tree. Holding on to a limb with one hand, he parks his shield on a branch and stabs the water with his sword. The swamp is dark, and the water is darker. The stench is disgusting, and the shrill noise has not stopped. After a minute, he re-enters the water and presses ahead, though he still feels tired.

Wait, a clearing ahead. Mark moves a bit faster. The water becomes shallower. When he sees he's on land, he sits down. Why should he already be so tired? In theory, he is still in his room and has not moved an inch.

Out of the corner of his eye, he notices something flashing and turns around. It's the green beacon on the pole. He has returned to the starting point.

Mark begins to laugh and lies down. He then hears a noise behind him. He jumps up and flips around with shield and sword extended.

When Mark sees that it's Mikhail, he relaxes.

"I guess I'm not doing so well on this level." Mark tries to laugh it off, but Mikhail says nothing.

Finally Mark looks at him more carefully. His expression does not change, which doesn't seem like him. "An avatar?" Mark wonders. He realizes the truth almost too late. Mikhail, or whatever it is, slashes at Mark with a sword. Mark strikes at him apparently doing him no harm. He slashes at Mark, knocks him down, kicks him, and even spits on him.

"Mikhail! Is this part of the game?"

Mark is *en garde*, waiting for the next move. Suddenly a sword bursts forth from the center of his opponent's chest. He falls to the ground. Behind him is Mikhail, at least Mark hopes it is the real Mikhail.

"You called, captain?"

"I guess so."

"Hmm. It seems you haven't made much progress." Mikhail laughs and slaps Mark on the shoulder.

"Okay, you're the real Mikhail."

"Surely you weren't fooled by this...thing?"

"It was pretty convincing. I guess it just lacked your charm. Look, I've spent a lot of time on this game so far, and as you can see, I'm back to the starting point. The swamp was—"

"A dead end? Who said you had to go through the middle of the swamp?"

"I don't?"

"You could climb just a bit and move along the edge of the mountain side. It's pretty steep and rigorous, but after a time, the topography will change."

"Now you tell me."

"Carry on, captain. And again, call on me if you need me."

Mark begins moving along the edge. He has to climb a bit and slips several times, and occasionally he has to put his legs down in the sludge. He hopes no creature will attack him here, as it would be difficult to fight without something firm to hold on to. He reassures himself now and then by climbing up just a little to be certain he can still see the red beacon in the distance.

At length the terrain changes and becomes flat and firm. He still sees trees, although a fog is settling in.

Note to self. Avoid the swamp.

The high-pitched shrieking sound has gone, as has the stench. Mark hears rustling in the trees ahead. He proceeds with caution. Suddenly he is challenged by an enormous spider in his path.

"Ex-cel-lent!" Mark mutters. He thinks, "*I've battled giant spiders in other games.*"

The insect backs away as he advances. Mark turns around and looks behind him and notices that retreat is blocked off by a massive web. He runs forward and engages the big bug, which climbs a nearby tree and tries to wrap him in a web and sting him.

Mark jumps on a bent-over tree trunk to leap up close to the spider so he can slash it or wound it.

As he jumps, something from above grabs both his arms and carries him over the trees up to a considerable altitude. He tries to look up and to each side. It looks like a pterodactyl has him in his claws and is transporting him somewhere. *It's only a dream, right?* So he cuts into the creature's legs with his sword. It drops him, and he begins falling to the ground.

"Bad idea," Mark says to himself.

Mark falls for a time and tries to look down. The wind is blowing strongly. He sees waves and foamy crests below.

Mark hits the surface and plunges deep under the water. It's almost impossible to swim in his armor. He struggles for some time and becomes even more tired.

"MIKHAIL!" He shouts underwater, creating a torrent of bubbles.

Mark is brusquely pulled upward to the surface. He coughs and spits as he is being dragged on to the shore. He looks up. It is Mikhail, and again, he hopes that it's Mikhail.

Mikhail laughs exuberantly. "Once again, captain, I have raised you from the dead!"

"Okay, thanks again. I'll try not to make a habit of this."

"You still have a long way to go, captain. Call me if you need me again." He runs to the side of a nearby mountain and begins climbing.

Mark looks at the large river and ponders how to cross. He moves over to the mountainside and locates the red beacon. It seems the shoreline moves along the side of the mountain and that he can keep moving ahead.

Mark proceeds, although he is even wearier. He is not accustomed to losing at anything, and so far he has not beaten a single step of this level. If he only had just a little technology, even one item from his operations belt, one of his side arms, or his lightning boots.

Just over a mound ahead, Mark spots someone approaching. He stops and drops to the ground. The figure disappears. He raises up, and sees the figure do the same. He stands up, as does the figure.

"What kind of stupid game is this?" He mutters to himself.

They draw closer to each other, and Mark begins to understand. He is about to be challenged by himself: a mirror image. He has no doubt. This "warrior" is a döppelganger, except in reverse. Mark raises his sword and holds up his shield. His mirror image does the same, in reverse, at exactly the same time. Something is missing; there is no mirror, at least none that Mark can see.

Mark taunts his opponent, "So is this called 'Monkey see, monkey do?'" He strikes out at him with force. But this time Mirror-Mark does not do exactly the same but meets the sword, as if he knew exactly where Mark would strike. Mark likewise senses his next move and matches it precisely.

He is literally battling himself.

And the struggle continues for what seems like hours. It's a stalemate. Both warriors are exhausted and finally fall on the ground.

"What's the point here?" Mark thinks, keeping his eye on his opponent. He gets up and begins walking away. Mirror-Mark does the same.

"Hmm," he mutters, "remember this in the future when fighting with yourself. Just walk away."

Mark climbs the steep side of the mountain just enough to make sure that the red beacon is still in view, but he sees no beacon at all. He walks over to the other mountain and does the same. No beacon. He looks at each mountain, which now seem identical, and he finally decides just to continue the same direction and hope for the best.

After several hours, Mark encounters ruins. Ancient ruins, stone buildings that have crumbled and fallen. Perhaps like Rome in an early era. Various structures have partially collapsed. The streets are full of what look like statues. As he moves along, a thought occurs to him.

"Pompeii?"

He stops and studies the sculptures and discovers that in fact they seem people who have been frozen in flight, including three warriors.

Mark instinctively knows what is going to happen next. He draws his sword. As he expected, the three warriors come to life, but not as human beings. They are stone warriors who strike with stone swords. Mark defends himself against their blows. He is fatigued, but he welcomes the new, more traditional challenge.

After several more clashes, he quickly discovers the catch: his sword cannot wound them, and they do not bleed. Their blades look like they are made of stone, but they are sharp.

The trio first circles him, like a pack of wolves who are studying and stalking their prey. He manages to evade them and strike, but without inflicting any serious damage. This continues for what seems like several hours. Mark now believes that all matches on this level last that long.

He starts to feel stiff. He shakes it off and continues fighting. He then quickly realizes that he is slowing down. His opponents see this as well, and they stop striking at him, as if waiting for something.

In just a few moments, Mark is paralyzed. He is standing there with his sword raised; he has turned into stone. The statues move in for the kill and begin striking him repeatedly. At first, his now stone armor holds, but in short order their blades begin cracking it.

Searing pain. He has never felt pain in combat or in a hologame. This is too much.

He is barely able to move his mouth and cry out, "Mikhail!"

As Mikhail shows up, the three warriors return to stiff stone, and Mark collapses on the ground. He thinks he is bleeding, and the pain continues. Mikhail kneels beside him.

"Search and Rescue, at your service, captain!" He pulls out an electronic device and begins making some type of adjustments. Mark's pain leaves quickly, and his bleeding stops.

"I thought I was a goner! How did you do that? You don't have your medical kit with you. What is that?"

"What, this? It's the game genie. It comes in handy to have one here on the inside. Hey, it's only a game. You are not really wounded."

"Not like any game I ever played. What moron designed this level?"

"You did, captain."

Mark stares at him in disbelief. "I'm afraid to ask for an explanation of that. I guess I lost again. I was hoping to face off with the Ultimate Dragon Boss, but obviously I'm not ready. Just give me a little technology and—"

"On the contrary, captain. You have succeeded."

Again, Mark looks at him in disbelief.

"You endured without quitting, and you called for help three times. Each time, you realized you could not prevail alone, something I think you are accustomed to doing or trying to do. You pilots tend to be loners. Personally I prefer to be part of a team."

"Okay, personally, I prefer to be part of a team, a winning team."

"Oh, captain, you are!"

—20—

DRAGON SLAYER

Out of his mouth go burning lamps,
and sparks of fire leap out.
Out of his nostrils goeth smoke,
as out of a seething pot or caldron.
His breath kindleth coals,
and a flame goeth out of his mouth.
Job 41, "Leviathan."

Mark just shakes his head as he gets on his feet. He turns, looks up, and sees the red beacon flashing.

Mikhail slaps him on the back. "Welcome to Dragon World."

They walk toward a large mount laced with crags and caves. The mount is still fairly distant, but Mark can see that on top is a glass case, or what looks like glass, glistening in the light of the setting sun.

"Is Dominique in that case?"

"This is your dream and your game, captain. For all intents and purposes, it is Dominique, held prisoner by the dragon."

"And where is this ultimate seven-headed emerald-green dragon with crowns?"

"It's coming. You'll see."

They are soon joined by Iqhawe, who is still wearing his Zulu warrior garb. Mikhail prepares Mark, "You have only your sword, shield, and basic armor. I have increased your ability to jump high. We'll be falling back for a time. You'll have first crack at the beast."

"Roger that," answers Mark. He then moves ahead running, looking for some sign of the dragon. As he approaches, he sees a reptilian head appear in the distance just over the summit behind the glass case.

Strauss's Also Sprach Zarathustra is playing in Mark's head. The enemy serpent began as a small shadow in a red sky and is now growing larger. Soon Mark can see huge wings flapping slowly but violently. The dragon flies in and lands. It is indeed emerald-green and is mesmerizing, strangely beautiful in a wicked sort of way.

Mark snaps out of it and looks again at the glass case. He begins to feel fear. This is not like when he confronted the cloaked assailants to protect Dominique. Now he has only a sword and shield to defend her against harm from a far more powerful assailant. The dragon is massive and awesome, the incarnation of humanity's worst nightmare. Mark fears that he cannot save Dominique or even protect her from harm. It's only a game, but he is taking this game very seriously.

The serpent spots the crystal box and appears to discern its contents. It raises up and exhales hell on the case but seemingly without any destructive or harmful effect. There's no way to know how much heat the glass can take.

Mark runs faster. *Eyes on the prize, and eyes on the enemy.* He quickly jumps to the top of the mount and confronts the dragon, taking a stand between it and the would-be casket. The dragon is large, probably two stories tall. He stares into its red, fiery eyes, his sword before him, waiting for it to make a move.

The dragon lurches forward, trying to devour him in one gulp, but Mark quickly leaps out of the way. It then tries to snatch him in its claws. Mark jumps over the left claw, sword in the air, and comes down with a hard, decisive blow, severing the head from the long neck.

That was too easy.

He is right. The dragon raises itself and stretches. It now has two heads.

"Oops! Mikhail did mention the multiplying head thing." It is now four stories tall. One head breathes fire, and the other spits out hail. Mark lifts his shield high in anticipation. The head on the left breathes a blast of fire. The head on the right spews out small hailstones that knock him down the slope of the mount. Mark gets back on his feet, shield up, waiting for the right opportunity, possibly between blasts.

Mark runs, jumps high, and somersaults in the air. In the process, he severs the two heads with precision.

"I've done this before with other virtual beasts," he remembers.

But now, the dragon has grown to ten stories, and Mark has to deal with four heads, breathing smoke, fire, hail, and acid in large quantities. Everything spews from them like out of four high pressure hoses. With four heads towering over him, the flow is nearly continuous. The dragon blasts Mark back down the mount and keeps him pinned, sword and body behind the shield. The dragon doesn't seem to run out of hell or hail and keeps up the pressure. It's hard to see through all the smoke, and he struggles to keep his shield steady to protect himself from the acid. Finally, the dragon lunges and strikes his shield repeatedly with its claws, knocking him back and forth across the plain.

Mark picks himself up and faces the dragon again, but now it has grown to twice its former size and has seven heads, each with a golden crown. Mark feels like an insect.

The dragon pauses its attack and raises itself to its full height. Mark is again mesmerized looking at it. He lowers his sword and shield. This is only a game. What's to be worried about? He's never seen anything quite like this dragon.

Suddenly the serpent begins to knock him around, as if toying with him. Mark is falling, rolling, and trying to recover his stance. He is blasted into the air and smashed against a rock face. If he were being judged with points, so far he would have a "zero."

This pounding goes on for some time, and Mark is becoming annoyed. It's just a game, but how can he win?

"Mikhail!"

"Yes, captain." It is Mikhail's jovial voice. "Do you think that it's time for us to help?"

"That would be welcome!"

The smoke, flames, acid, and hail abruptly cease. Mark looks out from behind his shield. The dragon has retreated back to the mount, still huffing and puffing and carefully watching the approach of Mark's companions. As they come near, it backs up even more.

Mark welcomes his allies to the battle. He looks at them, and then he looks at the dragon. "He's afraid of you two?"

Iqhawe declares solemnly, "He should be."

Mikhail clarifies, "Remember, we've played this game before."

"But this one is somehow my dream? Shouldn't I have a chance to beat the beast and be the hero who saves Dominique?"

"You will be. As I told you, you just need the minor assistance of your team, shall we say, a little help from shock troops."

Mikhail and Iqhawe move toward the dragon, who continues to back away. Iqhawe hurls his spear with deadly accuracy right into the mouth of one of the heads, which slumps over, dead. Its crown falls to the ground. Mikhail mysteriously disappears, apparently leaving Iqhawe to face the dragon alone. The Zulu continues walking toward the serpent, undaunted and unarmed. The remaining heads roar and discharge only fire like huge, improbable blast furnaces, but the flames have no visible effect on the advancing warrior.

As Iqhawe moves toward his opponent, the serpent shrinks to one-fourth his original size, and when the Zulu reaches him, the African warrior is twice the serpent's now much smaller size. As the dragon cowers before him, he grabs it by the tail, flips it, and slams it on the ground upside-down. Mark is emboldened by this turn of events and runs to join the battle. Mikhail appears suddenly from nowhere. He is now twice as big as the dragon and is holding a huge chain, which he wraps around it, completely binding it.

"You may slay the dragon now, captain."

As Mark continues to move toward them, the dragon bellows and squirms furiously to escape the chains. Up close it does not seem quite as terrifying.

Mark pulls his sword from its sheath but notices that it looks quite different. Its handle is solid gold with six large rubies inset. The blade is radiating a strange power, shimmering, as if it had been polished in some ethereal way. The dragon is still fighting and thundering.

"Now, captain!!!"

Mark plunges the sword deep into its chest about where he thinks the heart will be, if such a creature has a heart. It struggles, kicks, and squirms but finally exhales its last.

Mikhail and Iqhawe strip the corpse of its crowns. Mikhail drags it to a large hole in the ground, a pit with no visible bottom, and hurls it down into inky darkness. Iqhawe picks up a boulder many times his size and slams it down to seal the opening.

Mark is slightly stunned while observing this bizarre burial of the defeated creature. He asks, "It looked huge and kept getting larger, but when you two approached it, it shrank. Why didn't it do that before, when I was fighting it?"

"Ah!" responds Mikhail, "Its size? It's all in your head, captain. It helps to see it done by experts."

Mark nods and continues to try to process the battle that he has just witnessed.

Iqhawe picks up one of the crowns and hands it to Mark.

Mark examines it and jokes, "Wow! Gold! Can I keep this after the game, like as a prize?"

Iqhawe scoffs, "It's fool's gold. Keep it if you like."

Still a little dazed, Mark looks over at the transparent case. The crystal shell has disappeared, and a woman is lying there currently unprotected. He rushes to her side.

It's Dominique! He looks back at Mikhail, "Nice touch!" and leans over and imparts the magic of a lover's kiss.

Dominique's eyelids flutter, and she wakes up. At first, she is a little startled, but when she sees Mark, she smiles.

"Is this a dream?" She asks.

"Yes, my love, and you're going to be okay. Thank God that it's only a dream."

GAME OVER. Your awesome team has rescued the Princess!!!

The world suddenly goes black. Mark sits still just for a moment but finally removes his helmet. Mikhail and Iqhawe already have removed theirs.

Mark shakes his head, stretches, and blinks his eyes. "Intense," he remarks.

"We like the intensity." Mikhail responds. "It is excellent training, don't you think?"

"A little humbling," which is a hard phrase for Mark to utter. "I prefer more technology and a wider choice of weapons."

"Ah!" Mikhail laughs. "That approach tests only the weapons, not the warrior. We can play it again if we get the chance. We are all busy now. But should you play it alone, remember, you can increase the difficulty of any or all levels."

"Up to...?"

"Up to the power of infinity. There's always room for improvement, and there always will be. And we do love a challenge?"

"Absolutely," smiles Mark, looking over at Iqhawe, who, unlike Mikhail, rarely changes his facial expression.

Iqhawe stands up. "Captain, it was an honor and a pleasure to do battle with you. I hope we will fight together again."

They all shake hands, and the two visitors depart.

Mark decides to lie down for a while and rest. He tells Pinocchio to play Mahler, Symphony #2 and a list of other soothing classical pieces. He sleeps for several hours.

He is awakened by a holocall from Dominique. He knows from the expression on her face that something bad has happened. Her eyes and cheeks are gleaming with tears.

"My love, are you okay?"

"Mark..., oh, Mark, *Papa est mort*. He is passed on." She breaks down crying with her face in her hands. Mark wants to hold her, but this is not possible with hollow holograph technology. She is only a grieving image, well defined but empty, insubstantial, like a sad, beautiful ghost.

"I'm so sorry, *chérie*. I wish I could have spent more time with him, to get to know him. He was a great man, and he had a huge impact on me in a short period of time."

Dominique nods, "Yes, he was." She wipes her eyes. "I wish you could be here. I know that things are happening to the south, *n'est-ce pas?*"

"There will be a memorial service."

"On Friday. It will be at Notre-Dame, with burial at the Cimetière du Père Lachaise."

"That's a high honor."

"He honored his country. His country will honor him, as will the European Federation. I believe that some heads of state will be there and many high-ranking military. It's been planned for some time."

"You must tell me more about him."

"I will. It's hard not to talk about him, hard not to think about happy memories, especially now."

"Can I attend via HoloVision?"

"I believe so. Some of the dignitaries will be in holographic attendance. I'll clear it for you and see if we can have a holographic seat placed as close to me as possible."

"I'll be there in spirit, for sure."

"*Papa* will be looking down from heaven, smiling."

"Yes, I'm sure he will be."

Mark leans forward to kiss her, and she leans forward as well. Their lips meet in holospace.

"*Je t'aime*, Mark."

"I love you, Dominique."

Dominique disappears, but Mark has saved the image. He lies down in his bed and views another slide show of her. He always enjoys reviewing the file. Memories of the general pass through his mind.

PART III

—21—

THE ENEMY BELOW

"Captain Knutson! Bandits at two o'clock!"

Mark makes an evasive move and then goes into a steep dive only to pull up and attack the bandits' underbellies. He fires, and he does not miss. He easily takes out the three enemy planes and resumes his mission.

Below him is his target, a train that is racing toward a tunnel in the side of a mountain. His objective is to stop it before it enters. He decides to try to slow it down a bit first.

Mark goes into another sharp dive and begins strafing the train, car by car all the way to the engine, but it's still running. No matter. He moves ahead over the track and heads straight for the tunnel opening.

Mark waits until the last second and releases a bomb. As he pulls up, he hears the bomb explode. Even if he didn't hit the tunnel directly, he knows that he definitely did hit the side of the mountain, which will cause a landslide and demolish the train when it collides with the fallen rocks.

Problem is that he hasn't pulled up in time. His Red Baron bi-plane crashes into the side of the mountain, as well.

Mark is frustrated as he pulls off his helmet and shakes his gloves on to the floor. "I used to be good at this one!" Mark hates to lose. He can't go to work today with a loss on his mind, even in a hologame.

Mark again puts on his gloves and helmet. Once in, he upgrades his plane but does not replace the enemy planes. He selects an F-35 Super Hornet with an extra spread of missiles.

Start.

"Captain Knutson! Bandits at two o'clock!"

Mark does not take evasive maneuvers. He releases three small rockets, which easily knock the single-engine bi-planes out the sky. He then dives for the train, which is headed for the tunnel at full speed. With canons and rockets, he destroys it car by car and finally launches his biggest smart bomb to take out the engine. To add the icing on the combat cake, he fires four rockets toward the tunnel; two go inside, and two hit the hillside. The explosion practically levels the whole mountain. Mark pulls up comfortably as train, mountain, and tunnel are completely demolished.

The game voice proclaims, "Congratulations, Captain Knutson! You are Top Gun! You are awesome!"

He takes off his helmet. *Now I can go to work.*

Mark is still relishing his cybervictory as he patrols the Mediterranean Sea at a much slower speed than usual and at a lower altitude, just above shipping lanes. Destroyers alone are insufficient to protect against the present wave of subversive subs. Supply ships are equipped for limited self-defense and frequently have an inadequate number of escorts.

In recent days, the enemy subs have taken a toll. Somehow pirates are acquiring more subs and more sophisticated weapons, scanners, and jamming devices. Mark is searching for cloaked warplanes, surface ships, and subs. Current EuroSecure standing orders are "Shoot to kill. Territorial incursions are authorized if in pursuit."

The sea is calm today, and the Haze is light. No Rogue Storms are in the forecast. *Awesome day for hunting and fishing.* He turns his planes south, toward the edge of the buffer zone. As expected, his prey come to him. Four bogeys appear on his scanners. He marks them, and then he turns both warplanes to investigate.

Mark orders: "Daughter, kill the four targets marked."

The drone daughter craft pulls away, increasing speed and altitude. The four bandits begin firing and separate. Mark decides to sit this one out. He sometimes enjoys watching his drone daughter craft take out enemy fighters. It's like watching a hologame that plays itself; it can be entertaining.

In a short time, the targets disappear from the screen. The daughter drone returns to his side.

"Confirm kills," orders Mark.

The drone daughter craft reports: "Two targets were holograms previously validated by sensor ghosts. The other two blips were drones, which were eliminated."

Just as well I didn't waste my time. But then, they may have been testing us, trying to draw us away from the ships. Their new ghosting technology is impressive.

An hour later, eight fighters take off from a hidden underground base on the northern coast of Africa and appear on his scanners; all are approaching his position at a high rate of speed. Mark turns mother and daughter toward the targets to intercept.

"Let's see what we're dealing with." He launches a spray of Acer-6 missiles that will seek and destroy all real targets, but the missiles all detonate prior to reaching the warplanes.

They've also improved their shielding technology. He immediately separates from the daughter drone, and the two turn opposite directions and then attack from different angles.

"A little plasma should do it." Both fighters release a deadly dose and then veer away. The enemy fighters attempt desperate evasive maneuvers to escape, but the plasma overtakes three of them, and they explode in mid-air. The remaining five fire at Mark's warplanes and shoot straight up, gaining altitude rapidly.

Mark and his daughter give chase.

"Lock on targets," Mark commands. Suddenly he hears a high-pitched, shrill sound, similar to what he had heard in the *Sleeping Beauty* game and to what he heard just before his recent crash-land. He cannot lock on. They must have even more advanced disruptors.

Mark says under his breath, "Well, it's time to use the good ole Gatling gun. Let's have an old-fashioned dog fight. Ex-cel-lent." He leans hard on his stick and pursues one of his opponents.

The dog fight begins. Mark's warplanes are pursuing and alternately being pursued. Hunters and hunted switch roles in the twinkling of an eye. They make sharp, dangerous turns in every direction possible. It is a war of nerves and response times. Mark is sweating. Mark is loving it.

"Let's see you disrupt .50 calibers," Mark mutters as he squeezes the trigger. His drone daughter follows suit and fires bullets on the enemy planes.

The mother-daughter team takes out two of the remaining fighters, but three continue the battle.

Mark receives a radio transmission, "Hey, Knutson! Do you need any help there?"

"Nope, everything under control here."

Nonetheless four additional European Federation fighters come into view and engage the remaining aircraft. The enemy fighters again send out a disruptive beam, but this time it is to no avail. They are hit.

As the defeated fighters fall toward the sea, Mark and the other warplanes receive a distress call from the convoy in their sector.

"May Day! May Day! We are under attack. Undetermined number of submarines have just uncloaked and are firing torpedoes. Counterarmor is holding for now. Request immediate assistance."

The warplanes turn back toward the shipping lanes. Mark and his drone daughter craft, along with two other pilots and their drone daughters, fly just above the white caps. They decelerate and land gently on the water's surface. Mark is watching his scanners. "Definite targets down there. On my mark," says Mark to the other pilots.

"Submerge!"

At this command, the six craft streamline and transform, disappearing beneath the surface of the sea where they have been converted into submarines, or better said, stealth submarine hunters. Once under the water, they have an improved picture of the challenge. In an area of nine square kilometers, they scan more than twenty enemy subs of various sizes, and many are firing torpedoes at them.

But Mark and his fellow pilots have some torpedoes of their own. They spread out like sharks, ready to move in for the kill. The rebel pack flees in a panic in all directions, like fleet-footed gazelles being chased by lions, except under water. Some are able to cloak, while others can dive deep. BattleNet links the warplanes-made-subs' systems and assigns each fighter three initial targets.

Mark's daughter drone quickly picks off the smallest target. Mark pursues the larger one down, down deep amidst large rocks and caves where it is dark and darker still. He is operating by advanced sonar imaging, but the enemy sub is attempting to disrupt his sensors and with some success.

The target vessel moves through the caves and crevices with stealth. It disappears into one cave and emerges quickly from another. It then drops into yet another fairly narrow, dark cave. Mark is reluctant to follow. He wants to return to Dominique. For the first time in his life, he has a real reason to live. He fires several torpedoes, which explode inside, collapsing the entrance, but the enemy craft emerges on the other side of a large mount.

Mark continues the pursuit, discharging more torpedoes, which follow the vessel into yet another cave and detonate.

He notices no motion or activity. Mark waits and tries to scan, but his scanner is being disrupted. He sends in a probe to view possible wreckage. Black, thick oil emerges from the cave opening. Images from the probe are blurred and dark.

Mark waits, moving closer to the entrance, which is partially blocked. A different enemy sub comes out of another cave nearby, and Mark is in pursuit.

The vessel suddenly comes to a stop. Mark tries to decrease speed as well, but before he can, the sub blows up, apparently set to auto-destruct.

The shock wave sends Mark's warplane-sub reeling back and turning over, hitting its hull repeatedly on the craggy sea bottom. When he comes to a stop, he is upside-down and shaking his head.

He tries to regain control of his craft. Mark is finally able to turn it right-side up and start to surface.

When he comes up, he sees the other warplanes and other aircraft hovering.

"Captain Knutson, are you okay?"

Mark checks with his daughter drone and discovers a record of two kills.

"I'm fine. Four targets confirmed killed. And you?"

"All targets eliminated, captain. I guess these people just love to get their butts kicked. HQ has ordered us to return to our patrols. Call us again if you need us. Hey, that was fun! Let's do it again sometime."

Mark and his daughter drone surface and transmute back into warplanes, rising off the sea and blasting off to the south. They return to patrolling but pick up no further activity for several hours. Mark spends the time listening to music from the *Nutcracker* and thinking about Dominique.

Something is different inside him. He has been experiencing fear recently, and he has never been afraid of anything in his life. But this is a new kind of fear, similar to when he was confronting the Ultimate Dragon Boss in the game. He's afraid that something will happen to Dominique, that he won't be there to protect her, and that he won't be there at all so they can spend the rest of their lives together.

Three blips appear on his sensors. Four bogeys approaching the neutral zone. They are probably trying to lure him into following them. His warplanes turn south. In just a few minutes, all three cross into the buffer zone. His orders are to pursue them and take them out.

"Daughter, engage and destroy."

The drone daughter craft accelerates without asking any questions, and the targets retreat. Mark monitors the activity through the drone daughter craft's cameras and sensors. He decides to take over the system and manage the battle from a safe distance.

The targets are confirmed to be real, not holograms. As he crosses into the African continent, he notices that the disruption level has increased. His screen image is tearing, and the sensors are becoming erratic. Through the daughter's weapons systems he targets the three bogeys and fires.

He destroys one, but the other two take evasive measures. He fires again, but again, they escape destruction. He accelerates to join his daughter.

As he approaches, his stick suddenly becomes unresponsive. The daughter drone begins losing altitude, and so does he. He fights with the controls of the mother craft and manages to pull up. The exact same tractor beam that caused the mother and the daughter to go down before. This time, only the daughter drone has gone down. Mark has pulled away to a safe distance.

"What kind of technology do these people have?"

Mark notifies HQ that his drone has apparently been forced to land. He increases speed. He must somehow rescue the drone ship and protect it, but he can't let the mother get caught in that tractor beam again.

As his forward cameras zoom in, he sees that the daughter drone is on the ground, paralyzed. The drone's forward cameras show a dozen or more robed figures approaching. He notes that they are each carrying something, probably tools with which they can strip the warplane and pirate its technology.

Mark studies them carefully, half-way expecting to see a chieftain in a purple robe with a scimitar.

He is preparing to try to approach again and fire on them, but he notices that his stick has again become sluggish.

"Oh, no!" He decides to pull up and turn back, and as he does, he feels control of his fighter returning to the stick.

Mark warns off other pilots. On the remote screen, he sees that the robed figures are starting to work. One approaches the drone's forward cameras and sprays them with a dark liquid.

Black screen.

He tries other counter measures and sends a report to HQ. "Lost control of daughter drone. She's on the ground without power. Nothing is working. Cannot effect rescue due to dangerous tractor beam encountered previously." *We cannot allow them access to our technology.*

Once he receives official authorization, Mark initiates the self-destruct sequence. He then pulls up and turns back north. A counter appears next to the screen image. After ten seconds, a violent explosion registers on his sensors.

Mark files a report. He'll be called before a panel to explain this one, no doubt.

—22—
EIN FESTE BURG IST UNSER GOTT

Mark is in full dress uniform. He sits quietly and waits for Dominique's call while viewing the memorial service via HoloVision. They are not transmitting in 360-D, so he can only watch it on a flat screen. The cathedral is completely full, with one section reserved for holomourners. Via the HoloVision camera angle, he can see Dominique sitting in the front row. She is dressed in black. To her left is General Vaillancourt. In front of her is her father's casket lying in state.

On one side is a French flag and on the other, a EuroSecure flag. The coffin is surrounded by flower arrangements and sprays. Around Dominique, Mark sees a sea of dignitaries, many in military uniforms. All are wearing black armbands. Above her and to the rear is the magnificent rose window, which is noticeably pale today. He remembers his last visit to Notre-Dame. He was impressed by the architecture but annoyed by all the tourists flooding the place and buying souvenirs.

Dominique wipes her eyes with a handkerchief and takes out her portapack to make the connection with Mark and tying into the empty holoseat across the aisle from her. The holomourner section is specially equipped with projectors. The images are clear; however, the quality is not quite as good as holograms in Rome. He responds, activates his projectors, and instantly she is sitting beside him in his apartment, but only in 2-D. His system extrapolates and converts her 2-D image to 3-D but a 360-D resolution is not possible. On the screen, Mark is sitting across the aisle from her in the cathedral in full dress uniform.

Mark cannot move or do anything to distract from the gravity of the occasion. He looks up at his apartment's flat screen and studies himself sitting in 2-D across from Dominique. Her avatar is sitting next to him in his apartment. She's really all he needs to see or wants to see.

On the screen, he watches Dominique lean over to her right and look at his avatar across the aisle. She whispers, "I love you. *Je t'aime.*" In Mark's apartment, her avatar looks to her right, but he can read her lips. He looks to his left, and his avatar on the screen follows suit, and he replies ever so softly, "I love you. I wish I could hold you." She smiles faintly at his avatar and then looks forward again.

The organist begins playing Bach's Ein feste Burg ist unser Gott. When she is finished, General Vaillancourt walks up to the front and proclaims in a loud, forceful voice: *"Aux grands hommes la patrie et EuroSecure reconnaissants!"* Marks translates in his head, "The fatherland and EuroSecure recognizing its great men!" At this, all in attendance stand, and the military officers in full dress uniform salute. Mark and his avatar stand with them. He engages Universal Translator.

"We welcome you to this memorial service, distinguished guests in person and via HoloVision."

There is a short intentional pause and silence, after which all again take their seats.

The general reads from a small screen before him: "Emmanuel Gérard Lécuyer was born on August 7, 1980, in Nice, France. He is preceded in death by his wife, Jacqueline de Bonne Lécuyer and a brother, Ives-Michel Lécuyer, and a sister, Miriam Lécuyer de Carpentier. He is survived by his only daughter, Dominique Miriam Lécuyer, of Rome, Italy. General Lécuyer served in the French military for thirty years and in EuroSecure for an additional twelve years. For his participation in campaigns in Iraq, Afghanistan, Nigeria, Angola, Syria, the Ivory Coast, and others, he was awarded the Legion of Honor, the War Cross, and the Legion of Merit from his native France and numerous other awards from eleven other countries."

Mark watches Dominique on the screen beside his avatar in 2-D and then looks at her in his apartment in 3-D. He feels a sense of pride to be engaged to the daughter of a great man and hero. He is proud of her but feeling sorrow at her grief. He is still concerned that she is in Paris and that Paris has been hit. He looks at her in his apartment and again looks at her on the screen. *What a strong woman she is. Breathtakingly beautiful in word and deed and appearance. Such a treasure.* All these feelings are new to him.

Mark tries to appear attentive as various dignitaries who follow General Vaillancourt give remarks and tributes. As the service concludes, the holomourners vanish. Those in real-life attendance file past the coffin to pay their last respects. Many come and say kind and comforting words to Dominique. Mark has vanished for the moment.

A smaller group will go to the burial site at the Cimetière du Père Lachaise. Dominique leaves the church and gets into a long black limousine and sits in the back seat alone. She reactivates Mark's avatar on her left by tying her portapack in with the limo's cameras and projectors, which produce a better image for her and a vastly improved image for him in his apartment.

"Are you okay?" he asks attentively.

"With you on my left, and God on my right, I'll be okay."

"Right." Mark looks over at her right side.

"What will you do now? When are you going to come back to Rome?"

"I have a number of matters to attend to with regard to *Papa's* estate. I'm not sure how to handle the house. I know that things are becoming more intense at the base in Naples. They've been wonderfully understanding, but I have to return to my job as soon as possible. That's what *Papa* would want, for me to continue to be part of the effort."

As they arrive at the cemetery, Mark disappears and then reappears next to Dominique on the front row; the image quality is again not good. General Vaillancourt continues to officiate. He steps forward and presents a folded French flag and a EuroSecure flag to Dominique and repeats: *"Aux grands hommes la patrie et EuroSecure reconnaissants!"* He then salutes her. Dominique squeezes the flags close to her chest and holds her head up high.

General Vaillancourt steps back and addresses the crowd, explaining that General Lécuyer had requested the reading of a scripture at the memorial service. He begins to read, but Mark has not reengaged Universal Translator. He picks out most of the words. "I tell you a mystery.... We will not all die..., but we will all be changed..., in the 'something' of an eye. The trumpet will sound...." Then he loses the thread.

Once the passage has been read, a short procession of EuroSecure military aircraft fly overhead, tilting their wings in tribute. A saddled, riderless horse passes nearby. An honor guard of seven fires three volleys into the air, after which a trumpeter plays "La Marseillaise." All those in attendance stand. When he is finished, Dominique walks to the casket and picks up a flower and a clump of dirt to throw on the coffin. Mark remains seated, his avatar disappears, and from his apartment he continues watching via HoloVision in 2-D.

Dominique tosses the clump and the flower on the casket and says, *"Cendres aux cendres, de poussière à la poussière."* Ashes to ashes, dust to dust.

Mark vanishes, and the screen goes blank.

After a week, Dominique boards the hypertrain to return from Paris to Rome. Mark is tense, full of anxiety. He cannot protect her on the train. Who knows where the terrorists will strike next? He rushes to the station to meet her. When she steps off the train, Mark embraces her tightly and kisses her.

"Never leave me again!" he whispers in her ear. They are both smiling as they walk down the platform to the exit, where they are scanned and cleared.

Later, they have dinner together at Mark's apartment and discuss the past and the future.

"What news from EuroSecure?" asks Dominique. "I'm sure I'll be briefed when I return to work tomorrow. What do you know?"

"It's been strange. No new terror attacks on Rome or on Paris that I know of."

"Nothing new in Paris."

"It's been relatively quiet again. We had a massive submarine attack on shipping lanes not long ago, but it didn't last. Things are calm again in Rome, for the time being."

"You were part of the defense against the submarines?"

"Yes."

"You were not injured?"

"I'm fine. I wish I could say the same for my daughter drone. We had to destroy her. I can't really explain what happened. We ran into that invisible tractor beam, like before. It grabbed hold of us and caused the daughter drone to crash land. The mother craft and I managed to escape. I got authorization for a self-destruct sequence, and we blew some pirates to the infernal regions."

"I'm glad you're okay."

"Well, again, they've initiated an investigation, but I won't be furloughed this time. They need all qualified pilots available. We're back to doing extended shifts as of last Thursday."

"I'm looking forward to getting back to work and to some kind of normal routine and to some romantic dates perhaps?"

Mark smiles. "I think that can be arranged. What else?"

"What else?"

"When can we talk about a wedding date?"

"You are eager, *monsieur*?"

"I am eager to marry the woman of my dreams."

"And she is eager to marry you. But the times, they are uncertain, Mark."

"I know. And that's all the more reason. Loving you is the one thing I'm certain of."

—23—

UNLOCKING THE MYSTERY OF LIFE

After Mark finishes his shift and files his comprehensive report, he returns to Rome and to his apartment to discover that Angela has left a voice message. She is excited. "Marco! The Lumena, it is meeting late tonight in a larger theater outside the Bolla. The crowd will be larger, and that which Seren will do will astound you! There will be none doubt in your mind that this is the future, right in front of your eyes!"

Though he is tired, Mark decides to attend. He is no longer officially attached to the *Guardia Pretoriana*, but he has been advised to pursue any suspicious activity and is still wearing his gear.

He arrives slightly late and is surprised to see several thousand in attendance. He cannot find a seat and so begins recording while standing on the right side of the theater along with dozens of others. Seren is talking. He is looking for Angela among Seren's assistants, but he does not see her. He initiates Universal Translator.

"And why did Rome decline and fall? Because along the way some of its leaders have lacked vision. For example, Julius Caesar himself saw the next step, while the senate worked only to prevent that step. They were nest of vipers and traitors!"

Seren continues with the most inflammatory rhetoric against the Roman senate that Mark has heard yet.

Whenever Seren pauses, it is as if the audience has stopped breathing.

"But my friends, you did not come here to listen to me criticize the senate. I'm sure that all of us engage in that recreational pastime on a regular basis." He smiles.

Mark hears murmurs of laughter from the audience.

"That is old news. No, you came because you want to see something new and different, perhaps something world-shaking, as my followers have suggested to you. You will not leave disappointed, I assure you."

Big talk. Let's see you deliver.

"For tonight's meeting, I have invited a number of guests, all of whom have one thing in common. As advanced as modern medical technology is, it cannot cure them. It cannot restore or heal them except with pitiful devices that sometimes malfunction or wear out. These special guests have been left without hope, until tonight."

Seren's first guest is in uniform and is helped up on the stage. He is obviously crippled. His legs appear to be twisted and maimed.

"Please, corporal, have a seat." He helps the soldier sit comfortably.

"Ladies and gentlemen, you have seen this before. It is sad that soldiers have to pay any price, but to lose the use of their limbs? In order to compensate, what does Rome give in return? My brother, how were you injured?"

"I was on patrol thirty kilometers north of Rome when a terrorist bomb went off."

"And what hope have doctors given you?"

"Reconstructive surgery didn't work quite as they hoped. They are planning to amputate my legs, but they're going to give me state-of-the-art prosthetic limbs. They actually look pretty good, and I know several fellow soldiers that have already been fitted—"

"My friend, I'm sure those artificial limbs are the best Rome can do. What if I offered you something better?"

"Well, I...uh..."

Seren turns a nearby scanner toward the sergeant's legs and activates it. A 360-D transparent image is projected above them, showing just how twisted and maimed they are.

"Ladies and gentlemen, technology is not required for what we are about to do. The scanner will only verify for you skeptics that what is about to happen is real."

Seren puts his hands on the sergeant's knees and begins chanting under his breath. After a moment, Seren's fingers begin to glow, and the veteran's legs glow; a radiance spreads and finally reaches his hips and his toes. The soldier seems agitated; his body is shaking. Some in the crowd gasp and most all lean forward. The people around Mark are whispering, and many are taking video with small devices.

Mark looks up at the 360-D image of the legs. Something is happening. The man is trembling. Mark looks at the man's real legs. They are straightening and filling out. Mark looks at the holographic image; the same thing is happening there. Mark activates his oracle glasses and zooms in, trying to discern evidence of some type of optical illusion or trick. He is astonished to see a physical rebuilding in progress.

Finally Seren steps back and commands him, "Stand up, my noble friend, and walk!" The man has calmed down but still seems a little dazed. He looks down at his legs and up at Seren in disbelief. He sits up, rocking his feet back and forth. Then he stands and smiles as he lifts his legs up and down. He almost begins laughing as he then bounces up and down lightly. Finally he jumps up and down several times and grins. Soon he descends the stairs of the stage and runs up and down the aisles, shouting. The audience is shouting with him and clapping.

Mark is in shock. His oracle glasses reveal no holographic activity in the legs, no technological illusion of any kind. The hologram above is frozen; the last read-out of the man's legs is still suspended in mid-air and shows a normal bone structure.

Impossible!

Finally Mark spots Angela. She is helping a woman to the stage. Apparently the woman is blind.

The audience calms down only because they are eager to see what is next.

"My good woman. What need brings you here today?"

"I have been blind since I suffered a facial injury at a very early age, bone fractures that damaged my eyes and severed the optic nerves."

"And what has medical science told you?"

"They called it 'bi-lateral traumatic optic neuropathy.' There is no treatment. But they've implanted a chip in my brain that allows me to see outlines of things, some light and shadow." She points to a small box that she carries hooked on to a belt around her waist. "In this box is the hardware that makes it possible."

Seren uses the scanner and creates a holographic view of the affected area inside her head. Mark can see the damage to her eyeballs and the nerves.

Seren abruptly pulls the box from her waist and dramatically casts it aside. "You will need this no longer!" he cries, and again the audience gasps.

"Spit into my hands!"

The woman looks astonished, confused.

"Spit, I say!" She finally complies.

Seren places his spittle-covered palms over her eye sockets. His hands and her face begin to glow. She cries out.

"What do you see?"

"Light!" Then she screams, "Light!!!"

Seren removes his hands, and the woman rubs her eye sockets. She begins blinking. The 360-D image has changed. Mark is not a doctor, but he believes that the eyeballs and the optic nerves now look normal.

The woman stands and looks around the auditorium. She exclaims: "Oh, my God! Is this what the world looks like?" She tries to take a step and almost falls, but Seren catches her. She sits down and begins laughing uncontrollably. She continues to look around and waves at various spectators. The crowd joins her in her laughter and applauds enthusiastically. Mark studies as much as he can see through his oracle glasses. He is recording the whole thing including the analytical read-out images.

Seren continues to heal all kinds of diseases, injuries, and deformities, each one more stunning than the previous one.

After a time, he pauses and addresses the audience, "But you say, these are mere illnesses or physical damage to the body. Technology will soon be able to duplicate all you have done here tonight, and you may be right. For this very reason I have invited some special guests."

A man and woman approach. The man is carrying a little girl in his arms. She appears limp. The woman is wiping away tears.

"Please, my friend, lay her down on this table." The man obeys.

"Your daughter is dead."

"Yes, my Lord Seren."

"How long ago did this happen?"

"She died yesterday. Here is the death certificate." An assistant projects the certificate on a screen to his right.

Seren touches the little girl's face and hands. "She is cold, blue, and stiff. Rigor mortis has undeniably set in."

Most spectators in the audience are on the edge of their seats.

"Good parents, I have hope for you in this Path I have been teaching. Bring the scanners so that all can see what is going on inside her." The scanners are adjusted and a hologram of her entire body appears above her physical body. There is no sign of life.

"Because I have steadfastly followed the Path, I have grown in power. Many of you saw the earlier days and manifestations. I am indeed glad that you have come tonight to witness the power of the Path, the power of Life. Good people, please, watch carefully. You decide."

Seren places his hands on the little girl's head, then on her shoulders, then back on her head. Finally he puts his hand on her heart. Mark is waiting for Seren to make a mistake, to slip up. There is a trick to all this. Mark just has to figure out what it is.

As Seren continues to press firmly on the little girl's heart, the radiance appears again, but this time, the brilliance is so intense that all have to shield their eyes with their hands, just for a moment.

Mark looks at the hologram. He sees activity. The heart has begun beating. The little girl suddenly sits up, her eyes wide open; she is gasping for air. Many in the audience likewise gasp; some are almost choking. Her parents are astounded and trembling.

"My friends, behold, a true miracle. Technology does not and cannot create life. Only life begets life. The life within! The light within! Lumena!"

The little girl's eyes flutter. She looks at her parents and holds out her arms for them. They quickly run to embrace her. They are crying, along with most in the audience. Some in the crowd are still standing, their mouths hanging open. And Mark is one of them. How will he report this to HQ?

"We have a madman on the loose."

"Is he killing people?"

"No, he's raising the dead!"

"What technology does he use?"

"He uses no technology!"

"Does he have weapons?"

"He has no weapons."

As Mark ponders this, he spots Angela and moves forward to try to talk to her.

"Marco!" Angela seems thrilled to see him. "I'm so glad you came. I know how you are thinking. You hear about such things, maybe even you dream about them, but then you see them with your own eyes! And you become so...so excited. Is this what you are thinking?"

"I'm not sure what to think."

"Which means that you do not believe. You believe only that this is all a big fake. Go closer and talk to that little girl! She doesn't think that it was a big fake."

"Well, I...uh..."

"Marco, what did I tell you? This is going to change the world! Think of this power Seren has. Think of the power we all can have. The difference is that he knows how to access his, and he is teaching his disciples how to access theirs."

Mark is thinking about what his dad would say. "I may look like a moron, but I ain't."

"You know, Mark, Seren is looking for people like you. He needs help with security, not for himself of course, but for his growing number of disciples. Look at the crowds here; they are growing, too. Who knows what evil groups are out there? Seren's intentions are only good, but you know how is this world; it's full of hate and violence. People attack things they don't understand. Please consider to being a part of this!"

Mark replies, "I'll think about it." He leaves.

Mark is actually still pondering his report on what he has seen. He returns to his apartment to take a nap before leaving for work.

Mark lies down and closes his eyes. He opens them again suddenly. He's not sure if he slept or not. He checks the time on the display. An hour has passed. He closes his eyes again and drifts off.

He once more jerks awake, but this time, he is in the desert alone. He cannot feel his legs. He reaches for his side arm, which is not there.

This has to be a dream. He struggles to wake himself up. He cannot.

Wake up.

He raises himself and looks at his legs. He has no legs, which should upset him, but he somehow knows that it is just a dream. But he still struggles to wake up.

He looks around and begins pulling himself along the sand.

Suddenly the sun is blocked out by something flying overhead. He looks up. It's a dragon. His worst nightmare. Where's Dominique? He can't see Dominique anywhere.

The dragon lands in front of him. Mark has no weapons of any kind.

"Mikhail! Help!"

—24—

A PRISONER OF VIGILANCE

Three days later, Mark is returning from work and passing through security scanners as he enters the Bolla. It is late, and he does not see many people in the tunnel.

As he walks along, a large transparent tube suddenly drops down from the ceiling and traps him. He reaches for his side arm, but the newly formed chamber quickly fills with some kind of gas. He instantly drops to the ground, unconscious.

When he wakes up, he finds himself in a virtually blank room, sitting in a metal chair, his hands and feet bound by magnetic cuffs. A flood light is shining into his eyes.

"Captain Knutson."

"Who are you? Why have I been gassed and bound up like this?"

"Patience, captain. We need to ask you some questions." Mark discerns four shadowy figures behind the flood light.

"Then why don't you come out into the light and ask me? You seem to know who I am! If you're official, identify yourselves!"

"All in good time, captain. We need answers to questions about your recent activities."

"Who are you people? Are you official? Praetorian Guard? If so, I've served recently as a guard."

"We know that. And that you are now serving as a pilot for EuroSecure."

"You know so much. So you are Praetorian Guard?"

"Not exactly."

"Look, you can contact my former supervisor, Colonel Valenza. He can vouch for me."

"Colonel Valenza is dead."

"What?...Whaaaaat!?" Mark begins to shout.

One of the shadows comes forward and gives Mark a shot in the arm, after which he calms down.

"What kind of nightmare is this? What do you mean, Valenza is dead?"

"Colonel Valenza is dead. He was assassinated. We're looking for the murderer."

"So you are Guard members?"

"No, captain, let's just say we are agents of the Roman senate, commissioned and empowered to watch the watchers, so to speak, to monitor Guard members and seek out moles and other potentially treacherous groups."

Mark scoffs. "I had nothing to do with it. Valenza was a friend and a man I respected greatly. Who would murder him?"

"Captain, Valenza is dead, we believe, by treachery, and possibly from within the Guard."

"You're crazy! How does that involve me? Get to the point."

"The point is, captain, that we have been reviewing your reports and have found some irregularities that need to be clarified."

"Everything is in the reports. I explained everything to Colonel Valenza, and he was satisfied."

"The colonel did not have full access to all your information. We have just compared your reports to data on your own personal recorder and have found a certain amount of editing that troubles us. Moreover, you seemed to be amazingly close at hand during terrorist attacks on Rome, and you have been visiting a number of groups outside the Bolla, some of which you did not report on. All these things cause us to wonder and have prompted us to continue the investigation—"

"I believe regulations do not require a detailed report of everything we do while on patrol, only those things that might be of a potential concern. There's all kinds of flaky stuff going on outside the Bolla, you know that."

"Indeed."

"As for the attack on Rome, I was headed toward the exit when the attack occurred. I wasn't all that close, but when I heard the explosion, I got there quickly. I worked with others to pursue the terrorists. I wounded one of them and was wounded myself. You know, I already explained all this to Colonel Valenza."

"And Paris?"

"I don't know what you're talking about. The Sûreté called me in as a consultant. I was summoned to the scene and pursued suspects. The explosion was on the other side of the city from where I was."

"We are also investigating Ms. Lécuyer—"

"What are you assholes, Nazis? She's done nothing. Don't you know who she is? If you so much as—"

"We know you are in a relationship with her."

"You people are vile. This is the glory of Rome? You spend your time watching other people's love lives? What does that have to do with Roman security?"

"Speaking of your relationships, Ms. Angela Pesce, your former domestic partner, is now heavily involved in the Lumena organization. You have contacted her each time you attended a meeting, no?"

"I was there on official business. I recorded and reported everything."

"Everything except the demonstration with the wine?"

"That didn't seem significant. None of it did. The man is a harmless lunatic and so are his followers, all nuts. They're not even armed. It's just a rehash of other fringe activity we've seen before, maybe just a little more theatrical than the average."

"That is what we thought for a time as well. But now we have concerns. We think that Seren's influence is far more widespread than we have previously believed, and even within Rome herself."

"You have proof?"

"That is why we have brought you here, to help us."

"I'm afraid I can't help much, beyond what you've seen in my reports. I haven't had any contact with Seren or Angela for several days, no encounters beyond what you've seen."

"That may or may not be true, however, we need to push things a little further."

Two dark figures approach Mark and blindfold him. He protests: "What is this? What are you doing?"

"We regret this, captain, but we believe a brain scan is indicated."

"Do you have a warrant? Who is in charge of this?"

"We receive our orders directly from the Roman senate. We need no warrant. The future of Rome is at stake."

Mark feels a tight rubber cap being fitted around his head.

They're going to scan my thoughts!

"Please, be still, captain. I'm sure we will find nothing incriminating. We are only seeking to protect Rome."

"Interface between neurons and A.I. is still in its infancy. It's not reliable, and you know it!"

"We are looking for clues, perhaps things you did not even notice."

Mark feels the device activate. His mind is being scanned. He tries to resist, tries not to think about anything, but to no avail.

"Relax, captain, please. Let's start with a suggestion. Angela and Seren." Against his will, Mark begins remembering the meetings, his conversations with Angela. It's a jumble, a blur, and undefined forms appear.

"Please try to concentrate, captain. We're observing everything on a screen. You can help us to make this short."

Mark remembers the first meeting. The grapevine, the wine, some of Seren's remarks.

The shadowy figure studies a screen on which Mark's thoughts and memories are being displayed. "Very well, captain, this matches your report, except that you failed to include the last part."

"And you think it looks dangerous? Maybe he has a point. Most of the world is starving."

"Now please remember the second meeting."

Mark thinks about the transformation of metal.

"A cheap parlor trick. That's what I thought. That's what I said in my report. The third meeting was the same."

They continue prompting memories of his encounters with the terrorists and his other surveillance activities. They are scrolling through his life, calling up images with the power of suggestion, but random images and associations appear.

"Who's the chieftain with the scimitar?"

"That was a dream, drug induced."

Mark blacks out.

He wakes up later and is alone. He has no idea how long he has been out. He is no longer restrained. The cell is blank. He sees a sink, a cot, a toilet, and the chair in which he was sitting while being interrogated; the restraints have disengaged. He can see no door or light source. He stands up, stretches, and begins walking around, pacing. He is sure that someone is watching him.

"Anybody there?"

No answer. He continues to walk around restlessly. After a time, a table folds itself down from a wall and a small opening appears. Inside, he finds a drink and a protein square, which he eats.

"Hey! You forgot the little 'EAT ME!' and 'DRINK ME!' signs! So what, will I get bigger or smaller now?"

No response. In the room, not a sound, no music, and no technology, at least none that he can use. Mark is powerless and alone. *I'm in hell.*

Suddenly the room begins to vibrate. Then, nothing.

"What's going on out there?"

Nothing. Mark lies down on the cot. He wonders about Dominique and fears that they may have arrested her. He cannot imagine why they would.

For a time, he remembers her and alternately worries about her. He wonders what will happen next. He falls asleep.

—25—

THE UNRAVELING

Mark is abruptly awakened. His room is vibrating again, trembling. The cot, the chair, the sink, the toilet, everything in the room is shaking. The quaking becomes almost violent. Mark sits on the floor, away from the vibrating objects.

"Hey, is there a problem out there?" he shouts.

The room becomes calm again. Mark gets up and paces for a while. When more tremors start, he is near the chair so he sits down. As he does, the magnetic restraints are engaged around his wrists and ankles, and they snap him in.

"What the...? Hey, are you there? Why have you cuffed me again? I'm not going anywhere!"

No answer. Mark just sits there. He has no knowledge of the actual passing of time, only that a lot of time has passed. He is cut off from Rome, from his world, and from his life.

Mark falls asleep again. His head slumps over. He is awakened again by more violent shaking. Everything is the same, except that now in his cell it is pitch black.

He suddenly feels some kind of strange power surge. A door opens from a blank wall, and light floods into the cell. He squints but can't shield his eyes. He only sees the silhouette of someone unusually large surrounded by a brilliant halo of light.

"Ah, Captain Knutson."

Mark replies sarcastically, "I'm sorry. Have we been introduced? Who are you?"

His eyes get used to the light, and he is stunned as he looks at his visitor and realizes who he is.

"Iqhawe!"

"Congratulations, captain. I believe your pronunciation is improving. Come, we must leave here quickly."

The magnetic restraints fall off of Mark's wrists and ankles.

"Sorry, I didn't know who you were. In fact, I don't know anything much right now."

Iqhawe is wearing a Search and Rescue uniform with gear.

"I'm really glad to see you, but how did you know I was here?"

"Mikhail has a friend who works in this facility; he told him that you were in custody. Mikhail asked me to look in on you."

They walk down a hallway. People in the building are hurrying about almost frantically in and out of rooms and offices.

"What's going on?"

"I've come to set you free. By the way, here is all your gear and your portapack. You will need to reactivate most of them if they allow you to do so."

Mark eagerly collects them and straps them on. "Thanks! How heaven's name did you get them?"

"Connections."

They walk out of an unmarked building into a courtyard and proceed toward a security gate. The guards are distracted; they are looking up, nervously watching the tall buildings all around. Mark realizes that they are not far from the Arco di Constantino. As they approach the gate, it seems to open by itself. No one protests their departure.

"You are needed, captain. You felt the earthquakes?"

"That's what all that was?"

"Yes, they have been increasing, and things are becoming quite serious. Vesuvius is active. Many buildings outside the Bolla have collapsed."

"Could the terrorists have caused the quakes? Do they have that kind of technology?"

"No, but they and others will take advantage of the chaos."

"Do you know anything about Dominique?"

"Dominique is safe, I assure you."

"And Mikhail?"

"Mikhail is busy, as I am. As you will be soon. As the earthquakes increase, there will be greater confusion and panic. Please return to your apartment, if your building is still standing, get whatever you need, and, again, please try to reactivate your PG equipment."

"But what about those...those people who were interrogating me?"

"They have much bigger problems right now. You are of no interest to them. You must do what you can to save lives."

"How long was I in there?"

"I'm not sure, perhaps several days."

"Several days! Who were those people? I have so many questions. How did you get in? And how did we get out so easily?"

"It wasn't hard. The earthquakes have triggered random power outages and brown-outs. They are quite serious. You may or may not have power when you return to your apartment."

"Do you think the quakes are caused by Vesuvius? Have you heard reports from EuroSecure about quakes in other countries?"

"I heard rumors that the quakes are widespread and that tsunamis may have resulted. We do know that in Italy alone hundreds of thousands of people have died, and many more will die soon. Captain, this is all the more reason that I must leave you now. I regret that I cannot answer more of your questions. I have others in need of rescue."

"Okay, but just one more. Is this a dream?"

Iqhawe smiles. It's the first time Mark has seen him smile.

He replies, "Life is a dream."

Mark watches him walk a little ways down the street, and he calls out to him:

"Is this a hologame?"

Iqhawe continues walking away, raises his right hand, and waves without turning around.

Mark stands in the street for a moment, scratching his head. He looks in all four directions. The Bolla seems intact, but the buildings are all blank, no holographic enhancements. It is still daylight, so it is hard to tell where there might be outages. People are running in all directions. Aerocars and aerobikes are flying overhead in a haphazard fashion; obviously the synchronization program is off line. Cars are randomly racing down streets. Unrest is in the air, and the disorder seems to be spreading.

Mark makes his way back to his apartment building, which is still standing and still has power. He immediately checks his messages. Dozens are from Dominique. He opens the most recent, from this morning.

She appears before him, sitting on the side of her bed.

"Mark." She seems overcome with emotion and is wiping away tears. "Are you all right? Please call!"

Mark freezes the message and places the call.

She answers, but only 2-D is available.

"Mark, is it really you?"

"Yes, baby, I love you."

"I love you, *mon bébé*. Where have you been?" Her voice is distorted by static, and her image is constantly tearing.

"I'm not sure. It's a long story. But Rome is in deep trouble. Are you okay?"

"Now that I have seen that you are all right, I'll be okay. I have been sick with worry."

"Dominique, we have to get you back to Paris."

"No! I want to be here, with you!"

"Look, I'm coming over to your place. I'm going to put you on a hypertrain."

"Mark, I desperately want to see you, but it is dangerous outside. People are in a panic. Many of them are trying to leave, and I'm not sure Paris is any better off. My apartment is secure. You need to go save lives and help maintain some kind of order. I've been listening to reports on the emergency radio channel, and they've called out all PG and other rescue workers. Some small buildings inside the Bolla have collapsed. Please take care of yourself."

Mark gathers his operations belt, utility wristbands, side arms, and lightning boots and reactivates them. It was easy. *"They must*

ignite, each emitting a blue flame, boosting it higher into the air. As he rises, he gains a panoramic view through his oracle glasses of the smoldering debris that was recently called "Rome." The city looks like a war zone, and there hasn't even been a war, not a shot fired, not a bomb dropped. He is still not entirely sure if the buildings turned to rubble were in fact bombed by anyone.

Mark receives an update on the channel restricted to emergency workers.

"Emergency workers, continue your efforts. We regret to report that most, perhaps all of the Roman Senate has been assassinated. Surviving administrators are attempting to form an interim government."

Mark is stunned again. The world as he knows it is disintegrating before him.

As he flies low, he notices more seismic activity and random explosions. He still cannot tell if they are caused secondarily by the quakes or if they are bombs. Another earthquake seems to be rocking the city. He sees pandemonium in the streets below.

The sky is continuing to darken, and the wind is picking up.

Mark is cruising toward the newly constructed two hundred-story Hotel Impero near the Coliseum when he sees a massive explosion at the base of the hotel. As he zooms in with his oracle glasses, he sees that the hotel's foundations are trembling, and now collapsing.

"NO!" Mark shouts, but he is helpless, powerless to stop what he sees happening. The tower starts to shake, then to wobble and tip. Mark quickly ascends to a higher altitude. He can see people below, near the building trying to escape the inevitable.

The tower leans even more and slowly begins its inexorable toppling. Mark tries to put more distance between himself and the falling building. He watches it come apart at its foundations, fall, and crash, demolishing about half of the Coliseum, which is no match for its weight and force of impact.

Other explosions follow from all around the city. Mark is certain that the dead and injured in Rome alone now number in the tens of thousands, maybe even more.

Mark presses on to Dominique's apartment. Below he sees more blasts, more anarchy, and more panic.

He notices several more explosions around the perimeter of the Bolla. Flashes like lightning fire all over the bubble, followed by more blasts that seem equally spaced. The fusion plasma generators for the energy bubble are detonating in sequence, one by one. *These have to be bombs.*

He sees increasing lightning-like static on the dome, followed by random flashes and a sizzling sound, and then Bolla disappears completely. The Haze and the ash from Vesuvius rush in like a dark, shadowy plague to fill the once magnificent city.

Mark quickly dons his breathing mask. His oracle glasses allow him to see through the ash and the Haze. Below him, multiple crowds are running in many different directions. Buildings are not guaranteed safe shelter, but people know they will not fare well in the newly polluted air which is even more toxic with the volcano's recent addition.

Mark can see waves of people all around the perimeter, climbing over the rubble and pouring into the city. The looting has begun, unrestrained, and violence seems to be escalating. Mark cannot stop to protect anyone. He continues trying to contact Dominique, but no answer. He presses on to her apartment complex.

He looks to the eastern sky. A Rogue Storm is fast approaching to add to the misery. He sees angry black clouds boiling, gigantic thunderheads, and dark sheets of rain. Powerful winds are swirling in every direction. The fire of lightning fills the storm center making the clouds look like fiery coals, and there are lightning flashes all around.

Mark decides to descend and proceed to Dominique's apartment at a much lower level, closer to the ground. The panic continues as people are seeking shelter. But how to flee from falling buildings, poisonous winds, vandals, and a Rogue Storm?

As Mark approaches Dominique's building, a powerful, rushing wind suddenly knocks him off his bike and throws it and him violently to the ground. At the same time, a blinding bolt of lightning strikes close by and temporarily knocks out his oracle glasses. The flash is followed almost immediately by an ear-piercing thunderclap, then the sound of a strange trumpet blast and numerous people shouting. The ground continues to tremble for several seconds afterward.

Marks sits up and checks his oracle glasses; they are working again. *That was unusually powerful, even for lightning, and even for a Rogue Storm.* Mark wonders how many people were killed by the electrical charge alone. He cannot even imagine the current death toll, plus the count of the missing and displaced.

Finally he reaches Dominique's building; it is dark outside and inside, and he must apply power where needed from his wristbands and operations belt. When he enters her living room, it is in shadows. He sees her message indicator light flashing faintly. Her systems seem to be running on batteries. He scrolls and discovers that the messages are all from him. Dominique is not there. Where could she have gone?

Mark remembers where she keeps her holojournal, and he rushes to activate it.

Dominique appears in full flower before him, but she is not looking directly at him. He sits down and relishes this technological ghost of her presence. The last journal entry is for him.

"I love you, Mark. I always will. I hope you will somehow be able to access this. I don't understand all that is happening, but I can see that our world is coming to an end. Rome will never be the same. Perhaps Rome will never recover. What will happen next? Only God knows."

Mark pauses the program and rubs his eyes. He starts it again.

"I have just lost my father. And now I fear that in all this devastation, I will lose you. I'm not sure how much power I have left here. I've tried to reach you, but the communications system doesn't seem to be working."

Dominique pauses to dry her tears with a handkerchief.

"I don't know what will happen. I wonder if EuroSecure can cope with all this. I'm not sure if this is affecting other cities of the Federation. I am cut off from news about the outside world, about my job, and about you. I can only pray."

Mark continues to listen, hoping for some clue about where she might have gone after leaving the apartment. But the message abruptly ends. He can't tell why.

Mark is exhausted, so he lies down to rest. Perhaps she will return shortly. He closes his eyes.

Mark realizes that he is in Paris, on the Champs-Elysées. He looks in one direction and sees the Arc de Triomphe. He is relieved not to be in Rome, but Paris is deserted. Where are the people? He looks up. He sees no Bulle, only blue sky with real puffy white clouds. There are no sounds, only the sounds of his footsteps.

But he hears something, the clip-clop of a horse! He looks down the boulevard and spots a rider coming toward him.

"Hello!!!" He shouts out, hoping to make a connection and find out what has happened.

No answer. The horse continues to approach. At length he sees that the rider is a female, riding side-saddle. But the horse is strange. It is red and has large wings, like Pegasus.

The rider is Dominique! She is wearing a white veil and a long white dress. She has never looked so beautiful.

He cries out to her, "*Chérie!* I am so happy to see you! Are you okay? Where have you been? I've been looking for you everywhere! I should have known you would be in Paris."

Mark tries to approach her, but the horse rears up before him. He backs off. He tries to find his operations belt, but he cannot.

"What's happening, my love?" he calls to her.

Dominique smiles at him and begins to speak, "I love you, Mark. I always will."

Mark calls to her, "Come down! We need to get married now. We need to stay together!" He begins crying uncontrollably. He has never cried so much in his life.

The horse rears up again and spreads its wings, and, accelerating to a full gallop, leaves the ground. Dominique blows him a kiss, and the flying horse takes her up into the clouds. Mark looks around for an aerobike and spots one. He enters his PG codes, but the bike will not start.

He looks up again to try to see which direction Dominique went. The sky has become dark and red. He sees three small black dots that are growing larger by the second and descending.

The dots grow and start to look like huge, surreal vultures. One begins diving toward Mark. The other two continue in the direction Dominique went, seemingly in pursuit.

"Nooooooo!!!" Mark runs and jumps up in frustration. One vulture swoops down and picks him up, carrying him the opposite direction.

"Nooooooo!!!" Mark shouts and sits up on the couch. To his relief, it was only a dream. He lies back down and rubs his head.

The relief does not last long. He begins reflecting on the nightmare that his world has become. How to wake up from this?

Mark closes his eyes, until he hears a sound at the door. Someone is trying to enter. He grabs his operations belt and draws his side arm.

The door opens. It's Dominique!

"*Chérie*! You're okay! I've been worried sick." Mark begins crying and runs toward her.

But he passes right through her and falls on the floor, which begins trembling. Another quake is in progress. He tries to get up and turn around to grab Dominique.

The floor splits open. Dominique looks terrified and begins shouting, "Mark!!! Mark!!! Save me!!!" She stretches out her hands, but the floor of her apartment falls as the building is disintegrating. Mark reaches out desperately, trying to grab her hands and pull her toward him, but he cannot. He watches her anxious face slip away and fall down, out of sight.

Mark tumbles off the couch on to the floor. He wakes up.

"God! How much more? I can't take this!" He sits up and rubs his eyes. "I've had enough sleep for a while."

Mark gets up and puts on his operations belt and other gear. He has to go out and do something, search for Dominique, save lives. He has to go out and face the nightmare in the streets of Rome.

—27—

THE DECLINE AND FALL

"Terrified by her torment, they will stand afar off
and cry, 'Alas, alas, Babylon! O great and mighty
city, for in one hour your doom has come!'" –
Revelation 18:10

Mark leaves Dominique's apartment. As he walks outside, he is
hit with a stench, perhaps tens of thousands of dead bodies, wet,
rotting corpses everywhere, mostly untended. Many have died
in explosions and in the resulting fires and collapse of buildings;
some have inhaled too much toxic smoke, and a fair number have
been murdered. Mark puts a small filter mask over his nose and
mouth. He finds the aerobike that he had left hidden and activates
it. The storm has ended, but visibility is low, so he adjusts his oracle
glasses to help him navigate.

Mark scrolls through his records and finds the visit to the
catacombs. He then programs "return" into the bike's navigational
system, at which he begins seeing a read-out of the path to follow,
and the aerobike begins moving toward that precise location.

As Mark rises into the air, he gains a panoramic view of
the progressive obliteration of the Eternal City. Yet another
megabuilding has fallen, taking other smaller structures with it.
Fires are burning and smoldering everywhere. Rescue workers are

still gathering the injured and taking them to area hospitals, which are heavily guarded.

In the streets, anarchy. Mark sees what look like small armies marching down roads and staking out territory. In other zones, there is no semblance of order, just plundering and violence. He must proceed to the catacombs in the hopes of rescuing Dominique or of finding someone who might know where she is. He resists the temptation to think that he might instead find her dead body.

As Mark cruises over the new, disfigured face of Rome, he sees only more of the same.

He hears a familiar voice calling to him. "Knutson! Is that you?"

At this, Mark turns and looks around beneath him. He sees Massi on an aerobike ascending. Both have used their oracle glasses to identify each other. They switch their aerobikes to hover mode and take off their helmets.

"Massi! Fancy meeting you here!" jokes Mark. "How did you find me?"

"My PG transponder is still working. I'm trying to locate PGs and get them all together."

Mark asks, "You think we can fix this?"

"Yeah, it's some pretty sorry shit, isn't it?"

"Do you know what's happened? Who's responsible?"

Massi replies, "Take your pick of the crazy groups we've been monitoring. Probably all of them plus Mother Nature being pissed off."

"I'm just trying to save lives. I guess there has been an interim government formed. You know anything about it?"

"There is no interim government, and there won't be. I'm only interested in the answer to one question, 'who's next?' That's a question you need to be asking, *amico.*"

Mark asks, "Oh? And you know?"

"You heard about Seren?"

"Uh, a little. I went to a few meetings and reported what I saw to HQ."

Massi answers assertively, "*He's* next. And I'm with the guy who's next, the only one who actually can be next."

"What do you mean? He can be next only if he can fix all this."

"Yeah, he can fix all this. This dude has real power. I've seen it! Have you?"

Mark shrugs his shoulders. "I saw a few things. I wasn't sure."

"Knutson, I like you. But wake up. 'Seren' is the name of tomorrow's reality. There is no more senate or PG or HQ or interim government. It's all gone now. A new order is about to arise."

"What about those other groups?"

"Come on, Knutson! You know they're all a bunch of *idioti*, and all they have are traditional tech-weapons."

"I like traditional tech-weapons. They get the job done. And Seren? I wasn't sure about what I was seeing. I figured he was faking it all."

"Sure, that's what I thought at first, but I hung around and checked things out in private, met with some of his assistants. He has been looking for PG members to be a part of a new order, one backed up by power, a power way beyond what we have or know. I tell you, I've seen it in action. It's for real."

"Really? Massi, I went to three meetings. In the last one he was healing people."

"Then you've only seen the low-level stuff."

"Really."

"Knutson, Seren could use a guy like you. A pilot and a PG. You would rise through the ranks quickly."

Mark is listening to Massi, somewhat stunned. He thinks, how quickly allegiances shift when the wind changes direction.

"Massi, you know the senate has been assassinated."

"Well, most of the senate. Get this, quite a few of them were already on board with Seren."

"Quite a few? You mean the ones who weren't killed?"

"Okay, maybe three or four."

"They weren't hit? Why not? And do you know anything about Colonel Valenza's assassination?"

Massi says nothing.

"I know why not. Because the pro-Seren senators assassinated the others. Did they have help? Were PGs involved in killing Valenza?"

Massi remains silent. Mark doesn't need to ask the next question. He thinks that Massi may have had a part in all the murders. He wonders who else was involved in the massacre.

"Massi, I'm sorry. I'm trying to find my fiancée, Dominique. That's my priority right now."

"Okay, sure, but think about it. And don't jump to any wild conclusions until you learn more for yourself. I'll put in a good word for you."

"Where do I find you or Seren?"

"Trust me, *amico*, very soon we will find you and everyone left alive in Rome."

They part company. Mark's aerobike retraces his route and follows the red arrows on his oracle glasses to a precise point, marked now by an *X*.

Mark lands and locks the aerobike. The wind is blowing, dispersing the smoke and ash somewhat. As he turns around, he realizes that he has company. A small gang of six young toughs has appeared from nowhere; they have made a semi-circle around him. They are wearing masks and goggles. Three have clubs, two have metal rods, and one has a large hammer.

"*Cosa?*" he asks in Italian.

"*Lo sai,*" one answers. They begin closing in. Mark laughs to himself as he thinks about old 'spaghetti western' movies he watched as a kid. He even hears the theme songs of a few in his head. With both hands, he pulls back his smock, revealing his operations belt and two side arms. He stretches out his hands like one of those legendary gunfighters and wiggles his fingers briskly.

As he does this, the toughs stop in their tracks and begin walking slowly backwards, showing less cockiness than before.

Mark slaps his hand on his side arms and bellows, "*Guardia Pretoriana!*" At which the gang disperses with blinding speed.

Mark turns and continues to follow the red arrow trail, but when he arrives at the entrance, he finds that someone has moved the stone to the side. He walks in and continues down the passageway, descending deep. The light on his operations belt illuminates his path.

Mark is hopeful because he cannot see any damage in the passageways, just a few more pebbles and rocks on the floor and the steps. The trail leads him to where he passed out. He explores surrounding tunnels and finds the entrance to the room where he had seen Mikhail, Dominique, and the group. The room is empty. He turns around and looks at all the walls. He only finds the stone benches and a few burnt-out candles, but not much else. He sits down.

Mark doesn't believe in ghosts. He nonetheless feels a certain sense of presence, somewhat like what he feels in Dominique's apartment. The place where she lived and moved and breathed. Where she spoke, laughed, and loved. Where she ate, slept, and danced. Here, where she sang. Mark recalls that he has never heard her sing. He'll be sure to ask her to do that when he sees her again.

Mark hears the wind howling in the tunnels. They may soon be full of polluted air and ash. For now the room is a quiet refuge.

Eventually he emerges from the catacombs through the opening. The streets are still empty. He finds his aerobike and ascends for another view of the ongoing, progressive fall of Rome. It's now hard in places to tell the difference between inside Bolla and outside. Vandals have defaced buildings and artwork, smashed glass, destroyed storefronts and looted what was in them.

Mark sees numerous brutal fights as he passes over neighborhoods. He briefly considers intervention, then decides against it. He checks the emergency channel, which he finds is now dead. He then thinks about the hospitals and sets a course to the nearest one.

When he lands at the gate, he is met by security and is quickly cleared. Overhead he sees three helicopters that seem to be guarding or patrolling the area. He estimates over a hundred guards around the perimeter of the facility.

"What's the situation here?" he asks one of the guards.

"They're treating patients as quickly as they can with the few resources that they have left. We're on emergency power, so we're not sure that we can handle more injured. No one wants to leave after they're treated, so it's become a sort of refugee camp as well, overcrowded."

"Do you have a list of those treated?"

"We have a list of all patients at all hospitals in the area. It's hard to know if it's completely accurate. There's been a lot of interference." He pulls out a device with a screen.

"May I?" Mark takes screen and scrolls down, looking for Dominique's name. He does not find it.

"Thanks." He returns it to the guard. "Have you seen a rescue worker named Mikhail? Large, Russian fellow, with wavy blond hair?"

"Sure, he's brought patients here several times today. He might come back yet today, but he's taking them to other hospitals, to wherever they can squeeze them in."

Mark looks at the horizon and as he adjusts his oracle glasses, he sees new billows of black smoke everywhere. "I wonder what that new smoke is."

The guard answers, "We're starting to burn cadavers. It could be coming from that or from God knows what."

"I don't suppose you might have a comprehensive list of the dead?" Marks asks, though it seems a futile hope.

"Not a chance. There have been too many, especially in the last day or so. We're just trying to save the living. The patients that have died in the hospital are on that same list you just looked at."

Mark thanks the guard and takes off again. A stronger wind is blowing, and the Haze and the ash from Vesuvius have diminished slightly, but the black smoke of death is worse in places. He sets down near the French restaurant where he and Dominique had dinner and danced.

Mark walks inside and sees that it is empty. It looks bombed out; all the glass is broken. He sits down and looks around, remembering. How is it possible? They laughed and loved there. They drank wine and danced. Another part of his world, gone.

He continues to retrace the steps of their courtship. He goes to the Trevi Fountain, which is now hardly recognizable. He then flies to the Tiber, which is full of debris and some dead bodies washing on its shores. Finally he returns to the Parco Centrale, which has become a picture of destruction with wreckage and trash, instead of a place of peace, happiness, and natural beauty. He lands and looks at the lake, now polluted with debris and bodies, and walks around it.

Mark spots a small group on the other side. It appears to be a woman and some small children. They seem frightened and are running frantically, so Mark engages his lightning boots and speeds around the water's edge to meet them.

"*Guardia Pretoriana!*" he shouts through his amplifier, hoping to reassure them, but they don't seem reassured. They continue to run. Suddenly a lion emerges from a nearby wooded area and is in pursuit of the small group.

The zoo. It must have been damaged. This lion is not a hologram; it's the real thing.

The lion is now between him and the woman with the children. Mark has only a split-second and one shot. He stops, kneels, and fires a focused flash-plasma burst at the lion and takes him out. But the woman and children are still running.

Mark turns around and sees that two more lions are upon him, and one is about to jump. He raises his weapon and fires a flash plasma burst while attempting an evasive maneuver. He wounds the closest one, but it manages to knock his side arm out of his hand as it falls. He rolls on the ground as the other is about to jump. He pulls out his other side arm and fires a bullet right into its heart. It bellows and falls to the ground.

A third lion is upon him. He fires and wounds it, but it swipes his hand with its claw, knocking away his last gun.

Mark jumps to his feet, and as he does, he notices that yet another lion has emerged from the trees and is bearing down on him. He takes off running, calculating that his lightning boots should enable him to outrun a lion. He hopes his calculations are correct because he can't quite remember how fast lions run.

"Female lions are efficient hunters." He remembers this line from his high school biology teacher.

The wounded cat seems unable to move fast, but the remaining one continues the chase. Mark circles and runs back into the wooded area hoping not to meet any more wildlife.

The trees offer some protection but slow him down. Even though the lion has also slowed down, it's getting closer. He can almost hear it breathing.

Mark again runs out into the open. After a burst of speed with his lightning boots, he realizes that he cannot outrun a lion, even with the boots. The remaining cat is upon him and knocks him to the ground. From his operations belt he quickly extracts a knife and the spy-pin.

Mark confronts the lion, who is pacing and prowling, studying its now almost powerless opponent. It charges and leaps. Mark falls back and stabs the lion's underbelly with the spy-pin and the knife blade and rolls to the side. The cat howls and lands hard on the ground, struggling to get back on its feet. Mark rolls back over, pulls out the knife, and stabs it again, but the lion catches him with a claw on his right arm. Ignoring the pain and warm blood, Mark continues to stab it.

Mark wishes Mikhail would show up about now. He wishes this really were a hologame.

Finally Mark pierces the lion in the heart, and it collapses completely.

He sits there for a while, checking his injuries and scanning for other lions or escaped zoo animals. Nothing. He looks around for the woman and the children, but they are nowhere in sight. He pulls a small first-aid kit from his operations belt and dresses his wounds.

The sun is going down. Maybe it's time to call it a day. Mark recovers his weapons and leaves.

—28—

THE CITY OF GOD

"The invaders carry off young girls and boys. They
tear children from the arms of their parents, and
for their own pleasure, they rape the mothers.
They sack temples and homes. There is fire and
murder everywhere. The streets are full of fighting
men, dead bodies, spilt blood and weeping." – Cato
Uticensis, quoted by Augustine in *The City of God.*

As Mark returns to Dominique's apartment, he flies over every place
he thinks she might be. He still hopes that she has returned home,
but when he arrives, he sees that she has not. Her room becomes a
sanctuary for him. He finds some limited power in her apartment
building, although with occasional brown-outs. Between that, her
batteries, and his own power pack, he should be able to stay there
for a fair length of time.

The next morning, Mark accesses the external cameras, knowing
what he will probably see outside. The media wall becomes a
window on the world as it currently is, a sort of strange visual news
report. Columns of smoke are billowing up, and scattered fires
are still burning. He sees more toppled buildings. Random groups
of people are running, sometimes colliding; some are fighting.
Pointless, endless anarchy. It's depressing. He cuts access, and the
wall goes blank again.

Mark sits and thinks. He calls up a hologram of Dominique and freezes it. The image enhances that sense of her presence that he craves, and it brings back many happy memories. He remembers that he can access her picture files, so he begins calling them up and projects them into the room. He initiates a shuffle slide show; some are 2-D; most are 3-D or 360-D.

The first picture is 2-D projected on the blank media wall, Dominique as a little girl, smiling at the camera, looking uncharacteristically shy. *A beautiful child.*

The next is 3-D, Dominique graduating from the Conservatoire in Paris, wearing regalia with diploma in hand, and looking young, thrilled, and gorgeous.

The next picture is back to 2-D. Dominique and her parents with the White House in the background. She couldn't be more than eight or nine. She stands between them, squinting her eyes. The general is not a general yet; he is a captain. This was probably when he was on an exchange with the U.S. military. Her mother has her hands on Dominique's shoulders. *Maman* is a spectacularly beautiful and projects a quiet, gentle spirit.

Mark decides to re-run Dominique and *Maman* playing the duet of 'The Prayer.' He projects it in front of the media wall, to the right of the real baby grand piano and mirror. He initiates the program and again watches Dominique playing the piano along with her reflection playing the piano in the mirror. Opposite is *Maman*, who is playing her piano with no mirror beside her. He sees a total of five pianos, but only one is real, and the real piano is silent.

As Mark takes in the performance, he studies *Maman*. In her he sees a glimpse of Dominique, who resembles her physically, but he sees much more than just physical resemblance. *Maman* was a major force that shaped Dominique into the musician and into the woman she now is.

When the program concludes, the two women both freeze. Mark walks over and kisses Dominique on her virtual cheek. He then does the same to her mother.

"That's from your daughter," he tells the image.

Then Mark calls up new holograms and watches himself and Dominique in 360-D near the Eiffel Tower, embracing and smiling, in love. Warm tears well up in his eyes. He remembers a quotation from Lucretius that he had to memorize for Latin class in high school.

Nec sine te quidquam dias in Lumenas oras
Exoritur, neque fit laetum, neque amabile quidquam.

He never believed that he would need to utter those words again. He never imagined that he would meet someone who fit that description so fully. Mark whispers the translation as he gazes at Dominique's hologram: "Without you, nothing emerges into the divine shores of light, and without you there is no love or happiness in the world."

"You have been the last dream of my soul."
Charles Dickens, *A Tale of Two Cities*

Now his world is no more. He will likely not be a pilot again anytime soon. Rome as he and Dominique knew it, where they fell in love, does not exist. He wonders about Paris and other cities of the Federation. He cannot access any news broadcasts. He hears only static and some strange audio interference that he has never heard before.

Mark fears that Dominique is also...no more. Before, he worried that he would not be able to protect her. Now he fears he will never find her again. He has never known so many fears. He has never cried so many tears.

He feels a tightness in his chest. He hits the wall with his fist repeatedly and wipes his eyes. He is shaking almost uncontrollably, like a man with a strange illness whose cure would be effected by the appearance of one woman. That would not solve any of the world's current problems, but at least he would not be alone. He never wants to be alone again. Mark sits down and entwines his fingers and clasps them around his knee. He rocks forward and backward. A pressure rising from deep in his throat is almost choking him.

Mark looks across the room at Dominique's antique desk. He walks to it and rolls up the top. He sees an open book with a pen lying in the middle. He picks up the book and reads. It's in French. He regrets not having dedicated more time to his French studies. He turns the book over to look at the spine. *La Sainte Bible.* It's Dominique's Bible.

While holding his place, he flips through it, looking at passages she has marked. He turns off Universal Translator on his oracle glasses. He sees notes in the margins. He opens at 'Psaume 23.'

This one, I know. He reads over the underlined verses.

Mark looks over on her bookshelf and spots a *Larousse French-English/Anglais-Français Dictionary*, which he pulls from the shelf. He sits down and reads his translations out loud.

"The Eternal One is my shepherd."

Moving down to the next underlined passage, "When I walk in the valley of the shadow of death, I will not fear any evil, for You are with me."

Further down, "Yes, happiness and grace will accompany me all the days of my life, and I will inhabit the house of the Eternal One until the end of my days."

Dominique has written to the side, *"Pour Papa."*

Mark continues to flip through the Bible and to try to read her marginal notes. He turns to the right of where she had opened it and reads aloud the underlined verses. 1 Corinthiens 13:4-8. Mark translates what he knows. "Love is patient..., full of goodness..., never envious..., does not vaunt itself..., inflate itself..., does nothing dishonestly..., does not search for its own interest..., is not irritated..., does not suspect evil..., does not... —Hmm, not sure— ...does not rejoice in injustice but in truth..., she excuses everything, believes, hopes..., supports? Love never perishes."

In the side margin, Dominique has written *"Mon amour pour Mark."* Mark loses it. His grief is unbearable. Reading what Dominique has written brings her closer but only increases the pain. He weeps and wails for some time. He cannot just stuff it or make it go away. He has never had to deal with anything like this, except possibly when his mother passed away. Dominique so reminds him of her.

He turns back to the place where she had it open and reads the underlined verses. Romains 13:11-14. Mark translates: "It's the hour for you to wake up." Ironically, that's what Angela told him to do. "Salvation is closer now than when we first believed. The night is advancing, and the day approaches." Mark has to look up *"rêvetez"* in the dictionary. Now he completes the reading: "Clothe yourselves with the Lord Jesus Christ."

He shuts the Bible and looks at the floor for a moment, thinking deeply about what he has just read. Praying is a new experience for him, but as he whispers a simple prayer, his heart is strangely warmed.

"Certitude. Sentiment. Joie. Paix." – Blaise Pascal.

Pax.

Peace.
He has no need to read further.

—29—

DEATH OF AN ANGEL

"A glooming peace this morning with it brings;
the sun, for sorrow, will not show his head."
Shakespeare, *Romeo and Juliet.*

Mark leaves the building and activates the aerobike. His oracle glasses still enable him to navigate through the smoke and to see more than he really wants to see. He is again overcome by the stench of rotting flesh, which is worse than before. He is sickened to see even more piles of burning cadavers.

Mark ascends and takes in a more panoramic view of Rome. From there, he watches another installment in the relentless disassembling of the Eternal City by everything from spontaneous militias to small gangs. He has somewhat limited vision, even with the oracle glasses, but he can still behold the fall, from order to disorder, from civilization to its discontents, from design to chaos, from life to death. Once again, Rome is besieged by barbarians and vandals.

On one street, plundering. On another, a gang is toppling a statue. A small group nearby has hijacked an emergency food truck and is eating the spoils. Mark climbs higher. Most buildings are being ransacked or burned. The smoke drives him higher still. He sees fire coming out of the several megabuildings. At this point, he has not spotted any victims fleeing. All are doubtless locked in their rooms or in any room they can find, as he was, fearing the inevitable invasion, rape, and murder. He still hopes that he can locate Dominique and rescue her, but there are so many bodies.

> "Treason and terror were there, along with cruel wrath.
> There I saw first the dark imagining of felonies.
> The cruel Anger, as red as any glowing ember.
> Pale fear, and the stable burning with black smoke.
> The treachery of the murdering one lying in a bed.
> Strife, with bloody knife.
> Cold death, with mouth gaping upright.
> Madness, laughing in his rage.
> Armed complaint, alarm, and fierce outrage.
> A thousand slain, but not killed by the plague.
> The town destroyed, there was nothing left.
> I saw conquest, sitting in great honor
> With the sharp sword over his head.
> Also depicted was the murder of Caesar,
> Of great Nero, and of Antonius."
> – Thoughts and images from the Temple of
> Mars, Chaucer, "The Knight's Tale"

Mark looks up at the sky and sees two Prochain Mirage fighters circling Rome. *What can they do now?* It occurs to him that they might be committed to Seren. Nothing would surprise him at this point.

Mark accesses a message that he has just received from Angela. It is brief, and the transmission is garbled. She seems to be having difficulty talking. She sounds hoarse, even discounting the interference.

"Marco, Seren is responsible for what is happening! His people have killed most of the senate. His people are everywhere, more than I before thought. Be careful! Marco—"

The communication is abruptly cut off. She has confirmed what he suspected during his conversation with Massi.

Another storm is moving in. Mark hopes it's not a second Rogue Storm. He makes his way to Angela's apartment house, which looks intact. Still some power there. The security system allows him to enter.

As he opens the door of her apartment, he sees Angela lying on the floor, stretched out, a cup just out of her reach, and the cup's contents have spilled on the floor. He quickly checks her.

Angela is dead.

Mark is in shock, disbelief. He picks up the cup and smells its remaining contents. He's sure that it is Seren's wine.

Mark sits beside her and leans back on the couch.

Impossible. He wipes away tears, and looks at Angela's face and body.

He suspects foul play, but what can he do to avenge it and bring the murderer to justice? Seren killed her, whether directly or indirectly. He picks up Angela's body and puts her on the couch. He then finds a sheet and covers her with it.

He kisses her forehead before he pulls the sheet over her head. "*Ciao, Bambolina.* I'm sorry, so sorry."

Mark leaves with a knot in his gut. He walks back out into the street. Some emergency workers are continuing their efforts, but the tremors are continuing. It's raining, and the winds are increasing in force.

Mark feels exhausted. His building is still standing, so he returns to his apartment, lies down on the couch, and closes his eyes. He sleeps until morning.

When he wakes up, he accesses an external view, and the wall dissolves before him. The rain has stopped, and everything looks calm; the air is relatively clear. He senses no tremors, and the streets appear peaceful. Mark feels relieved, but he wonders if things could ultimately get even worse.

He zooms in on the square below and sees a group of people filtering into it. They are not running or fighting. This group seems a little strange, out of place. Time to go outside and check things out. Everything appears peaceful, but he wonders if this could be the calm before another storm.

Mark straps on his operations belt and other gear. He pulls out his hunting rifle and slings it around his shoulder. He descends to an open balcony of the building down at the ten-story level. He is now fully armed and ready for any situation...he hopes. He decides to cloak himself, even though it will drain more power from his operations belt than he would like. He activates a scan-blocker, just in case someone still has scanning capabilities. Mark again spots the group and zooms in with his oracle glasses.

It's a small crowd of about thirty, all dressed in white garments and...dancing? And singing? He hears a strange music that sounds like an organ or synthesizer. Some are playing flutes and tambourines. The music is soothing and incongruously upbeat. Everyone in the group is laughing as they dance, in stark contrast to the destruction and death all around them. Absurd. He scans the buildings and sees quite a number of strategically positioned armed guards, who seem to be looking around carefully while watching the group, apparently guarding them. They are dressed in dark robes and move in the shadows. Mark sees through his oracle glasses that they have weapons.

One of the dancing troupe steps out and begins to speak; his voice is magnified. Mark turns on Universal Translator. He links his hunting rifle to his oracle glasses. Cross hairs appear in his visual field.

The young man is dressed in a white toga and wears a laurel wreath on his head. In fact, they are all wearing small wreaths, Roman style. It looks like a young version of the senate.

"Friends! Romans! We have come bearing good news! Come out! You have nothing to fear." After a short time, a few curiosity seekers appear here and there. The group does not look dangerous if you don't notice the guards.

"Friends, Romans!" His ringing voice is amplified even more and can be heard in the surrounding streets, probably even inside some of the buildings.

"I have good news! Amazing news! You look around you, and you see death and ruin. Before new life appears, there must be death! A dead seed must be planted before it can give life. I tell you, the seed has been planted, and new life is springing forth!"

They're all nuts!

"We are on the edge, the beginning of a new dawn for humanity. The Age of Aquarius has begun! This is not a revolution, rather, it is evolution!"

His cohorts applaud.

"What you are witnessing is a transformation, indeed, the beginnings of transhumanization that will prepare us to rise from the ashes, yes, like the phoenix. When this happens, you will see the world change in many ways. But this change I am announcing is not new. We seek and promise only what Rome has sought for these last two thousand years, the sweet life and a true Roman peace!"

Mark thinks of Angela and of her last message.

"And one is coming, soon, even today, to lead us to this quantum leap into the future. No, don't be discouraged by what you see around you. We bring good news. Rome will rise again! Though it seems impossible, our new leader, Lord Seren, will make it happen. You will witness it with your own eyes. Perhaps then you will believe."

The crowds are growing. More people are coming out of the buildings, still wearing masks. Members of the dance troupe are not wearing them and don't seem to be affected, even though there is still some smoke and pollution. The Haze is light, but Mark can still smell the ash and odors from dead bodies.

—30—

PAX ROMANA, THE RISE OF SEREN

Mark descends to the ground floor, finds his aerobike, and takes off. As he flies over the wreckage of the Hotel Impero and what's left of the Coliseum, he notices a mounted troop, making its way up Esquilino Hill on the other side of the half demolished amphitheater. He descends for a closer look and zooms in with his oracle glasses.

Several hundred horsemen wearing black capes are riding down the streets, clearing the way for their leader, who is wearing a scarlet cape and hood and is mounted on a shiny champagne-colored Arabian with an elaborately jeweled saddle. The horsemen seem to have no armor under their capes, at least no armor is visible. Mark thinks it's probably some sort of invasion force. *Hmm, take a number, gents.* To him they don't look adequately equipped to take over Rome by military force, even in its current state.

Mark feels he must move in closer and possibly intervene, even with the odds overwhelmingly against him, a lone combatant. He decides to land on a relatively low building that is still standing and observe. He is about a dozen stories up and a block and a half away. He finds a good spot among several large metal ventilation hoods and pulls out his hunting rifle. He again cloaks himself, zooms in, and watches carefully.

The troop stops in an open area and forms a circle around their leader. At length, he rides out of the circle, and the horsemen give him a wide berth. Down the slope of the hill, many groups have gathered and are watching him apprehensively. Some seem defiant and ready to fight but don't have weapons of any sophistication. The rider does not appear to be afraid of them. His horse is restless and dances back and forth. He finally pulls back his hood, revealing his identity.

It's Seren.

Mark zooms in on Seren's assistants. He can see that they have weapons under their capes, armed guards. He checks them out one by one until he sees Massi, no surprise there, but he also spots Lorenzo and Gregorio. Traitors? Impossible!

Mark readies himself to take out Seren. The bullet is in the chamber.

Crowds of people begin pouring into the area and populating the hillside. Hundreds of them are Seren's followers, all dressed in white. There now seem to be even more curiosity seekers, maybe a thousand-plus at this point. Seren's young followers have done well.

Mark zooms in on the crowd, trying to figure out who is there and what their agenda might be. He tries to be systematic in his coverage, but everyone seems restless for different reasons. They are all milling about and talking. Mark activates audio magnification, linking his operations belt and oracle glasses. With a long-distance audio amplifier, he tries to listen in on some of the conversations. He goes from group to group; some of them are large, and some are small.

Then he sees two men from the back. They seem to be just standing there, watching events unfold. One of the men is tall and blond, the other is black and slightly taller. "It's Mikhail and Iqhawe!" Mark blurts out. "It has to be! Who else?"

They never turn around so he can be sure, and they are not talking. The two are walking along and eventually turn down a side street out of view.

Suddenly the crowd becomes restless. A few begin yelling and hurling insults. Then, Mark notices another group approaching several streets down. He adjusts his oracle glasses to zoom in for a closer look. It seems to be a small military force wearing uniforms that he does not recognize. They come armed with mostly high-tech weapons but also a few traditional armaments. He recognizes all of their guns and larger plasma cannons. This group could definitely do some damage. Mark then zooms in more closely. He sees a logo on each of the vehicles, an eagle with a hatchet in each claw.

Mark shakes his head. "The Neo-Fascists. So they really do exist. I guess this is their big day, their big chance." Mark decides to watch an inevitable battle. *Maybe those clowns will knock off Seren and do us all a favor. Or maybe they will both just kill each other off and do us an even bigger favor.*

The crowds are making way for the arrival of the opposing army. Many are fleeing the scene, frightened, and with good reason. Seren does not seem concerned as dozens of vehicles and hundreds of soldiers line up about fifty meters in front of him.

Once they are assembled, a man who seems to be a leader walks out to address Seren, his army, and those who might be able to hear. He seems confident, perhaps a little cocky. He reminds Mark of video footage he has seen of 'The Duke,' Signor Mussolini.

As the leader turns and is about to speak to the crowds, Seren raises his left hand and then points directly at him. A blazing column of fire suddenly falls from the sky and consumes him. Immediately armored vehicles and soldiers begin firing at Seren and his entourage with flash-plasma blasters of various sizes, but Seren again has raised his left hand and has created some sort of invisible force field that the energy bursts cannot penetrate. Civilians scatter and scream, but Seren's troops do not move or try to defend themselves. The opposing force eventually stops firing. They look both shocked and confused.

Seren's army moves back, giving him an even wider berth. They seem to know what is about to happen. Suddenly Seren again raises his left hand and in an instant grows—or appears to grow—to the height of a ten-story building. Mark can tell because he himself is atop a building close to that size less than two blocks away.

Another cheap trick. Holograms can only scare people, but they're about as scary as ghosts, which don't exist.

Seren's horse moves toward the vehicles and rears back on its hind legs, shaking its front hooves in the air. As his hooves come down, they land on two armored vehicles that had followed the Neo-Fascist leader who came to confront Seren. They smash them flat. Some of the nearby soldiers flee in fear.

In an amplified voice, Seren calls out to the crowd: "People of Rome. Hear me! There is no cause for alarm! I come in peace to benefit Rome and for the good of all humanity! What you see happening is part of Rome's destiny. We will certainly rise from these ruins. Do you remember your history? Julius Caesar understood the destiny of this great city, but traitors in the senate stopped it. This time, the senate has failed, but look! A new Caesar has arrived."

Ecce homo.

Mark was thinking that Seren is holographing himself, except a hologram can't smash armored vehicles.

Seren continues: "People of Rome. People of the world. You may ask, how can Rome ever be better than it was? How can it rise now from these ashes? How can the Eternal City be rebuilt from this devastating destruction? These are the obvious questions, but I assure you that it will happen before your very eyes. Let me begin with a demonstration of the first step."

Seren dismounts his horse and looks up at the sky, the smoke, the Haze, the ash.

With a thundering voice, he commands: "Let there be light." He waves his left hand skyward, and suddenly the Haze, the smoke, and the ash are all swept away, not by wind, but by some invisible force.

For the first time in a decade, Romans can now see a real blue sky and pure sunlight shining on their faces. The people are in awe and begin talking excitedly.

Mark's audio amplifier picks up the shouts of one of the spectators, "It is the voice of a god, not a man!!!" And many in the crowd, including some of the Neo-Fascist soldiers, fall on their knees; a few fall on their faces before him.

Seren looks to the east and declares, "A New Age has begun!"

As the multitude roars praise for Seren, Mark presses his cheek against his hunting rifle. He squints his eyes and brings Seren's smiling face into his cross hairs. Seren is waving at the cheering masses. *He's distracted, and at ten stories high, he makes an easy target.*

As he wraps his finger around the trigger, Mark mutters: "An old-fashioned bullet should do the trick..."

—To be continued

Printed in the United States
By Bookmasters